Broken Vessels

By

Shellie M. Saunders

ISBN: 0-615-54739-7
ISBN-13: 978-0-615-54739-8

This is a work of fiction. Names, characters, places and incidents are either the product of the author's imagination or are used fictitiously. Any resemblance to actual persons, living or dead, businesses, companies, events or locales is entirely coincidental.

To order additional copies of this book, go to www.shelliemsaunders.com.

Acknowledgements

Thanks be to God for his awesome power! He planted the seed for me to write *Broken Vessels* when I was only 21, and I am grateful that he has kept open the door for me to pursue this dream. As I've written and edited this book, God has shown me so much about His goodness and mercy, and the resilience of human nature.

I am grateful to my husband who has supported my dream from the moment I told him I was writing a book. Charles Jr., you are my best friend, the father of our miracle baby and my biggest cheerleader. Thank you to my parents who never discouraged me from chasing my dream of being a writer. Thank you to my grandparents; I was privileged to have three of you in my life. Though two of you have passed on, each of you has influenced me through your own talents and strengths.

To all of my friends and family who've asked, "How is the book coming?" know that each time you uttered

4

this question, I felt renewed in my goal of completing the book. I'd like to extend a special thank you to Vivian—a mighty prayer partner—and "My Misha" for providing early feedback on the manuscript.

Thanks to those who've helped turn my manuscript into a book, including editor Nikki Andrews. To author Heather Neff—thank you for your feedback on my manuscript and steady encouragement.

I hope that *Broken Vessels* touches you in a way that you did not expect and will not forget. I pray that you find strength in Trinity's story and the courage to press on through your own brokenness.

Prologue

When I was a little girl, I watched my mother drink out of her favorite coffee mug—a carrot-orange, protuberant mass of ceramic that she had fashioned into the likes of a medieval goblet. The ghastly hue choice—suitable for agricultural products alone—was exacerbated by three progressively slumping textured rings that shadowed the rim.

Over the years, the mug had become her connection to both self-awareness and the world. It brought her to a tolerable state of being by serving as the only mug worthy of her morning coffee. A constant companion to her daily *Detroit Free Press* paper, its base was notorious for marking its territory on the front page of the Sports section. My father, a late riser, rarely had the privilege of getting to the paper before Mom's mug lined it with an irregular brown circle.

Morning after morning I would watch my mother flip through the newspaper, browsing national and local news stories with an extended pinky and three fingers slipped through the thin, half-heart shaped handle. I was drawn to that handle. It was the most delicate thing on the clunky mug and appeared out of place. Amazingly, it continued to hold the weight of the mug for more than a decade.

Sipping from the misshapen cup as if she were among England's elite at high tea, my mom and that cup would have been dismissed even by the Queen's lowly subjects. Yet she held that unsightly lump with pride and dared anyone to say a negative word about her precious mug.

I remember my curiosity about the mug's power over my mom. Surely it had *some* sort of power. After all, it called an otherwise reasonable woman to drink from its core every single day, without regard for appearance or functionality.

One brisk day in fall, I decided to look for the mug's secret. I figured that if I drank from it, I might discover its mesmerizing power. I had been watching snow flurries hover over the city for hours, while I was trapped in the house with my parents and brother. The day before, my dad had picked up apple cider and donuts at The Franklin Cider Mill. The family was watching a movie in the basement when my thoughts settled on warming a cup of cider. I slipped away and treaded up the steps to the kitchen.

There were cabinets all around—low and high. The refrigerator was the source of the only noise coming from that level of the house, humming until it hacked to a silence. The cabinet holding all of the household mugs was directly over the sink. I approached it and stretched to my utmost to open the cabinet door. A subtle creak preceded its separation from the cabinet box.

The screaming orange mass sat on the second shelf among the stale grey, white and navy sameness of the other, demure mugs. I eyed it for a moment, trying to tap into whatever my mother saw in it. Reaching for the mug, I wrapped the fingers of my right hand through the handle and gripped the left side with the other hand. I slid it toward me, and inevitably, I lost my grip. The mug tumbled and crashed into the sink below. Four large pieces blasted to each corner of the sink and microscopic fragments scattered about.

I stared at the broken pieces, trying to will the mug back together. It lay there, useless in its new form. There was no resemblance to the mug I'd briefly held in my tiny hands just seconds earlier. I tried to fix it, but my efforts were futile. Not even Super Glue could return the mug to its previous state.

Fearing my fate, I ran upstairs to my bathroom and feverishly unraveled every roll of fluffy toilet tissue under the sink, stuffing it into my underwear and down the legs of my sweat pants. I waddled into my room, paper protruding from each pant leg. Plopping onto the red bean-bag chair in the corner, I picked up *Charlotte's Web* and pretended to read. I decided to convince my mom that a loud truck went by when I was in my room reading. The vibration was so strong that it forced the cabinet door to open and the mug to plunge from the cabinet, crashing into the sink! That story was wayyy better than trying to glue the pieces back together and getting caught when Mom's morning coffee seeped through... or I thought it was a good story. Moments later, my bedroom door opened.

The anger on my mom's face led to a desire deep inside to jump in a time machine for a do-over. Despite its hideous appearance, I wanted nothing more than to see the contentment on her face as she drank coffee from her favorite mug with her paper. All I wanted was for things to be as they once had been.

Bits of spiraling toilette tissue, a two-inch wide leather belt, flailing arms and my own piercing screams are all that I can remember of the moments following the opening of the door.

Since then, I had come to know brokenness as little more than the remains of something that was once whole but is now measurable only by the pieces that remain. Once something was broken, the pieces no longer made sense by themselves. Once something was broken, it could be equated to defeat, emptiness and insignificance. Once something was broken, we could express our anger or sadness about its demise, but when we were over our feelings, we were often quick to toss it aside.

Sometimes I feared that I would become that mug—cast off and abandoned. On the surface, my mug looked flawless—no cracks, no superglue, no missing pieces. My fear was that the flaws on the inside would soon become evident to those on the outside. I had done an admirable job of faking my way to wholeness, but the truth was that I was far from infallible. It amazed me that I was the only one who seemed to know it.

At times I awaited the moment that someone would look deep into my eyes and figure out that the true me was somewhere deep inside—only a trace of her was evident on the exterior. But so far, no one seemed to notice.

Maybe it was because my façade had become part of me—so much so that the line between fact and fiction had blurred. I wanted to be like the girl that everyone else saw in me; I wanted to be her so badly that I sought her, studied her, and ultimately became her. I sought her so intently that I forgot who I really was. The cost of becoming her was more than I had ever expected. I'd retained my value, but I'd lost my identity.

The only difference between me and the remnants of that orange mug is that my damage was internal. I would do anything to keep it that way, but there was one problem: I knew that I, like all people, was a conduit, designed to take in and pour out. Like a vessel, I was filled with life's experiences and lessons. Ultimately, I would become so full that I'd have to overflow, pouring out what was inside of me. I feared that when my own cup began to overflow, it would leave nothing but secrets and wounds. My past would rush through the cracks and over the brim, exposing me, contaminating others, and overpowering my self-worth. My walls would shake until, piece by piece, they'd crumble, and I'd become a useless remnant of my former self. I would be left with the choice of embracing the life I contrived or accepting the one I left behind. I would have to face the past I worked so hard to conceal. I would have to confront the people who helped paint the image of the woman I am *supposed* to be.

Facing the past was not an option and vulnerability wasn't my strong suit, so I would have to uphold my façade at all costs. After all, faking it was the only way I knew to get through. It had worked for this long. Surely, I could muster the strength to keep up the make-believe.

Chapter One

Dense winter skies and snowcapped pine trees withdrew, making room for sprouting tulips and green tree limbs that emerged from deadened bark. Chirping birds returned from travels south. People rushed to corner car washes to cleanse salt and dirt from their vehicles. Tigers fans emerged on the downtown streets, clad in navy blue and orange. Self-proclaimed gardeners geared up for Eastern Market's annual Flower Day, hoping for bragging rights on great deals for flats of their favorite blossoms. Spring was shaking Detroit awake.

This was also the time of year that my best friend Shawna celebrated her birthday. In high school, she had some sort of celebration every year, from skating parties to deejayed parties in the basement where we danced until we sweated out our perms. For Shawna, those days had been replaced by just about any place with a bar and an assortment of men. Today was her twenty-seventh birthday, and her pleasure was going to TGI Friday's, where she could get plenty of free drinks. I picked up my cousin Toya and drove to the restaurant, where we found Shawna had arrived with four other girls—three from work and one she'd grown up with.

Friday's didn't have the fastest service on a Friday night and it would only be slower because the weather was breaking and Detroit was full of people with cabin fever. Friday's was a good place to socialize, drink, get hit on by trifling men, and catch up with people you hadn't seen and probably hadn't thought of since high school. Well, that's what it was to me—minus the drinking, anyway.

Bikes, boats and random novelties were affixed to the ceiling and posters of forgotten celebrities hung on the walls, while two hundred people attempted to talk over the 1980s tracks that were booming from the overhead speakers. It was so crowded that we waited nearly an hour for a table while dodging tray-balancing waiters and waitresses who looked more like Foot Locker employees with button fetishes than restaurant workers. By the time we took our seats, I had talked to nearly a dozen people—mostly guys—I knew from my days at Cass Technical High School. We engaged in the usual "hey, how ya been?" and "looking good" exchanges. Most of the conversations ended with the insincerity I hated. We exchanged business cards, said we'd keep in touch and parted ways, knowing neither of us would ever make a phone call.

We had already ordered Shawna a couple of drinks from the bar before we were finally seated. She made it quite clear that she intended to be nothing less than incapacitated on her birthday. After another hour, I'd finished a couple glasses of pop and a plate of greasy fries. My stomach was in a slight twist and my bladder was full. I had to visit the ladies room. I didn't want to because it meant passing a flock of drunken beasts at the bar, but I had to pee!

I was almost to the bathroom when a two-hundred-fifty-pound boulder jumped up from his stool and backed right into me. He bumped me so hard that I was surprised he did not hurl me into the bathroom. A guy on the other side of me intercepted my inevitable flight.

"Why don't you just knock me out?"

My question was lost on the beast who continued in a loud, vulgar conversation. He seemed totally unaware of the fact that he had contacted another object, animate or inanimate.

"Are you okay?"

In my anger with the drunken buffoon, I did not realize that I was practically resting in a stranger's lap.

"I'm fine." I regained my posture. "I apologize for bumping into you, but he didn't give me much of a choice," I said, smiling at him. He chuckled at my icebreaker.

He's cute.

I couldn't help but notice his long eyelashes and his smooth, milk chocolate complexion that was only challenged by his black, tapered hair. His pale-coral, long-sleeved linen shirt was neatly pressed and tucked into his indigo jeans. Brown Calvin Klein loafers and a matching belt made the entire ensemble one that could grace the pages of a Banana Republic catalog.

"I'm Caleb." He extended his hand.

"Trih—" was all I could say before being distracted by a boisterous laugh across the bar. The sound of it sliced through the jumbled cheers, conversations and bad music. There was something so familiar about this laugh—something that drew the breath from my mouth. The source tugged my line of vision, and I could not believe whom I saw.

Without even turning back to look at Caleb, I lowered my hand, said, "Excuse me," and walked away. A magnetic force gave me no choice but to follow the laugh to the other side of the bar. As I passed through the thick crowd, the beating of my heart gradually drowned out the pick-up lines and voices that had been so loud. I thought I heard someone call my name, but it did not matter. I was on a mission.

Inching my way to the source of the laugh, I could see that, physically, he hadn't changed much. A few extra pounds stuck to his solid, stocky build. As always, his caramel skin was vibrantly clear, his hair was cut low and he was wearing the latest sportswear. Tonight he posed in a Carolina blue and white jogging suit with matching Nike shoes.

Finally, I was behind him. He must have felt my presence. Before I could say a word, he stopped in the middle of his conversation and turned around. When his eyes met mine, I realized that I'd forgotten what a beautiful shade of hazel they were. We locked stares for a brief moment. Then he was zapped back to reality. His eyes nearly defied the boundaries of their sockets, and his facial expression suggested that acid was tumbling in his stomach. With a grin and a tone of slight disappointment he said, "Hi, Trih—" but before he could finish, I slapped him across the face as hard as I could.

"Coward," I said calmly, without breaking eye contact. I hoped my stare would burn Tony's cold soul.

"Damn!" the guy next to him yelled. I spun around to look at him, and he dropped his head like a puppy that had pooped on the new carpet. Tony held his face and stared at me in disbelief.

Without another word, I spun back around and walked through the thick crowd once again—this time with no problem. I returned to the table and grabbed my purse, which was hidden in my seat. My blood was boiling. I looked at Toya, who was talking to two of Shawna's friends.

"Let's go!" I demanded.

Oblivious to what happened at the bar, everyone at the table turned and looked at me as if I were crazy. I repeated myself, only this time more slowly and forcefully. "Let's go, now."

Normally Toya would have made a smart comment or picked an argument, but not this time. I looked at Shawna and mouthed, "I'm sorry. I'll call you." Shawna just nodded her head. She was so drunk, I wasn't sure she realized what was going on. "Who's taking her home?" I addressed the rest of the girls at the table.

"I picked her up," one of the girls responded. She was Shawna's coworker. "I'll get her home safely."

"Thank you." Even though I was shaken by the run-in with Tony, I would not have left without making sure that Shawna was well taken care of.

On the walk to the car, I heard chatter coming from Toya's mouth, but I was so consumed by the rapid thump of my heart beating that I could not decipher the meaning in her words. My hand shook uncontrollably, making it difficult to get the key in the ignition. Finally, I started the car and threw it into reverse first and then into drive before peeling off as if the ground were crumbling behind me.

Toya prattled on until I reached a stop light and slammed on the brakes. I gripped the wheel as if I were trying to prevent it from getting away and looked to Toya, whose jaws were still flapping. I used the strength of my inner mom and looked Toya directly in the eyes. "Look. I really need you to be quiet, *right now.*"

Like magic, she stopped midsentence and allowed me to drive her home without listening to her blather. I knew she was uncomfortable and it must have been more than a notion for Toya to actually sit in silence, but there was so much going through my head, I didn't even notice the stillness of our voices. When I pulled into her apartment complex, Toya looked at me and said, "Do you want to stay here tonight?"

"No, I'll be fine." I smiled with my eyes to let her know that my anger was not directed at her. She opened her mouth and I thought she'd say something, but each time she tried, she swallowed her words. I knew she wanted to ask me what was going on, but was trying to respect my request for her to stop talking.

"Okay. Well, call me." She hesitated briefly, then got out of the car. Watching her disappear behind the security door, I breathed a sigh of relief and drove off. I could not tell her the truth.

I headed home, alone with my thoughts. I had never slapped anyone like *that* before. When I began to walk toward Tony, I didn't know what I would do. I certainly didn't plan to hit him. When I looked into his eyes, something came over me. I had not seen or talked to him since undergrad. The mere sight of him conjured up feelings I had shut down several years before.

My feelings weren't purely hateful, though. I actually felt sympathy for him. My heart told me that he had been battling his conscience all of that time, even though he had never been brave enough to talk to me about it. Still, I knew he'd pay for it for the rest of his life.

I wasn't sure that a stranger who'd watched my actions that night would be able to tell that I was a Christian. I doubted it. Still, I could not deny that it felt good to hit Tony. I had confronted him and let him know I thought he was the scum of the earth, even though I had only said one word. Besides, if it weren't for him, I might have discovered a connection with Caleb—the cute guy I fell on—but thanks to Tony, I only knew his name. To add insult to injury, I still had to pee!

Once upon a time, Tony and I were very good friends. Even he and my parents were close, which is much more than can be said for most of the men in my life—present and past. Tony and I had become friends during my junior year at Howard University. He was a senior. Somewhere along the way, Tony got attached to me. He became my shadow and always wanted to be in my company, whether I was watching a movie, studying or grocery shopping. When we were home for the summer, it was more of the same, but with the addition of his family. Tony's family was very close, and I was around them enough to form a relationship of some sort with each of them. They welcomed me with open arms.

My relationship with Tony was purely innocent—he had never even tried to kiss me. Though I was attracted to Tony and I thought he felt the same toward me, I liked the nature of our relationship the way it was. When we got back to school my senior year, he went into his fifth year. He had been in no hurry to leave collegiate life. We both had apartments, but he was at mine so often, my roommate referred to him as the third roommate who didn't pay rent.

One night my roommate's boyfriend was in town, so I left for Tony's apartment to give them some privacy. Tony and I were watching a movie in his living room when I felt my eyes get heavy. I rested my head on his shoulder and dozed off. I awakened to a kiss on my forehead. When I looked up to get my bearings, he caressed my face. His eyes were warm with adoration, and I could not pull away from his stare. There was no awkwardness or intrusion, only a feeling I could not explain that made me see him in a different light, instantly.

I closed my eyes and felt his lips press against mine. I felt like a teenager engaging in her very first grown-up kiss. It was passionate, comforting. When we pulled away, he kissed me on the cheek and pulled my head to his chest, letting his other arm embrace me. I fell asleep in his arms. As I drifted off, I thought nothing could be more perfect. I could not have been more wrong.

Chapter Two

The morning after Shawna's birthday, I forced myself to get up for my usual Saturday morning jog. It was an unseasonably warm morning, so I decided to jog outside instead of at the gym. I stretched on my porch, smelling the moist air. It was fragrant like wildflowers and freshly watered grass. I closed my eyes and inhaled slowly to draw in some of the microscopic droplets that bounced off the lawn's blades.

My two-year-old condo complex was between the University of Detroit's campus and the University District neighborhood—a historic community that was full of large brick and stone homes. I loved to jog the neighborhood just to see them. Each had its own character and style; a couple even had castle-like entranceways. Ivy climbed up the front of many of the homes, as if to mark a territory, letting passersby know that they were well guarded. The University District was a far cry from the cookie-cutter houses that were being constructed outside the city and selling for hundreds of thousands of dollars.

After I finished my run, I circled back home and showered to go to my standing hair appointment. Laila, my hairdresser, got me in and out in two hours so I stopped by the mall—just to window shop. Who was I fooling? I went home with two outfits, a pair of shoes and an ice cream cone.

It was 2:30, and I had absolutely nothing else on my agenda. I was a little tired from the day before because I'd worked late before going to Shawna's birthday outing. Still, I didn't want to take a nap—I was afraid I'd miss something. The next-best thing to a nap was to sit down on the couch and annihilate two Coney Island chili dogs... but I'd already had the ice cream. The second next-best thing was to choose a movie from my collection. I went with that option and popped a movie in the DVD player. After the movie, I would take a long bubble bath and give myself a pedicure. As I pressed play on the remote, I remembered I was supposed to call Shawna.

"Hello?" Shawna sounded so groggy that had I not known better, I might have thought she had the *flu*.

"Hey, it's me. Are you still asleep?"

"Girl. Ooh, I can't move. What time is it?"

"2:30."

Momentarily Shawna had some life in her voice. "Oh, uh-uh! Stop lying. I don't believe I slept that long!"

"I do... the way you drank!"

We both laughed.

"Look, I want to apologize for leaving early last night."

Shawna was silent.

"I knew you wouldn't remember," I teased.

"Girl, I'm sorry. I don't re—wait a minute. I—I remember you being pissed. What happened?"

"Tony was there last night."

"Stop playing with me!" Shawna yelled. "Ow, that hurt my head."

"I wish I *were* playing."

"Mmm. Well, did he see you?"

"Mmm hmm."

"Did you say anything to him?"

"Not much." I moved the battery cover of the remote control in and out of the locked position to an unheard constant rhythm.

"Dang, Trinity. Do I have to drag the story out of you? What did you—"

I cut her off. "There really isn't much to tell. I wasn't expecting to see him. He obviously wasn't expecting to see me. We caught each other's eye and he was drunk... and obnoxious. The whole thing just pissed me off."

"Did he say something out of order? Wait, did he touch you?" Shawna's voice squeaked.

"No, calm down. It was a brief... encounter."

"Mmm. All right then." She sounded unconvinced.

I put down the remote and walked to the kitchen to pour a small glass of water. I was starting to get upset about the incident all over again and hoped the water would cool me down. I gulped half of it and felt my body temperature begin to drop. "Well, I'm going to watch a movie, so call me later. I just wanted to check on you."

"Okay, Trin."

I did not feel the need to tell her exactly what happened, and I guess I didn't have to lie about Tony's intoxication, but the fib just rolled off my tongue. It was so much easier to say than, "I slapped the bastard and walked away." I think it was more believable, too. Well, except for the fact that, like me, Tony didn't drink. He usually just hung out at the bar with a plain Coke while those who surrounded him satiated themselves with beer and hard liquor, but Shawna didn't know that.

I never even told her about that night at school. It was not because I didn't trust Shawna; I had never told anyone. Why bother other people with my problems?

I tried to shake my thoughts by focusing on my movie, which was well past the opening scene, but I'd seen it so many times, there was no need to rewind it. I grabbed my Granny's afghan and settled into the couch. Fifteen minutes later, the phone rang. "Daggonit."

Why do people always call me when I am busy or sleeping? Why is it that no one calls when I'm bored out of my mind?

Realizing I'd left the phone in the kitchen, I rose from my comfort zone and tried to answer the phone before the voicemail picked up. Just as I pressed the talk button, I hit my knee on the corner of the coffee table. It felt as if a small drinking glass had shattered inside my knee, spreading miniscule pieces all about.

"He-llo?" I said, trying to mask the pain.

"Hi. What are you doing?" It was my mother.

"Watching a movie," I responded, rubbing my knee.

"Why do you sound upset?"

"Mom, I'm not upset."

"Are you sure? What's wrong?"

Bless her heart. She teetered on that fine line between pure pleasantness and bona fide irritation.

"Mom, nothing's wrong. I ran into the coffee table trying to answer the phone and hurt my knee."

"Well, what'd you go and do that for?" Her words were sprinkled with giggles, but a serious tone soon returned. "You know, you have such pretty legs. I don't understand why you've always been such a tomboy."

I ignored her comment about my legs. "So, what's up, Ma?" I massaged my knee, trying to alleviate the sting.

"I was calling to see what you're doing today."

"Oh, right now I'm watching a movie, but I don't know what I'm doing later. I'll probably just watch the basketball game."

"Okay. What movie are you watching?"

"Island in the Sun."

"You and those old movies." She chuckled. "Who's in that one? Dorothy Height and Harry Belafonte?"

"One for two. Harry Belafonte is right, but it was Dorothy Dandridge."

"Who did I say?"

"You said Dorothy Height."

"Well, who's Dorothy Height?"

By this time I was trying to hold back a laugh. "She was the tenth national president of my sorority. We saw the play about her at the Music Hall."

"Oh. I knew I'd heard that name somewhere."

"Ma, don't take this the wrong way, but why did you call me?"

"Excuse me for taking an interest in your life."

"I'm sorry. It's just that… I haven't figured out where this conversation is going."

"I just wanted to call my daughter. So, you don't have a date tonight?"

"Noooo, I don't." I tried not to huff into the telephone receiver.

"Well, Crabby Cathy, I did want to invite you over for dinner."

Ever since I was little, my mom had made up goofy names for me when my moodiness attacked.

"Lydia is bringing the kids over in about an hour, and we'll eat around five," she continued.

"Okay. I'll be there," I said.

So much for vegging out.

I lived only two miles from my parents' house. The unsynchronized Livernois traffic lights slowed me down along the way. I made a right turn on 8 Mile and another right turn at the white and green sign reading

"Green Acres." I was always drawn to the sign. There was a tree on it, and I always thought the tree top looked more like a cluster of clouds than foliage.

Mrs. Coleman, an elderly woman who lived in the yellow ranch-styled brick home on the corner, was tending to a flower bed in the front yard. I assumed she was weeding it, preparing it to plant flowers. Several doors down, four middle-school boys were shooting hoops clumsily in the driveway of a white colonial home. In my rear-view mirror, I could see a couple riding their bikes. A baby seat was attached to the man's bike.

I pulled into the driveway of my parents' home—a brown brick Tudor-style house—and noticed that the oak door had been painted the color of mahogany wood. I could smell the paint when I walked to the door. The odor was almost appealing. I rang the doorbell, then listened to my mother's laughter draw closer. She answered the door with a dazzling smile.

"Hi!" we both said in unison, kissing each other on the cheek.

I looked behind me. "The door looks nice."

"Thanks! Your dad painted it. Do you like the color?"

"Yeah. The mahogany works well."

"It's called 'majestic brown.' I wanted to match the wood chips. We spent half an hour at Lowe's holding wood chips up to paint swatches!"

Half an hour matching browns? I'd rather leave it up to my condo association to ponder issues such as whether one is brown versus really brown or reddish brown.

"So, where is everyone?" I asked, wiping my feet on the rug in the entryway.

"Your father is in his office. Lydia and the kids are downstairs."

Lydia was the oldest daughter of Aunt Georgia, my mom's sister. Lydia was seven years older than me, and though her mom and sister lived in Illinois, she had spent most of her high school days here in Detroit with her father. Lydia had been around a lot when I was younger and was like a sister—I loved her, but sometimes I wished she would just go away.

Lydia married six years ago and had two children—Autumn, who was five, and Aaron, who was four. Even at her wedding reception, Lydia talked about starting a family immediately. She said she didn't want to wait because she was pushing thirty at the time. It was as if she thought that when she turned thirty, some diabolical force would come up from the depths of hell and eradicate all of her eggs, rendering them useless.

I headed down the hall to my dad's office and peeked in the door, which was ajar. The ceiling fan was revolving at a moderate speed. Dad sat under the fan, leaning back in his leather chair with his left foot resting on his right knee. He was parallel to the oversized cherry wood desk that my mom had tried to convince him was too big for the office. A picture that fought the desk for attention hung above it on the wall. In it, I stood on Howard's campus in my cap and gown. My parents were at either side, their chests puffed out with pride. It looked like the three of us were intentionally standing according to height, with my father the tallest by far.

Hearing me at the door, my father motioned for me to come in. I kissed him on the cheek and his beard pricked my bottom lip. A couple of manila folders sat on one of his two filing cabinets. "Detroit's Soul, Inc." was crawling across his computer screen. My dad gave a number of uh-huhs to the person he was conversing with. He covered the mouthpiece and whispered, "How ya doin', sweetheart?"

"I'm fine, Daddy." I patted him on the shoulder. "I'll be downstairs."

He nodded his head and took his hand off the mouthpiece. "Okay, well, I'll check with Ron, but ten should be fine."

Ron was my dad's business partner. They had been friends since they were ten. Together they owned two of the best soul food restaurants in the city. Both were named Detroit's Soul.

I went down the stairs. Pictures of me lined the wall. With every few steps, I was able to observe my progression from infancy to my cap and gown picture from graduate school. There was something on the wall that I had seen time and time again, but never really paid attention to—my crooked smile graced every picture.

When I reached the last step, I could see Autumn, Aaron, Lydia and Chi-Chi—my mom's spoiled Shih Tzu. The kids were chasing each other around the couch, unaware that anyone had entered the room. Lydia was in the reclining chair, eating out of the candy dish—the culprit behind my first cavity. The Houston versus Chicago basketball game was blaring in the background.

"Who's making all that noise? I need to see some identification!"

Startled, the kids looked at me and their eyes lit up. "Auntie Twineedee!" they shouted. They couldn't pronounce my name. And though we were cousins, I guess they figured that since my mom was their aunt, I must be, too. It made sense to them—they called my father Auntie Charles.

"Heyyyyyyy! I didn't recognize you two! I started to call the rugrat police!"

"Nuh-uh!" they both yelled and ran to me.

"Uh-huh!" I responded as I grabbed them in a hug.

Autumn was the color of hot cocoa and had long, thick, jet-black hair like her mother's. She often wore four or five braids with big, marble-like ponytail holders like my mom used to put in my hair. Today Autumn only had two frizzed-out ponytails. Her eyes were big and dark as coal. A Kool-Aid ring lined her lips and a space separated her front teeth.

Aaron had the complexion of honey. Freckles spotted his nose, like his father's, and his eyes were dark brown. His lips were fuller than his sister's, but the gap between his front teeth was identical to Autumn's. Aaron's brownish-red hair was knotty and begged for a haircut.

"Play with us!" Autumn shouted as she pulled my hand and guided me in front of the couch. Chi-Chi did her imitation of a jumping bean at my feet. I put Autumn under my right arm and Aaron under my left arm then twirled them around until my biceps were sore and my breath was short. They had worn me out in all of ten minutes.

I sat down on the couch to catch the basketball game. The kids sat next to me—Aaron to my left and Autumn to my right. Houston had a six-point lead over Chicago and there was less than two minutes left in the half. Lydia and I made small talk and Chi-Chi fell asleep at my feet. The kids were quiet—too quiet. I looked into their faces. Both were asleep. Autumn was leaning on my arm, and Aaron was lying in my lap. They looked like angels.

"Ooh, thank you, Trinity! They have been live wires all day!" Lydia said.

"Hey, anytime."

"Dinner's ready!" Mom yelled from the top of the stairs.

Lydia pushed herself up from the reclining chair. "I knew that moment of peace was too good to be true."

I woke Autumn and Aaron and we all headed upstairs. Mom had set up a kids' table for them next to the kitchen table, which only sat four.

My mother cooked turkey, dressing, fresh green beans and cornbread. My dad prepared a tossed salad and a batch of iced tea that was just like the kind his father used to make in Mobile, Alabama. Both of my parents liked to cook. It was too bad I didn't share that sentiment.

I think that cooking did not appeal to me because there never seemed to be enough time to get it done. With a job as a senior account manager at a marketing agency, I often worked 10- to 12-hour days, and didn't get home until seven or eight at night. After an evening workout, I rarely had the energy or time to cook. Quick fixes had become my usual routine. Every week or two, I got a twinge in my bones and wanted some home-cooked food, so I did what most single people my age did: I went to my parents' house. On other days I picked up something from one of Dad's restaurants. Either way, I couldn't beat the free food.

My father said grace in his quiet but strong voice. As we ate, the conversation turned from Lydia's kids—who were having a discussion of their own—to other family members, to work, and on to the very topic I dreaded.

After taking a bite of her cornbread, Lydia turned to me and said, "So, Trinity, when are you going to get married?"

As I watched a large crumb of cornbread fall from her lips while she chewed, I felt myself trying to communicate with her through my stare.

Why would you ask me that, Lydia? You can't fathom that I can be happy with myself? Why be so anxious to know about my personal life? Is it because your husband works seven days a week, ten hours a day, and you're lonely? Are you trying to find out if someone is lonelier than you?

"Actually Lydia, I don't know if that's going to happen. It's not a priority right now."

"Oh, don't be so certain. You never know when love is going to come knocking at your door," she told me, devouring her dressing like a vulture feeding on a carcass.

The truth was that if love were to come knocking at my door, I'd probably hide from it the way my mom hid when Jehovah's Witnesses came to her door.

"What ever happened to that young man you were dating in school?" she persisted.

"Oh, things just didn't work out."

She knew that Diori and I broke up after I moved back home three years ago. Why was she doing this to me? I wondered if she had any idea how much she was irritating me.

"I told her the Lord meant for him to be her husband, but she didn't listen," my mother chimed in. "I could have been on my way to preparing for grandmotherhood right now. You know Diori's getting ready to do his residency."

"Sorry to disappoint you, Mom." I winked at her and glanced at my dad, who grinned but remained silent.

A thought occurred to me. "And how do you know what he's doing anyway?" I asked.

"Well, you know his aunt—Brenda—keeps me posted every time I see her at church."

I shook my head, then gulped down the rest of my food thinking that the faster I ate, the more quickly I could get out of this conversation. Lydia and my mother tag-teamed me, giving me blows between bites and miscellaneous table talk. After dinner, my mom made a phone call from the kitchen and Lydia and the kids went to the basement with Chi-Chi. My father invited me to join him in the living room to watch the rest of the basketball game. I accepted and took my indigestion with me. Dad never judged me or pressured me with a bunch of questions. Although I knew Mom and Lydia didn't mean any harm by their curiosity, I didn't want to be bothered.

After the game, I ventured up the stairs toward the bedrooms and stood at the doorway of one of them for what seemed an eternity. The rest of the house was still, though I knew no one had left. With my hand shaking, I twisted the knob and walked into the room. It was my brother Bashaye's room and this was the first time I'd been in it since the year after he died—fifteen years ago.

After his funeral, I would go into his room every day and pray for his return. Some nights I would slip into his room and sleep in his bed. My parents thought I was asleep in my own room, and I always sneaked back into my room before they woke. I hoped that when I awakened, Bashaye would be there and my nightmare would be over. Needless to say, it never happened. On the first anniversary of his death, I gave up on his return.

My parents knew nothing of my ritual. They told me that Bashaye was in a better place and that God took him home. Still, no matter how hard I tried, I could not bring myself to accept his death and became angry— angry with God for taking Bashaye and angry with Bashaye for leaving. After the first year of praying, I lost faith. I lost hope. His room was a grim reminder of how I had been let down.

Bashaye was five years older than me. He would have been thirty two this year. He had been the best big brother a little girl could have asked for. I remember being in afternoon kindergarten and seeing him waiting for me when I got off the school bus. Even though we were never close enough in age to attend the same school, he continued to greet me in that way until the very day he died. He thought he was my protector, my knight; and he fought for my honor. In fact, he called me Princess and he made me feel like one.

One of my most vivid childhood memories of Bashaye was on one stifling, summer day. All of the kids were in the neighborhood park, soaking up the sun, while our parents either tried to keep cool in the basements or barbecued in the back yards. I was on the park swings with two other girls while Bashaye played basketball on the courts with a few boys from the neighborhood. The basketball courts were behind the swings, so Bashaye was able to keep a close eye on me.

Bashaye played on the court with JJ, who lived on the street behind us with his younger brother, Lil Mike, the neighborhood nuisance. He terrorized anyone smaller than him because he knew everyone was afraid of JJ, who always rescued Lil Mike from any trouble he got himself into.

I was in a zone, swinging with a friend. I wore one of my favorite outfits—a yellow Hello Kitty T-shirt and matching shorts. The shirt was a favorite because Kitty's pink bow was metallic and puffed out in a 3-D effect. My mom helped me to look like the shirt by adorning each of my side ponytails with hot pink ribbons, just like Hello Kitty's.

My friend and I had just found our momentum on the swings. There was enough force to let the wind fly through our ponytails but not enough strength in our bodies to do a 360 on the swing set. I was leaning back, feeling at one with the swing when a force rammed me so hard that I went flying off the swing. I landed face down in the dirt. Pulling myself up, I tried to wipe the dirt from my face. It blurred my vision and salted my tongue. I could hear a heavy laugh echoing throughout the park. I rubbed my eyes, which only irritated them more. Rising up, I turned around to see the perpetrator.

Through my burning eyes, I saw Lil Mike, bent over with laughter. He hadn't noticed that I had regained my footing and was walking toward him. I crept without a plan. Still, he bellowed in his same position. Before I knew it, I kicked him with all of my might, right on his butt. I watched as his overweight, ten-year-old body slowly tipped like a buoy in water. He fell face down, mouth open, into the dirt.

"Ha, fat boy!" I yelled, as granules of dirt stalled on their way down my throat. Realizing that he could get up and kick my scrawny behind at any given second, I quickly straddled his back, grabbed a few of his matted cornrows and slammed his face into the dirt again, and again and again. "How do you like it, fat boy? Huh, fat boy?" I yelled as if I were possessed by a spirit sent to earth to take over the bodies of kids who sought revenge for the wrongs of bullies. Lil Mike started to cry and begged me, a frail nine-year-old girl, to stop, but his pleas only made me yell louder and slam his face harder. I continued to make him digest my original-recipe mud pie until I felt my sixty-pound body snatched from his.

"No! I'm not finished!" I wailed as I was carried away from the scene. I wanted to leave my mark, so I swished up enough spit to coat the dirt that remained in my mouth and used the spitting skills Bashaye had taught me to catapult a glob of saliva toward Lil Mike. It landed on his wide behind. "Bull's-eye, punk!"

"Girl, be quiet. What the hell is wrong with you?"

I was so worked up that I had not even looked to see whose shoulder I had been tossed over. I turned to see the back of my brother's head. Bashaye stopped at the sidewalk, put me down and squatted so that we were at eye level. He peered at me with his big doe-like eyes. I huffed like a raging bull. He grabbed my forearms. "Trinity, what is your problem?"

"Bashaye, that hurts!" He loosened his grip, but my attempt to avoid the question didn't fly.

"What was that back there? Answer me!"

Bashaye's interrogations could be so intimidating that I was more afraid to get in trouble with him than with my parents. I rambled on about the events that led up to my attack and by the time I finished, my brother was laughing, but I could not figure out why.

"What's so funny?"

"I can't believe you had the ba—the nerve to stand up to him. I taught you well, Princess." He tried to wipe the dirt from my hair. He swept his hand down my shirt and shorts, dusting off my clothes. Remembering that I'd been wearing my special shirt, I grabbed Hello Kitty's bow, as if trying to protect her, and it discharged a plume of sand. Bashaye tried not to laugh.

"Come on. Let's go home and clean you up. I'll think of something to tell Mom and Dad."

I never found out what exactly he told our parents. I just knew that they didn't know the truth, because they did not tolerate fighting. It wasn't the Christian way or the Porter way, they'd say. Even so, because I was so small, my brother had started teaching me how to defend myself when I was seven.

I laughed as I thought about that day. Looking around the room, I realized it had not changed since Bashaye was alive. My mother cleaned his room every Tuesday—dusting, vacuuming, making sure everything was in its place. She even changed the sheets regularly. When she and my father redecorated the house, she made it clear that Bashaye's room was not to be touched. It was as if she feared changing his room would deny the fact that he ever lived. Maybe she feared that changing it would acknowledge the fact that he was dead. Whatever her reasons were, I knew her behavior wasn't healthy and so did my father, but he said that was the way she dealt with losing a child. If it meant allowing her to preserve Bashaye's memory through his belongings and his room, that was what we'd have to let her do. The strangest thing of all was that if a visitor came to the house and never saw my brother's room, he'd never know that Bashaye existed. When he died, Mom removed all of Bashaye's pictures and awards from the living room and the basement. She transferred them all to his room. It was only in his room that his legacy came to life.

Football and academic awards lined the top of his bookshelf. Run DMC and Whodini posters still clung to the closet door. The tape that held them in place had yellowed. Inside the closet Bashaye's clothes waited for something that would never happen. As I glanced at the color-coded, pressed clothing, I spotted what had been Bashaye's favorite sweater—a forest green and black Bill Cosby sweater with green leather patches. They used to call them that because Cosby often wore that type of sweater on *The Cosby Show*. Before I realized what I was doing, I had pulled the sweater off of the hanger and over my head. Maybe it was my imagination, but it still smelled like Bashaye—the scent was an unlikely mix of eucalyptus and cocoa butter. I found myself lodged between the narrow walls of the closet, struggling once again with the anger that began so many years ago.

Why did God choose him? He was so young—only seventeen. He was so ambitious and he didn't even have a chance to live. He was supposed to play college football on scholarship and go on to earn a law degree. He was supposed to marry some girl I'd deem nearly good enough for him, and they would make me an auntie. We were supposed to get together with our families and tell them stories of our childhood.

How could he leave me when he knew how much I needed him? He should have been there to put fear in the heart of my first date. He should have been there to see me graduate from high school. He should have been there to see me off to college. He should have been there to share the joy of receiving my degrees. He should have been there, but he wasn't. I still could not forgive him for leaving this world. I still could not forgive him for leaving me.

I was clenching my arms so tightly that my armpits began to sweat. Still, I sat there, rocking, wondering, questioning. After all of those years, I could not understand. I could not accept it.

A distant voice penetrated my thoughts and brought me back to the present. "Trinity?" it called.

"Yes, Mom?" I answered trying to swallow all traces of pain.

"What are you doing? I have something to tell you."

"Just finishing up in the bathroom." I pulled the sweater from my body, hurriedly replacing it on the hanger. "I'll be there in a second." I slipped across the hallway and into the bathroom. After splashing some water on my face, I pulled a comb from the drawer and ran it through my hair, which was in disarray from pulling the sweater over my head. Staring into the mirror, I whispered, "Keep it together, girl."

I walked toward the stairs, taking a deep breath. When I reached the last step, Mom was waiting, her eyes aglow like a child on Christmas day.

"Caroline is coming to town!"

My thoughts drifted back to my childhood. "Oh, great," I responded without inflection.

My cousin Caroline was very smart and, well, beautiful. Her hair was long, curly, and the darkest of browns. Her creamy skin had never seen a pimple, scar or blemish, and as she matured, her body put many models to shame.

She had never wanted for anything—my aunt and uncle would not have it any other way. When we were kids, Aunt Georgia treated Caroline like a porcelain doll. She never bought her pants, and she dressed her in frilly dresses, keeping her hair pulled back in obscenely sized bows every single day. Her play clothes were the equivalent of my Sunday best.

"She'll be here in less than two weeks. I told Georgia you'd pick her up from the airport."

"I know you did," I said. "But, uh, why can't her big sis' Lydia get her?"

"Shhh. Do you want Lydia to hear you?"

Lydia and the kids were in the basement with my dad and Chi-Chi.

I looked at Mom as if to say I really wasn't concerned.

"Lydia's schedule is too hectic," Mom rationalized. "Do you *mind* picking up your little cousin?" she asked, talking as if Caroline were five years old.

"Of course not, Ma." I really didn't mind. It was not like I had a life... or anything like it.

Caroline and Lydia were half sisters, and I hadn't seen Caroline since my college graduation party five years ago. She lived in Barrington, Illinois, with Aunt Georgia and Uncle Jonathan. Uncle Jonathan was my aunt's second husband and Caroline's father. They used to send Caroline to visit us in Detroit for a week or two every summer.

When Aunt Georgia married up to Uncle Jonathan, Lydia got rebellious. After Caroline was born, Lydia all but wanted to disassociate herself from her new family. Eventually, Aunt Georgia and Uncle Jonathan sent Lydia to Detroit to live with her father, who'd gotten a job working on the line at Ford after the divorce. Lydia would go back to Barrington for the summers. Interestingly enough, when Lydia was in Barrington, Aunt Georgia and Uncle Jonathan sent

Caroline to Detroit to stay with us. I think it was my aunt's attempt to bond with Lydia without Caroline around to steal the limelight. But Lydia and Caroline never bonded. Still, these days, it seemed that Lydia was taking more interest in Caroline, so maybe there was hope yet.

Chapter Three

It was Sunday morning, and I had been looking forward to going to church all week. I'd missed the service last week because I was so burned out from work. That week I had gone in early, stayed late every day and even went in on Saturday to prepare for a client presentation. So when Sunday came around, I only wanted to recoup and do last-minute preparations.

But this Sunday was different. I really wanted and needed to receive the Word. As usual, I attended service by myself. My parents still went to the church I grew up in. That church had many good memories, but it could have used a breath of fresh air—a breath of youthful air. My parents were considered young folk in their congregation. If you asked me, their service looked more like Heaven's waiting room with all of the walkers, oxygen tanks and old women in hats—big, huge hats! I had nothing against their congregation. I just wanted something different.

Most of my friends attended church sporadically and went to either Hartford or Greater Grace. I had visited both, but Ray of Light was my church home. I used to ride home with a girl in undergrad who was a member at Ray of Light. She always invited me to visit. I had graduated before I decided to take her up on the offer. By that time, she had moved to the Grand Rapids area to practice law, but I began attending regularly, and became a member after about six months.

Most of the time I just attended Sunday service, but I also helped out on the Communications Committee as well as with advertising for events. The congregation was a considerable size—about eight hundred members. Like many growing churches, it had two services. I chose the second. Getting somewhere before eight in the morning on the weekend usually didn't work out for me.

This morning I arrived at church fifteen minutes early. That gave me enough time to speak to folks and to get a decent seat. I took a program and sat about ten rows from the front, on the center aisle so I could see the reverend.

The choir marched in and we sang the processional hymn, "Leaning on the Everlasting Arms." During the announcements I thumbed through the program and found the day's scripture lesson. It would come from 1 Thessalonians 5:1-11. As covertly as possible, I opened my Bible to the index. I knew it was somewhere in the New Testament.

As a little girl, my grandmother, Ma Lo, would make me recite the books of the Bible. I liked to do them fast and rhythmically—like a nursery rhyme. Gen-e-sis, Ex-o-dus, Le-vit-i-cus, Numbers, Deut-o-ron-omy.... But those days were gone and with them, my skill for finding books of the Bible. I quickly located the book of 1 Thessalonians in the index, entered the page number in my short-term memory, closed my Bible and rejoined the congregation in listening to announcements.

As testimonies began, I dragged out my bookmark, located the page number for 1 Thessalonians and stuck the bookmark at the beginning of the book. When the scripture lesson was announced and the congregation was invited to turn to it, I would simply open my Bible and do a brief search for the chapter and verse. I would create an illusion—an appearance that I knew my Bible. No one had to know. Well, no one except God, but I didn't think He'd tell. I listened to bits and pieces of a testimony from Sister Mary Washington who was having hip surgery, Brother John Moore who requested prayers for his wayward brother, and a teenage boy who shared his thankfulness after a brush with death.

We had altar call, after which I assumed my seat and prepared to receive the Word. The choir sang "I Love the Lord." I closed my eyes in reaction to the chills that permeated my body as the soloist sang. Moisture wrapped my eyes as memories of Ma Lo singing that very song entered my mind. I twirled her wedding band—a simple, gold band about one-quarter of an inch wide. I had worn it on my right hand since my sixteenth birthday. I clenched my eyelids tightly, so not to shed the tears. I found myself mouthing the words, rocking gently as I drifted into another world with only the lyrics of the song on my heart and my grandmother's sweet memory on my mind.

As the choir finished and the soloist hit her final, moving note, I stood to my feet and clapped, filled with emotion. It was funny how something as simple as a song could move people on the inside.

When the reverend approached the pulpit, I felt my heart begin to beat slightly faster. Just as the choir had the power to move me to tears, Reverend Smiley had the power to move me to act. The sermon title was "If You Died Today." The thought alone affected my nerves. Reverend Smiley began to preach, exploring all facets of the lives of "part-time Christians," as he coined them. He touched on those church folk who get up in the morning without thanking God, forget Him once at work, neglect his Word in everyday life and prance around with a holier-than-thou attitude come Sunday morning.

He then posed the question: "Considering the way you've been living your life, would you go to Heaven or Hell if you died today?" Again I had chills, but this time it was different. The excitement I had felt before the sermon was disintegrating as I questioned my own dedication to Christ.

At the age of eleven, my grandmother's death hurt me more than anything I'd ever known. A year later, Bashaye's death hurt worse. After dealing with both, part of me had become numb to pain. I often carried my problems on my own shoulders, deciding not to bother God with my issues. He had more important things to handle, like terrorism, the plight of the homeless and bringing people back to Him after living wayward lives.

As Reverend Smiley continued to talk about part-time Christians, I felt as if he were talking directly to me. The man sitting next to me must have felt the same way. He looked to be about thirty-five or thirty-six. He was attractive, with skin the color of sable and jet-black hair interrupted by a striking gray streak. He had small, slanted, brown eyes and a beautiful smile that he flashed when he sat down. He was impeccably dressed in what looked to be an Armani suit accented with an eye-catching teal tie with hints of gray that matched his suit perfectly. Despite his cool, dapper appearance, I noticed him squirm as the reverend continued to call out members of the congregation without the use of names or specific incidents.

I glanced around and was almost certain that as the sermon progressed, people were shrinking in their seats. I wondered how many other people wanted to get up and run out of the service. I even got so desperate to remove myself from the discomfort that I discreetly clicked my heels three times in hopes of being zapped back to my car. It didn't work. I was still in the pew surrounded by others who looked as miserable as thirsty dogs on a sweltering summer day. Reverend Smiley finished, after what seemed an eternity. I was relieved. It was a wonderful sermon, masterfully crafted and arranged, but I just wasn't ready to hear it. Apparently, many other members of the congregation were not ready, either.

At the end of service, the reverend invited those who had not been saved to approach the altar so their fate in Heaven could be sealed. I was christened as a baby, but I had never taken action on my own to be saved. I wanted to be saved, but I was not ready today. I had already been embarrassed enough for the day.

Reverend Smiley stood at the altar with his arms lifted to the Heavens, calling for any congregation member to save his or her soul. Several came, but he still called. It was as if he were waiting for one more to change her life; waiting for one more to confirm a final resting place.

As I sat, he still called.

I couldn't get to the exit doors soon enough when service was over. I felt like I had been exposed—the jig was up! I was a part-time Christian, unworthy of all of my blessings. I was God fearing and I loved the Lord, but did I truly live for Him? Did I always give Him the praise He deserved, or did I find myself on my knees more during the hard times?

I called my parents from my cell phone. I knew they'd be home because they always went to early service at their church. It had been more than a week since I'd last joined them for dinner and I hadn't seen them since then because of work. So in that moment, I decided to take the plunge and cook dinner for my parents. As much as I ate up their food, it was the least I could do. Lasagna, Caesar salad and garlic bread were on the menu. Since I didn't cook often and had minimal food in my refrigerator, I made a beeline to the grocery store.

I hated going to the grocery store. No matter how many people were in the line I chose, I always managed to get in the slowest lane. Half of the time I went to the store, there were no baskets. The other half, I ended up with a basket that had a bum wheel. Additionally, because I often broke the number one rule of grocery shopping and went to the store hungry, I went home with more than I needed and more than I could afford.

This day was no different. I wondered if the Apocalypse had been predicted while I was in service, because it seemed everyone within a thirty-mile radius was at my Kroger store. I grabbed only what I needed, for once, and proceeded to the shortest line—only twelve people were in front of me. The line wrapped past two other checkout aisles. Suddenly my religion was lost.

Great. I can't stand this crap. Uncle Jimmy is right. I was meant to be single. I don't like going through this mess even for myself. And you think I'd do it for a man other than my daddy? What-ever.

I picked up the latest issue of Essence from the nearest magazine stand and began to thumb through it to pass the time. There was an article on why men cheat. I skimmed through it and boasted internally as I read.

I don't have to worry about my man cheating on me.

I often loved being single. Then again, it had been so long since I'd had a man, sometimes I got curious about being in a relationship. However, this was not one of those times.

"Ouch!"

Some little rugrat mistook the six-inch space between my foot and the aisle for a track lane. In his quest for the finish line, he stepped on my toe, which was exposed in my open-toed shoes.

"Apologize, Ricky!" the woman in front of me belted out. Grabbing his arm, she looked at me and said, "Miss, I'm sorry."

"Oh, that's okay." My toe was throbbing, but I still offered her a slight grin. I looked down at Ricky and gave him a glare that could kill. He stared up at me with a stream of snot flowing from his nose.

Ieww. Disgusting.

A sticky blue circle surrounded his mouth. The front of his shirt was a patchwork of candy residue that never made it inside his mouth. He was so dirty that I just wanted to pick him up and throw him in an endless sea of bath water. However, that would require me to touch him.

Just then, he tactfully inserted his finger in his nose. I clenched my cart and tightened my shoulders in preparation for what I was about to witness. It was like a scary movie that I couldn't turn away from. He moved his finger around and I felt my stomach turn. What was he going to do with it when he pulled it out?

Pleasedon'teatit. Pleasedon'teatit. Pleasedon'teatit.

He removed his finger, which was adorned with the biggest, greenest, slimiest—

"Trinity?"

My booger research had instantly been cut short. I jerked around to find a tall woman smiling at me. She had dark skin smooth as silk, and salt and pepper hair that hung loosely on her shoulders. I knew her, but I couldn't believe I'd run into her here, like this, now. I realized it was expected that I respond.

"Hello, Mrs. Parsons. How are you?" As I smiled nervously, I felt the muscles of my mouth losing strength. My hands and my knees began to tremble. She opened her arms and proceeded to give me a hug. I reciprocated, but it was as if I were hugging a ghost.

"It's been so long! You look great!" she exclaimed.

"Thank you. So do you!" My heart rate increased and I felt as if a fireball had exploded in each of my organs.

"What's been going on with you? Are you just coming from church?" she asked.

I struggled for a coherent response about church, my job, family and anything else I could blurt out. We had a brief conversation that was erased from my memory the moment she said, "Tony's home for a few months!"

"Oh?" My voice cracked as I tried to sound surprised. Suddenly, my neck began to itch. "Actually," I scratched my neck, "I saw him... briefly."

"Really? He didn't tell me!"

Hey guess what, Mom? I saw Trinity, and she slapped me in a bar full of people. Then she tried to emasculate me by calling me out by my name. That was nice of her, huh?

"You know, you should join us for dinner before Tony goes back to D.C."

Okay. What was one to say in this situation? "Actually, I despise your son. If I'm in a room with him and sharp knives are in the vicinity, there's a great chance I may stab him... repeatedly."

"How nice of you to invite me." I tried to sound interested.

"Well, our door is open. Come see us! I'll tell Tony I saw you!"

"Okay, great!" My pasted smile weakened with each second.

"I hope to see you soon, sweetheart!"

Seeing her son's face in hers, all I could do was wave, as she pushed her cart away and turned down one of the aisles.

I had just put the bread in the oven when my doorbell rang.

I opened the door to find my parents standing on the porch. They looked like they were posing for a picture.

"Hi! Almost ready. Come on in," I told them, exchanging kisses on the cheek with both of them.

My mother immediately walked into the kitchen. "What do you need me to do, baby?"

"I've got it. You and Daddy can sit at the table."

That wasn't good enough for her. "Well, let me do something. How about—"

"Mom, just sit at the table. It's already set. Relax, my love." I grabbed her hand and squeezed it between my own.

Reluctantly, she went into the dining room and sat next to my father. Ever since I was little, she had to be a part of every aspect of my life. When I was twelve, we started my period together. When I was sixteen, we went on my first date. When I was seventeen, we decided where I'd go to college. When I was nineteen, we almost lost our minds trying to convince ourselves it was worth it when I pledged Delta Sigma Theta Sorority. When I was twenty-three, we went on my first real job interview.

Well, she wasn't actually experiencing all of those events, but she sure acted like she was. From the big things to the little things like dinner for her and my dad, Mom wanted to be a part of it and make sure everything was just right.

During dinner, I managed to forget the day's earlier events and enjoy the company of my parents. They kept complimenting me on the meal, and I had to admit that even though I didn't like to cook, I was good at it. We discussed a whole gamut of topics from work to politics. After dinner, Mom invaded the kitchen instead of allowing me to clean it up by myself. But I soon found out that she had an ulterior motive.

"Have you met any nice young men, baby?"

This was getting old.

"Ma, I've told you, I really don't have time to date."

"You have time when you're sitting on that couch watching movies."

A quick squint of my eyes said, "Please stop."

"I know you're busy, but you should consider making time. The Lord may just send you your mate. You don't want to miss out on an opportunity because you weren't paying attention." She explained that she had a coworker with a single son who was two years older than me. He was a lawyer who had just finished law school, had never been married, had no dependents, blah, blah, blah. I finished drying off the last dish as my mother went on about this man.

"Yeah, Mom, maybe we can arrange that some time." I sliced a piece of pound cake from the bakery around the corner and handed it to her on a paper towel. "Here. Have some cake."

"Oh, baby, I'm stuffed. I couldn't possibly."

"Daddy might want it. Would you take it to him?"

She took the cake to my father, who was watching television in the living room. As much as I loved her, I was glad to get my pimp out of the kitchen for a few moments.

My parents left around nine, and I got ready for bed, changing into a baby blue cotton nightie. My mind drifted back to my encounter with Tony's mother. Mrs. Parsons was such a sweet woman. She had taken a liking to me when Tony and I first became friends. I felt so bad knowing that I had lied in her face earlier that day. I had no intention of setting foot on her doorstep.

I was washing my face when the phone rang. After splashing some water on my face to rinse away the soap, I grabbed a hand towel before going to answer it. Pressing the towel in my face, I walked back to my room and answered the phone without looking at the caller ID.

"Hey, Trin. It's Angel."

With water still dripping off my lashes, I opened my eyes to see if the caller ID matched the caller's claim.

"Angel?" I said with the same tone my mom used when combining the words "happy" and "single."

"You don't have to say it like that, do you?"

Why is my heart racing?

"Oh. You just caught me off guard," I responded.

"What are you doing on Saturday, the twenty-fourth?" he asked.

Saturday the twenty-fourth? I didn't know what I was doing *this* Saturday. Outside of going to work, I didn't know what I was going to do tomorrow. At that point I had absolutely nothing to do on the twenty-fourth. My schedule was a blank. Tabula rasa, baby.

"Well, I have a few things on my agenda early, then I'm planning to go out later that night. Why?"

Just like that, I'd filled my plate with imaginary plans. I could never give the appearance that I didn't have a life.

"I'm giving you advanced notice—me and Johnny are having a barbecue at my place. Come by when you get a chance. Bring some of your girls if you want, too."

"Oh, yeah? What time?"

"We'll start cooking around four, but *you* can come whenever you want," he answered flirtatiously.

"Whatever," I said trying to hide the fact that I was grinning.

"See, that's why I don't like to call you. You're always turning me down. My ego can't handle it."

"Nobody forced you to dial my number. Besides, you're the one who sets up dates then falls off the face of the Earth before I can even get a meal out of it," I responded.

We both laughed.

I wanted to have the upper hand in the conversation, so I decided to end it. "Well, I appreciate your invitation. I'll try to make it."

"I hope you do more than try. I'd like to see you, Trin."

"All right," I said without acknowledging his comment. "I'll talk to you later."

"Don't forget!" he said.

"Bye, Angel." I hung up before he could say anything else.

He'd like to see me? What's up with him?

As simple a thing as it sounded, Angel had never directly said that he wanted to see me. I figured it was just something else his ego could not handle. I thought I had him out of my system. After all, lusting after him was the precursor to my deciding to be celibate two years ago. I hadn't even seen him since I ran into him four months ago at a fundraiser. But something unexpected was happening. I could feel butterflies in my stomach as I hung onto his words. Maybe I should have been mad that he had the nerve to call me after so long, but part of me was anxious to see him and show him that I was doing quite well without him. I wanted to show him what he was missing. Maybe I just wanted to see what I was missing.

Chapter Four

S everal days passed and I found myself waiting for Caroline in a baggage claim terminal at Metro Airport. Her plane had been delayed due to storms in Chicago.

I can't believe this. A fifty-minute plane ride, already postponed forty minutes.

It was 8:55, and I hadn't eaten dinner. I had a deadline on the next day, so I'd worked late with the hopes that I'd miss the rush hour traffic. What I hadn't accounted for was the accident in the never-ending construction zone on I-94. Still, I managed to make it just in time to mumble would-be expletives at the flight board, which displayed "delayed," among an assemblage of "on time" flight listings.

"Excuse me, Miss." I approached an attendant at the check-in counter. "Can you tell me when flight 4244 is expected?"

"Don't know yet," she responded without making eye contact.

"Does *anyone* know?" I persisted. She pointed to a woman at another counter who was helping a family check in their luggage. "She might," she muttered while cracking her gum.

I have never understood why people like you get jobs working with the public.

The attendant I'd been directed to had just finished helping the family of four.

"Excuse me?" I folded my arms and rested them on the counter before realizing I'd come in contact with a multitude of invisible germs. I lifted my arms like a doctor who'd just scrubbed into an O.R. and slowly let them fall to my sides.

Does the five-second rule apply to touching dirty counters?

"May I help you?" the woman responded while punching keys sporadically on the keyboard in front of her monitor.

"Can you please tell me when flight 4244 will arrive from Chicago?"

"Oh, baby." She shook her head and puckered her lips—not in preparation for a kiss, but in anticipation of dashing my hopes. "It's delayed. I don't know what time it'll get in, but you'll know when I know. They'll show it on the flight board."

She gave me a polite but dismissive grin before addressing the person behind me. "May I help you?" I stepped to the side as she reached for a woman's boarding pass who struggled to get her suitcase to the scale.

That was... not helpful.

I left the counter and stood in the center of the big metal box that was the "old terminal," as it had been unofficially named. It was the only wing that had not yet been remodeled. There were no sparkly floors, sophisticated light fixtures or airport trams running through psychedelic tunnels with transitioning shades of purple, fuchsia and green. This wing only offered the basics.

My stomach rumbled over the voice of the flight attendant, who announced that another flight had been delayed. I had to find something to eat, but even with the delay, I didn't want to go too far. I would never hear the end of it if the plane landed and Caroline got to the baggage area before me. Before September 11, my mom believed in greeting people as they got off the plane. It was some fairy tale crap she picked up in her youth and expected the whole family to adhere to. Post-9-11, she still had expectations that we were to wait for people as they rode down the escalator to the baggage area.

My watch ticked to 8:58—only three minutes later than the last time I checked. I decided to head up the escalator and down a corridor where I spotted a Burger King. Usually, I did not eat fast food that late, but BK was sounding pretty good. I could practically taste a Whopper Jr. To my excitement, there was no line. Then I realized there was no one behind the counter, only one of those signs that read, "Back at..." with a clock below the writing. The arms of the clock were set to 9:30.

How is everybody at Burger King going to go on break at the same time? Don't they know I'm hungry?

There was a souvenir shop a little bit further down the hall, but the line was long and the cashier wasn't handling the crowd very well. I spotted a vending machine near the shop.

Thank you, Jesus!

As I approached it, my stomach became increasingly noisy. I spotted a Twix—exactly what a premenstrual girl was looking for.

Just two feet from the machine, I was cut off by a man in a big hat and cowboy boots.

Okay. It's cool.

I ventured to the depths of my purse in search of loose change while he made his selection. I scrounged up ninety-five cents just as the cowboy walked away.

I began depositing my money and looked at the machine to see what number my Twix was.

"Oh, hell no!" I yelled. I couldn't believe it. That wannabe cowboy took my Twix, and it was the last one in the machine. I turned to watch him walk farther and farther away.

Bring back my Twix! You jumped in front of me, and took my candy? Could you be ruder? It's because I'm a black woman, isn't it? After all of these years, am I still invisible to you?

I turned back to the machine, realizing that I was overreacting. The number "95" was lit up in red numbers. I figured I might as well select something. A child-sized bag of Cheetos caught my eye.

Ninety-five cents for that? I can buy it for fifty cents in the dollar store by my house.

My stomach growled again, and I understood that this was not the time to be cheap. I pushed the button, watching the coil that held the chips turn and stop before my Cheetos fell. They were hanging by a small edge.

I glanced around the premises to see if anyone was paying attention to me. A few people raced by, pulling their suitcases, cooing at their kids, and chatting away on cell phones. They were all on their own agendas. I grabbed both sides of the vending machine and used all of my might to shake the chips loose. The colossal glass box barely moved.

I should increase my upper-body weights at the gym.

Digging through my purse again in search of more money, I found only a quarter. My wallet held a five dollar bill and a twenty dollar bill. I had used all of my singles getting stamps earlier that day.

I can't believe this.

I don't know if it was mental, but at that very moment I became faint. I looked to my right; the souvenir shop was still booming. I looked to my left; there was a bar. Surely, they'd give me change.

I sat at the counter, feeling the stare of a couple of drunk old men. Their eyes seemed to say, "Hey. I wanna get lucky. How 'bout you?"

Yuck.

I trembled at the thought.

"Excuse me?" I said to the bartender who was fixing what looked like a Bloody Mary. "May I have change for a five?"

She slammed the drink down in front of one of the old men then turned my way and said, "Want change, you gotta buy a drink."

She was missing her left canine tooth.

"All right, give me a Sprite."

"Don't have Sprite, only 7UP" she said, wiping the counter.

Do I look like I really care? I just want some damn Cheetos. Give me a pop before another tooth rots in your hillbilly grill.

"That's fine," I responded, enunciating both words. She pulled a lever on the fountain machine, which squirted a minimal amount of pop in a cup that quickly filled to the brim over the heaping pile of ice.

"Two-fifty."

"For that?"

"Yep," she replied with a grin.

Can you get your teeth fixed, though?

"Here," I said handing her my five. I sipped my drink. It was watered down.

Ain't this about nothing.

She brought back my change and told me to have a nice night.

"Hmm," I said biting my tongue and hoping the night could only get better.

I went back to the vending machine and got my two bags of Cheetos. One bag was history by the time I got back to the baggage area. When I realized I did not have any gum, I sucked down the rest of the watery pop and swished it around in my mouth, attempting to wash down all of the particles that were now evidence of my indulgence. I hadn't seen Caroline in years. I didn't want her to think my breath usually smelled like Cheetos. I flipped off the top and tilted the cup back, letting the crushed ice hit my tongue before chewing it up. With another swig of the cup, I chewed up a mouthful of ice and grimaced at the pain that shot through my sensitive molars. I tossed the cup and applied pressure to my jaw, hoping to diminish the pain.

I went back to the baggage area and took a seat to the left of the escalator. With my purse on my lap, I let my back melt into the chair. I slipped my hands in my jacket pocket and realized that each one held a peppermint. Immediately, I knew my mom put them there, probably when I was at the house the other day. She had been doing that since I was a kid, because there was "no excuse for having bad breath or dirty clothes"—that's what she used to say to me and my brother. It was also what her mother used to say to her and my Aunt Georgia.

I sucked the life out of that peppermint as I fought to keep my eyes open. I watched people go up, come down, go up, come down. Lovers reunited, kids ran into the arms of their parents and business people glanced at their watches. They moved in predictable shifts, stepping off the escalator, stopping at the over-sized screens to find their luggage carousel, and scattering like roaches to their appropriate locations.

Then Caroline appeared on the escalator. I knew it was her—she hadn't changed much. Her hair was pulled up into a ponytail in the middle of her head with long waves falling from a large barrette. She wore a conservative navy dress and matching four-inch heels. A Gucci luggage case trailed her steps and a matching shoulder bag draped her arm. When she noticed me, her pink lipstick seemed to illuminate as she smiled. I watched her ride to the end of the escalator and walk toward me with bags in tow. "Hey, cuz!" I said and opened my arms for a hug.

"Hi, Trinity! You look good!"

"So do you, as usual! Did you check any bags?"

"Two."

"Dang, girl." I looked at her carry-on luggage. You're only here for three days."

Caroline laughed. "I know. Even with college, I haven't learned how to pack yet."

I reached for her left hand to see her engagement ring. "It's beautiful!" I gave her hand a slight twist to the right. "Platinum. Princess cut. Two carats plus some. He's got great taste!"

"Wow." Caroline looked puzzled. "How did you know that?"

"Oh, I worked at a jewelry store in high school and during my summer breaks in college. I guess it doesn't leave you." I smiled and released her hand. "Come on. Let's get your bags."

We chatted in the car about her studies at Northwestern and collegiate life. She was in her last year of the undergraduate engineering program and was engaged to a young man from England named Simon who was in Northwestern's graduate engineering program.

It was almost midnight before we got back to my condo. I was exhausted. I had been up since six in the morning and desperately longed for the feeling of my pillow against my face. Though I was still hungry, I chose sleep over food. After showing Caroline around the condo and getting her settled in her room, I realized I was happy to have her around. Now that we were older, we had a little more in common, and I looked forward to spending some time with her.

I changed into my favorite red Victoria's Secret pajama set. It was cotton and was about as sexy as things got in my bedroom. After I wrapped my hair and tied a scarf on my head, I turned out the light, curled up in the bed and turned on the news. The news was usually depressing and tonight was no exception. Four kids died in a house fire, a little girl was abducted and raped, and five people were killed when a passenger on a city bus shot the driver, causing him to run off the road and slam into four other cars.

Tears filled my eyes as I thought of all the families affected by these incidents. They were babies, mommies, daddies and siblings. Pushing aside the desire to lie in bed and go straight to sleep, I peeled back the covers and kneeled on the floor. I thanked God for my family, my friends and my blessings, while asking for courage for the people affected by each situation. I climbed back into bed and clicked off the television, shutting off the subtle signs of Armageddon that would not come to light again until morning.

Chapter Five

Caroline had been in town for two days. She made her rounds between my place, my parent's house and Lydia's house, and this weekend she was back at my condo. She had been begging me to take her to a club on Friday, so I told her we'd go to the D-Spot. It was the hottest club downtown, and though I didn't like the club scene, I wanted to take her so she could experience Detroit's nightlife.

Since I took my shower after dinner and had already ironed my clothes, it only took me about twenty minutes to get dressed. Mother Nature was still smiling on Detroit with warm temperatures in the month of May so I had picked out a black-and-white top with capped sleeves that looked fabulous with a knee-length black pencil skirt. I had gotten a pedicure after work, so I pulled a new pair of black heels from my closet. They were peep-toe with a crisscross pattern, resembling a cage, and had a dainty zipper that ran through the middle of the shoe. When I slipped them onto my feet,

I wiggled my toes to see the shine of the white stripes that covered the tips of my toes. The heel was high enough to make the definition of my calves pop.

I checked myself out in the full-length mirror. My attention was drawn to my hips and thighs, which I had inherited from my mom. Running track in high school had only made them bigger and weight lifting sustained them.

If I stop working out, I am in trouble.

Moving from the mirror to the jewelry box, I selected a pair of oversized Swarovski crystal hoops and three matching bangle bracelets. After running a comb through my hair, I noticed it was time for a trim. I lined my lips with my Mac Currant lip pencil and followed with a nude lipstick and a lip gloss for a natural but shimmery look. I usually thought of maintaining lipstick as a chore, but I loved Mac makeup and I wore it when I went out or had meetings at work. However, during my day-to-day dealings, I went natural, to the chagrin of my mother.

"How are you doin' in there, Caroline?" I asked while spraying a little Michael—my favorite fragrance—on my collarbone. I walked into the guest bedroom where I found her fumbling through her suitcase. She still had on her robe and her long locks were pulled into a sloppy ponytail on top of her head. Random pieces of it bounced on her shoulder.

"Caroline."

She jumped at the sound of my voice.

"I didn't mean to scare you," I said.

She snapped around to look at me and bit her index finger—an old habit. She did it when she was frustrated or nervous. "Oh, my, God! I am so confused. I don't know what to wear." She glanced at me and threw up her hands. "You look so cute. You have so many nice clothes!"

"Caroline, you brought four bags full of clothes and shoes. How could you possibly not have anything to wear?"

"I—I just don't know. Nothing looks right. I think I've put on weight in the last couple of weeks. Maybe I can fit in some of your clothes. Do you have anything I can wear?"

No, she didn't! This chick insults me by asking to wear my clothes because her skinny behind gained two ounces?

"What are you trying to say, Caroline?"

"Oh, if you're not comfortable with lending me something to wear, I understand. I just thought I might be able to fit in something of yours."

It totally went over her head.

"No, hun. I mean that I wear a size six. You're a zero—at best."

"I *was* a zero, but I know I've gained weight. Look at my stomach," she said rubbing it. "Look how big it is. I can't believe I'm getting so fat."

Without another thought, I pushed her down on the bed. What is wrong with you? You could eat like a fat-assed country heifer and still look like a twig. Why don't you just shove your finger down your throat?

"Trinity—what should I do?" Caroline asked, interrupting my sadistic fantasy. She was still flipping through her clothes. "Maybe we shouldn't go."

"Oh, no," I said with authority. "You didn't get me dressed and ready to go for nothing—not if you plan on sleeping here tonight." I picked up a black sleeveless dress that was thrown on the bed. "What's wrong with this?"

"I don't know. I—"

I handed her the dress. "Put it on." I turned to walk out of the room and closed the door behind me. I went into the living room and popped in a Boney James CD to calm my nerves.

A few minutes later, I heard Caroline's voice. "Trinity, how does this look?"

I walked back into her bedroom. She was wearing the dress with black sandals that showed her bright pink toenails. She was fidgeting with her hair, which she had taken out of the ponytail.

"You look cute, Caroline." And she did, but she would have looked good in a fifteen-year-old beady and faded sweat suit.

"Are you sure, because I don't know what this club is like and I—"

"Caroline, sweetie, you'll be fine. I'm going to get my purse together and let you finish getting ready."

"Okay. I just need to do my hair and makeup," she said heading to the bathroom.

I *said* she'd be fine, but I wasn't so sure. It wasn't the outfit I doubted. Caroline had grown up with a bit of an identity crisis. She'd lived in the suburbs all her life and had gone to premiere private schools since kindergarten. When she was younger and came to Detroit to visit us every summer, she saw more black people in two weeks' time than she'd see all year in Chicago's suburbs.

I remember one summer when she came to visit. She had a favorite doll—a Cabbage Patch Kid. They made black ones and white ones. Hers was white. When Mom asked Aunt Georgia why she didn't buy Caroline black dolls to help her appreciate her heritage, she said she'd given her black dolls and Caroline wouldn't play with them.

My mother made it a point to buy me black dolls to help me with self esteem. She always talked about how they didn't make black dolls when she was a little girl and she wanted to see that I didn't have the same experience. It was something she really regretted about her childhood—especially growing up in the South when society taught folks that only white was right. Unfortunately Caroline's environment also taught her that dark skin, ethnic features and nappy hair equated to ugliness and inferiority. The fact that she possessed none of these features only complicated things.

My thoughts drifted back to a conversation we had one summer in the neighborhood park.

⁂

"I'm white."

"What?!" I said, giving Caroline a sideways look.

"I'm white, so I'm pretty."

"You're pretty, but you ain't white," I said with my hand on my hip.

"Yes I am. Look at me." She extended her arm and put it next to mine.

"Just because you're light doesn't mean you're white. You're black just like your mama, just like your daddy, just like me. And I'm your first cousin."

"I am white! Look at my skin. Look at my hair." She flipped her hair with her hand as if her name were Cindy Crawford. "Look at my lips."

"You know what? You crazy," I said and jumped up on the monkey bars.

I shook my head at my recollection and placed the glass of cranberry juice I was drinking on the coffee table. I went toward my room to get my purse. Caroline was bent over in the guest bathroom, wringing out her hair in a towel. She flipped it back like one of those picture-perfect white girls in the old Prell commercials.

"Caroline, what are you doing?" I asked as she violently tried to brush out the tangles in her wavy locks.

"My hair totally won't look right when I wear it down unless I wet it," she responded while playing tug of war with the brush.

"Oh," I said walking to my room. "I just hope you don't get sick. It's a bit windy tonight."

"I'll be all right," she said. "I do this all the time."

I giggled as I thought about what my hair would look like if I did that "all the time."

"Come on, girl." I flipped the light off in my room. "Let's try to get there before the club closes."

I slowed the car down as we approached the club so we could get a good look. The line was out the door and all the way to the end of the building.

The last thing I wanted to do was stand in a line.

This girl better like this stupid place. I'm getting too old for this mess.

"Oh my, God! There are, like, so many people here," Caroline said.

"Always on Friday nights," I responded. I glanced at Caroline in the passenger's seat to see if I could catch her expression. Her eyes expanded as she looked around like a tourist in a foreign land. I began to prepare myself in case she might chicken out, crawl under the dash and beg me to take her back to the condo.

I pulled into an adjacent parking lot. A scruffy man with an ungroomed beard and matted black hair came out of the attendant's box and was approaching the car. He wore a faded T-shirt with "Can't Touch This" written across the front, a pair of dirty jeans and some dingy gym shoes that were run over from wear.

"Can't touch this?" Caroline questioned. "Wasn't that MC Hammer, like, two decades ago?" I tried not to laugh because now he was at my window.

"Eighdolluh," he said sticking his hand in the car window.

"What did he say? Why is he in the window? Ieww," Caroline said.

"Eigh," he repeated abruptly holding out his hand, palm up.

"If you could back up just a bit, I'd be happy to pay you," I said.

He did, and I pulled the money out of my purse and handed it to him. He passed me a blue ticket for the window, and I made my way to a parking spot.

"How could you understand what he said?"

The truth was, I was fluent in ver-Black-ular. "It's a talent," I told her with a grin.

I parked in a spot and turned off the car. "Okay, let's go!"

When we walked toward the club, I spotted a promoter who had taken a liking to me some six months earlier at the annual holiday party my current sorority chapter hosted every year. He was chatting with one of the security guards when we approached him.

"What's up, Jay?"

"Hey, Trinity!" He leaned in and hugged me, and I introduced him to Caroline. Jay let us know that he was hosting the party and would get us in free. It sounded like a plan since they were charging twenty dollars at the door. We entered and walked up a flight of stairs to get to the dance floor. A mass of heat thickened with each step.

"It is crowded in there," I said to Caroline, who trailed me.

"How can you tell?" she asked. "We haven't even gotten within view of the dance floor."

"Body heat rises, and I am hot!" I said. I feigned heat stroke, holding the back of my hand to my forehead and pretending to be weak. Caroline's eyes got big and she pushed out a nervous giggle.

We reached the top of the stairs and looked around. "Dude, there are sooo many people in here," Caroline yelled.

Did she just call me dude?

I shook my head, then grabbed her wrist and pulled her through the crowd. The music was resonating and bodies were gyrating accordingly. There was a small area just large enough for us to observe our surroundings without too much friction. One of my favorite house music songs came on and I began to sway to it.

"I've never heard this kind of music. It's cool!" Caroline said.

"Don't you hear this all the time in Chi-town?" I asked.

She pondered for a second then answered, "I'm not sure."

Now, I knew we were talking about Chicago—a city that carried a huge house music following, yet she had no idea what she was listening to. Interesting.

"'Scuse me. Can I talk to you for a minute?"

My view of Caroline was suddenly blocked by the back of some brutha's head.

"Umm, I was kind of talking to my cousin," Caroline replied.

He was wearing an orange suit with a matching dob and gator shoes. He looked like The Great Pumpkin that Linus waited so patiently for in the pumpkin patch. If there was one thing I couldn't stand, it was a man who wore more flamboyant outfits than I did.

I could tell Caroline was intimidated by his app-earance. He turned to me and smiled apologetically. "Oh, my bad, sis." He turned back to Caroline and her figure, and proceeded to test his best "club lines" on my cousin. Anyone watching could see her disin-terest, but she politely continued to humor him with conversation.

Caroline tapped me. "I'll be right back, Trinity. He's going to buy me a drink."

"Want sum'in?" he asked me.

"No, thank you."

"I-ight," he said.

I wanted to hand him a phonics book.

"Watch your drink," I told Caroline. She nodded and followed The Great Pumpkin to the bar.

I was enjoying the music and taking in the scenery. Ballers, sophisticates, hoodrats—they were all here try-ing to be seen. They were all busy fronting like they lived a life they really didn't. My eyes fell upon a guy spilling money like water, buying bottles of Cristal.

He probably lives in his mother's basement.

"How you doin'?" A deep voice interrupted my observation. Before I could respond, a face was so close to mine that I had to step back to see it clearly.

"I'm fine, thank you," I responded and stepped back several more inches as a putrid odor burned my olfactory senses. He proceeded to try his hand at some tired lines that I paid little attention to. My concern was with understanding why this funky-breathed man felt the need to keep only four inches between his mouth and my nose. I heard his voice in the background, but all I was able to decipher were my own thoughts.

What... did he just chew a lump of shit and rinse with a shot of whiskey?

"So, uh, you think I could take you out some time?" he asked.

By this time I was taking short breaths and monitoring my breathing so as not to inhale any funk unnecessarily. "No, I don't think that would be a good idea," I said, then forced a smiled and stepped away so I could exhale. "Wow! That makes no sense," I said out loud.

"Girl, what's wrong with you?"

I didn't realize anyone was paying attention to me as I talked to myself. It was Jay, the promoter.

"I'm all right," I said and looked at him. He could tell I was a little embarrassed. "So what's been going on in your world?" I asked.

"Same ol', same ol', you know?" he said shrugging his shoulders. "You're looking quite nice tonight." His eyes followed the curve of my body.

"Thank you," I said, pretending not to notice.

"Can I get you something to drink?" he asked.

"I'll just take some cranberry juice, thanks."

"Straight?" He drew back and looked at me as if I were certifiable.

"Yes. Straight." I smiled and said, "Come on. I'll go to the bar with you."

I didn't trust men around my drinks, especially in public settings—even if the drinks weren't alcoholic. I wanted to see the transition from bartender to buyer to me.

The bar was ridiculously crowded. I touched my hair—the roots began to rise while the ends fell. Tiny beads of sweat formed on my upper lip. When Jay passed me the juice, I slurped it down, attempting to drench my insides. I felt like a replenished sponge, wet after being left out to dry for several days.

Jay and I chatted for a while. He was a cool guy, but he talked about his job as a promoter a bit more than I cared to hear. When it seemed we were on the verge of running out of things to say—or things for me to listen to—I thanked him for the drink and excused myself before the situation became too awkward. It was probably time to look for my cousin, anyway.

Getting out of the vicinity of the bar was a task in itself. I attempted to get back to the area where Caroline and I had settled when we first arrived, but it was occupied. I picked a nearby spot where Caroline could find me easily and glanced around the room looking for her.

I did some people-watching while I was at it. Spotting a female who was rather attractive, but obviously intoxicated, I watched her let some guy grope her from behind on the dance floor. She bent over, rubbing her butt on his thighs, revealing a white bra underneath a low-cut black dress. As she danced, her dress, which was barely longer than a T-shirt, rose up, revealing her stretch-marked thighs. The guy circled his hands all over her pouchy midsection. Their grinding was disgusting me, but it was so funny that I had to watch.

"Heyee!"

Caroline popped up at my side. I forgot that I was supposed to be looking for her.

"Hey, Caroline!"

Her eyes were glazed, and she held a drink that was filled to the brim.

"That's not the same drink you left for a while ago, is it?"

"No, this is my third," she said giggling. "These are good!" She looked like a little kid, pointing to the magenta-colored drink in a martini glass.

"Have fun, but know that it's been a long time since I've hauled a drunk friend or family member out of an establishment or held her hair while she tossed her cookies into a toilet. Quite frankly, it's not my favorite thing to do. Take it slowly, okay?"

"I'll be fine," she said smiling ear to ear. We chatted a while, mostly about the characters in the club. Bug-a-boos tried to make eye contact, but I ignored them by giving the appearance that I was engrossed in my conversation with Caroline.

"Trinity, why do you keep ignoring every guy who looks at you?"

I touched her shoulder. "Have you seen the guys who are looking at me, Caroline? I'm a jerk magnet."

Caroline laughed hysterically at my comment.

It wasn't that funny.

I tilted my cup, which held only a few pieces of melting ice cubes, and popped one into my mouth.

"Princess!" I heard a voice say. No one had called me Princess since high school. The sound of that name sent a chill up my spine, and for a moment I swore Bashaye's voice delivered it.

An overweight, brown-skinned man was standing at my side, grinning strongly. A tucked in, button-down turquoise shirt could not hide his stomach, which looked like it was regularly sustained with plenty of pork, beef and beer. He was clean. His cream-colored slacks were creased as if they had just been serviced at the dry cleaners and his turquoise Stacy Adams shoes and matching belt topped off his outfit. My eyes traveled back to his face, which was lined with a thin beard and moustache. A scar hovered over the bridge of his nose and intersected his left eyebrow. I looked into his eyes, and it finally clicked.

"Ah, *hell* no!" I said, louder than usual.

"Damn!" he said. "You look good! You *look* like a princess now, girl."

"Lil Mike," I said in a matter-of-fact tone.

He opened his arms and gave me a hug that if perpetuated, would have required my resuscitation. He pushed back from me, but his hands still grasped my shoulders. "Girl, I ain't seen you in a minute! Last time I saw you, you was still in a training bra."

"Shut up, Mike!" I said, stepping back slightly.

"Yeah, you still got that attitude. I can still see that same fire in your eye you had when you kicked my ass!"

"And I can see you still have that scar from when I busted you in your big ol' hard head!"

We laughed and hugged again. I hadn't seen Mike since he graduated from high school—after failing a grade or two before it was all over. I remember that he went off to Texas to go into the military. As I had heard through the neighborhood grapevine, he was dishonorably discharged.

"So what have you been up to, Mike?" I asked.

"Ah, you know, I'm just livin'. You know I just got out two weeks ago."

"Out of the military?" I asked trying to act like I didn't know about his discharge.

"Nah, girl," he laughed. "I was locked up for a minute. I caught a case a year ago, but you know...." He shrugged his shoulders. "I'm straight now." He nodded with satisfaction.

"Oh, okay," I said, trying to sound upbeat and appear as if his comment had not fazed me, but all I could do was wonder how I could have missed that major piece of information. "Oh. Mike, do you remember my cousin, Caroline?"

He looked at Caroline as if she were a smothered pork chop. "Miss Priss? That's Miss Priss?" he asked.

"Uh-huh, I remember." He sucked his teeth and tapped her arm. "You tight, you tight."

Seriously?

Caroline giggled then she leaned toward me. "Why did he call me Miss Priss?"

"I'll tell you later," I said, entertained by her cluelessness (or maybe it was forgetfulness). Everyone in the neighborhood called her Miss Priss when she'd visit as a child because she was like a walking, talking doll that had found its way down from a display shelf. Everything from head to toe was pristine, and her mother never let her wear a dress twice within a month's time. She was so very different from the kids in my neighborhood who dressed for play and didn't care if outfits were repeated week to week.

Mike and Caroline struck up a conversation about the summers she had spent here. He flirted with her shamelessly and for some reason she flirted back. I excused myself to walk around. I chatted with a few people I knew from high school, work and the gym. Bored with the scene, I headed back to where Caroline and Mike were. They were still talking in the same spot.

"I'm leaving with Mike tonight."

I looked around because I knew those words could not have possibly come from Caroline's lips.

"Mike who?" I said looking in her eyes for any sign of intelligent life. Caroline repeated herself.

"I'm having so much fun talking to him, and he invited me over so—"

"It's almost two in the morning. You think he invited you over to finish talking?"

"Oh, he's cool," she said flicking her wrist with unconcern.

"You're talking about a virtual stranger who hasn't seen hooha in a year. Are you stupid?"

"He told me about the whole jail thing, okay? But, I mean, I trust him. He's cool."

"Oh, so you established that in fifteen minutes, Caroline?"

She rolled her eyes and put her free hand on her hip. "What's wrong with having a fling?"

"A fling? You're sitting up here with that big rock on your finger and you're talking about having a fling with that—" I stopped myself and cupped my hand to my chin.

"Let's go, Caroline." I grabbed her hand and started toward the door. She stumbled behind me before snatching her hand from my grip.

I know this little girl is not about to cause a scene. I just know it.

"I take care of myself every single day and live by my own rules when I'm at school. Just because you're my 'big cousin' doesn't mean this is any different. I'm not that drunk! I know what I'm doing." She peered at me with the blood vessels in her eyes protruding. I gave her a once over.

What am I supposed to do with this mess?

"Caroline, you begged me to bring you here tonight. I did. I did not even want to come to this inferno. I'm in here sweating my hair out, getting hit on by cads smelling like funky cigars, just to get in my car and drive home by my damn self? Oh, no. We came together. We leave together," I said.

"Trinity. I'm a big girl. I'll be okay. See ya!" She turned to walk toward Mike. I grabbed her arm and her drink spilled in the motion. "Dammit! Look what you made me do. Now I've got liquor all down my arm," she whined.

"Be happy that liquor isn't running down your face! Don't test me, Caroline." I closed my eyes and took a deep breath. "Look, if you want to do me like that, it's one thing, but why would you do this to Simon?" I asked.

"I'm not doing anything to Simon. He'll never find out. It's not like I'm married yet."

Her words made my head spin. "Just like that?"

She didn't respond but her eyes showed her intentions.

I dropped her arm and cracked my knuckles to release the tension. "It's your life, Caroline."

With that, the drunken ding-dong bounced away. Mike was waiting by the door. He took her hand, and I watched them disappear.

Someone stepped on my toe, bringing my attention back to my immediate surroundings. "Ouch!" I looked up to see that funky-breathed brother from earlier. I looked toward the heavens.

Lord, will this night ever end?

"Sorry, sis," he said, then smiled at me. "Hey, cutie. I didn't catch your name earlier."

"That's because I didn't drop it." I walked toward the door with an angry switch added to my stride. I figured he had called me everything but a child of God by the time I reached the door, but I didn't think twice about it. I was fed up.

During my drive home, I wondered if I had done the right thing with Caroline. I could have chased her down, thrown her in my car and argued with her all the way home. That way I would have known she was okay and would not have to be concerned for her safety. I didn't even know where Lil Mike lived. But Caroline did have a point. She was grown. Grown and stupid maybe, but still grown. I couldn't help but feel sorry for Simon.

When I drove up to my condo, I pulled my phone from my purse and called Caroline's cell. It went straight to voicemail. I rotated the phone in my palm and looked to the star-dotted sky. "Lord, you take care of babies and fools. Caroline is no baby. Please watch over her with your mercy."

I walked up to my doorway and kicked off my shoes before I even got in the door.

I can't believe I paid eighty dollars for these sandals and they hurt!

The plush carpet soothed my feet as I walked to my bedroom. I flicked on the light switch just to witness the bulb burn out.

Wonderful.

Plopping on the side of the bed I rubbed my feet in darkness. A red light was flashing on my nightstand. It was the phone's voicemail light. I checked my messages, and the first was from Malik, my best male friend from high school. The second was from Lydia, and the third was from Simon. In his British accent, he said he had just come in from working late during his internship and wanted to hear Caroline's voice.

"Call me when you get this message, honey. I tried your cell, but kept getting your voicemail. I'll wait up. Goodnight."

I chuckled and hung up the phone. "You must not want to sleep tonight, Simon."

The next morning I awoke with an attitude. I still couldn't believe that little hussy left with Mike.

Well, I did tell her not to plan on sleeping at my place last night if we didn't go out.

I said that regarding her attempt to renege after I got dressed. Still, my words had come back to haunt me.

I left for my morning jog and did three miles. Glancing at my watch, I realized I ran the course in less than thirty minutes.

That's a first.

Feeling rather accomplished, I rounded the corner to my condo building with nothing but a glass of water on my mind. I wiped my forehead and pulled my

T-shirt away from my chest, allowing a slight breeze to dry the sweat.

An old, gray Impala was parked in front of the building but I thought little of it... until the passenger door opened. Out popped Caroline. She'd made her way right back to my doorstep. Before she could even reach the walkway, Mike pulled off. She hadn't seen me, so I thought about turning around to extend my jog while she rang my doorbell. I watched her bounce to my door and knock on it. I stepped back and around a corner. I could see her, but she could not see me. It was kind of funny watching her standing on my porch in last night's clothes and makeup and what was left of her hairstyle. I broke into a light jog and got close enough to be within her view.

"Oh, hi!" she said jovially as I approached the door.

"Morning," I replied dryly with heavy breathing, playing the part of an exhausted athlete. My blood pressure rose as I opened the door with her standing behind me. I couldn't stand to be in her presence, but clearly, she had not gotten the memo. Caroline babbled endlessly about how much fun she had at the club and what she wanted to do today. I downed two glasses of water while her voice chewed at my eardrum.

Would you please shut up?

I ripped my damp shirt from my body and headed to my room, wearing a sports bra and a pair of running pants. Caroline followed me. Her lips were still moving. I threw my shirt in the laundry basket, took off my shoes and socks, then turned the light on in my bathroom. She was still talking and followed me as I entered the bathroom. I twisted the shower knobs and gave Caroline a look.

"Oh, I'll let you take a shower." Caroline smiled and bounced off, tripping over her own feet on the way out. "Woops!" she said before rounding the corner to the hallway. I grinned mischievously.

Sometimes it's life's little pleasures....

The hot shower was so refreshing that I almost forgot I did not have my place to myself—until I opened the bathroom door.

"Mike is sooo much fun!" Caroline yelled from her bedroom. She went on and on about this loser so much that I actually began to listen. I even tried to find something rational in her thinking. I went to my dresser, pulled out the first shorts outfit that required little ironing and slipped it on.

"You talk as if you like Mike. What about Simon?" I asked.

"What do you mean?" she asked.

I stepped into the hallway. She stood in the doorway of her room.

"Caroline, you're engaged," I said.

She didn't seem to see any point in my observation. "Engaged... not married," she retorted.

I shook my head and bit my lip, allowing the disappointment to show on my face. Heading to the living room, I thought about our brief conversation. I never understood why people entered the institution of marriage if they didn't recognize its sanctity. Too often, people married for reasons outside of God's intention—yes, to procreate, but also to be an example to others on how to face the world's problems with Christ as the center of the home. Well, that was my interpretation of God's intention for marriage, but I was just a single person who was light years away from the prospect of marriage. Still, in so many places I looked, it seemed that marriage had been turned into a matter of sex, convenience, money or fear of loneliness. How did God feel when day after day, we made a mockery of such a wonderful gift to mankind?

I figured many people didn't feel the way I did. Apparently Caroline was one of them. Maybe her opinions were learned rather than innate. She and everyone in our family watched her father cheat on Aunt Georgia for years. As a partner at his law firm, Uncle Jonathan had many business trips and late nights at the office. Though everyone knew about it, not a word was ever spoken about his infidelity. He loved his family and took care of them, but he'd had a mistress for as long as I could remember.

Some women thought it was okay for their men to stray as long as the bills were paid and a warm body came home on most nights. I guess this is how my aunt saw things. Maybe it was easier for her to stay than to leave and risk losing the comfortable life she knew. Through it all, I think she still felt her life was better now than it was when she was with Lydia's blue-collar father, whom she'd married for love.

I think Caroline's parents' relationship shaped her understanding of marriage. What kind of relationship would she and Simon have if she were acting like a ball of hormones while wearing his ring?

"Lydia wants you to call her before you leave. And Simon called last night," I spoke loudly enough for Caroline to hear me from the bedroom. I took a Gala apple from the refrigerator and checked its firmness before taking a big bite.

"What did he say?" she asked. I grabbed the telephone from the kitchen and put in my voicemail code then walked the phone to her.

"Press one," I said and went to the living room couch with my apple and the television remote.

She was silent while she listened to the message but moments later I heard her say, "Hi sweetie! I'm sorry I missed your call," sounding so sincere. Then I heard her tell Simon that she forgot her cell phone at my place before we went to the loft apartment of one of my fictional friends who lived near the Detroit River. Apparently we'd stayed over because I'd had too much to drink and fell asleep.

This little biddy is too much!

I tried to tune her out, focusing my attention on the apple, but before I knew it, she was standing next to me.

"What are you watching?" she asked.

"Sports Center," I said without looking in her direction.

"Are you serious? That's what Simon was watching!" she exclaimed.

Woo hoo! What straight man doesn't watch Sports Center?

She plopped down on the couch and went on to talk about Simon's internship, before going right back to talking about Mike. The sun was peering into the window and revealed a hickey above her left breast. My head went into the same spin I'd experienced the night before.

"Caroline?" I cut her off. I turned off the television and faced her so I could look into her eyes. "Honey, do you really want to do this? Get married, I mean. Are you sure you're ready?" I asked.

Her eyes fluttered. "Well, yeah. I don't understand what you're asking. You're making a bigger deal out of this than it is. I love Simon."

I didn't say a word. Instead I looked into her eyes and searched for an answer there. When the gaze got tense, she looked away.

"Do you mind if I turn the TV back on?" she asked trying to remove herself from the spotlight.

"No. Here." I passed her the remote.

She flipped through the stations until she came to an old Brady Bunch rerun. I heard her laugh periodically and though I looked at the TV screen, my thoughts were elsewhere. She just didn't get it. Or maybe I didn't get it.

And my mother doesn't understand why I was unattached to a man and to the idea of being married.

The next day, I took Caroline to the airport. She called Mike before leaving my place to tell him good-bye, but he didn't answer. She left a message with her cell phone number. He didn't call her back—at least not before she got on the plane. In the car she babbled about getting back to Illinois, school and Simon. Her prattling continued right up to the moment I pulled up to the departure curb. Caroline got a skycap to help her with her bags. We hugged and I watched her hasten to the automatic sliding glass doors that led to the terminal. She turned around one last time and waved. "See you at the wedding, Trinity!"

She was out of my view, on her way to Illinois, where Simon was waiting for her.

Chapter Six

Caroline had been gone for a week, and the day of Angel's barbecue had come. He left a voicemail to remind me, but I had been debating about whether I was going. Confession: The only debate was over what I would wear.

My thoughts drifted back to a game of Spades that I'd played with Angel, Johnny and Ramona about a year earlier. Angel was my partner; Ramona was Johnny's. Johnny and Angel were best friends and Ramona was... I don't know what she was—other than always around. About half an hour into the game, Angel began to give himself the praises.

"I am the King! I can't be beat."

What-ever.

His self-praise didn't bother me. I let him live in his illusionary world. He was used to other females sweating him, but sweat him, I would not.

Still, he did look nice that night. The outline of his shoulders and biceps emerged from a T-shirt with the muscular precision I would expect to accompany the lost limbs of the Apollo Belvedere torso. His freshly cut hair was begging me to run my fingers through its uninterrupted waves. I watched his full lips curl around the brim of a beer bottle and release it before he lowered the bottle to the table. They curled once again to reveal the whitest, straightest set of teeth I had ever seen. When he laughed at a joke with Johnny, a small dimple spread on his right cheek just as he turned to me and said, "Right, Trin?"

"Yep," I said with little enthusiasm and no idea what I had affirmed. I did not make eye contact because I knew if I looked at Angel, I would surely melt like butter.

He is not that fine.

At least I'd never let him know I thought he was. My mind wandered back to the art-like structure of Angel's body, but Ramona eventually distracted me. I wasn't sure what had transpired between them while I was daydreaming, but Ramona began tearing into Angel like a knife.

"Please! You'll sleep with anything that walks. All she has to do is have a pair of legs and you'll have her in your bed. A name isn't even required."

They engaged in a back-and-forth war of tongues. Between her insults and accusations regarding his sexual activity, Angel let out a "whatever" or a sarcastic "okay." The rest of us responded to their dialog with laughter. Only, they laughed because they thought it was funny. I laughed because I felt the timing was appropriate. Outside, a storm was approaching. Thunder rumbled as Ramona continued to throw spears at Angel. On the end of each jab was another accusation, and she only got louder and louder.

"Playa, playa!" one of the guys yelled at Angel from the couch.

I wanted to crawl under the table, shrivel up and disappear. Was she doing this to make me jealous? Was she trying to make me feel stupid? Did she know that I had slept with him? Had she slept with him? Was she telling the truth? I didn't know the answers to any of the questions swirling around in my head. All I wished for was the power to reverse what had been done, to slap the shit out of her, to slap the shit out of him and to fly away. But all I could do was sit there and fake it.

What was I doing? Why did I want to go to the stupid barbecue? What if Ramona were there? Would he have invited me if she was going to be there? Ooh, I hate her.

The phone rang. It was Toya telling me she was picking up Gina—our childhood friend—and coming to get me for the barbecue. The plan was to stay for an hour and tell Angel we had to leave for some fabulous destination that was actually yet to be determined.

I hung up the phone and muttered to myself, "Trin, you're in now. You might as well roll with it."

It was eighty-three degrees outside so I figured a sexy sundress was the way to go. I chose a halter crimson sundress that tied around the neck. I would wear it with a pair of black T-strap sandals. As a bonus, I was having a "clear skin day," so flawless was the look I was going for... not that I was trying to impress Angel.

Toya and Gina got to my house about ten minutes after five, and I drove us to Angel's. His street was lined with Victorian-styled homes that, despite standing for the better part of a century, were well cared for. We parked across the street. Angel's house was sand-colored with beige trim and was one of the only ones on his block with a porch that had room enough for a swing. A couple of girls walked toward Angel's house and turned around when we opened the car doors.

"Sorry. Ain't nothin' anyone in this car can do for you, darling," Gina said to the girls as she got out of the car.

"You are a mess!" I told her.

The girls turned around again, and we all started laughing.

"Why are you trying to start something?" Toya asked as everyone got out of the car.

"I'm too old to be fighting. Besides, if your daddy found out you started this, he'd be on your behind quicker than that time you stole Apple Now and Laters from the corner store," I said to Gina.

Toya laughed.

"Why'd you have to bring that up, Trin?" Gina asked.

"Because I remember that... and it was funny!"

Two guys were leaning on a truck drinking beer as we made our way to the backyard. I could feel their eyes following us as we passed.

"Take a picture. It'll last longer," Gina muttered.

"Ooh. Is someone having a bad day? Who ticked you off?" I asked.

"Girl, I'm just tired of putting up with Justin's father," she answered.

After high school, Gina went to UCLA on academic scholarship. She met Kenny, who's from Toledo. He got her pregnant in her junior year. She and Kenny had been on again, off again ever since. Despite having Justin, Gina managed to finish school in five years and graduated from UCLA's School of Theater, Film and Television, although she hadn't yet used her degree.

"If I were big enough, I'd dropkick his pudgy ass," Gina said about Kenny.

"You can take him out. Remember what my mom used to tell us. Go for the nuts!" Toya said as she did her bob-and-weave impression. We burst into laughter, forgetting for a moment that we were among strangers who'd not been clued into our joke.

We made it to the backyard, where there were about twenty people and no more chairs. I spoke to those I didn't know before spotting Tim, Angel's housemate, just yards away, inside the detached garage. Strategically, he played the roles of both grill master and disc jockey.

He looked up after tossing a burger on the grill. "Hey, Trin! Glad you made it."

I waved. "Hi, Tim." I kept my distance so I would not interfere with his double-duty work. When I first met Angel, I thought it was a red flag that he had a house-mate at age twenty nine, but he explained that Tim's job required him to travel more than two hundred days out of the year, so he was rarely home and needed a steady place to stay when he was in town. The fact that he was willing to pay a decent amount of rent was gravy to Angel.

Angel and Johnny were nowhere to be seen. We made our way into the house to find somewhere to sit, but it was hotter in the house than it was outside. Johnny was in the kitchen seasoning chicken breasts and wings.

"What's up, girl?" he shrieked then kissed me on the cheek. Each time I heard his nasally voice, I got a vision of Bert from Sesame Street singing to his beloved pigeons.

Johnny and Toya spoke, having met before. When I introduced Johnny to Gina, his interest was obviously piqued, but her body language cut him off at the pass.

"Angel's upstairs. There are some seats in the living room," Johnny said.

Small sweat beads were rising from the pores on my chest.

"You know what—if you can tell me where some more folding chairs are, we'll just sit outside," I told him. Johnny pointed us toward the garage and we set up the chairs in a shaded spot on the grass.

"Would've been nice if he got the chairs for us," Toya said.

"Right, but he probably wouldn't have gone back to the kitchen," I added.

"Ooh. No, thank you!" Gina said.

They both went to the grill for some barbecued burgers and chicken, and I made my way to the cooler.

"Trin!" I heard someone yell over the music. I almost dropped the bottled water I'd just pulled.

"You could never be that loud," I said turning around to see Angel, who was standing there in a simple white T-shirt, long beige shorts and white-on-white Nike gym shoes.

He looked me up and down and nodded in approval but he said nothing about my appearance. I could have had a boob job and hired a Hollywood personal trainer to work with me three times a day, seven days a week, and I still wouldn't have gotten a compliment from Angel. At that moment, all I felt was overdressed. Thank God I had our fake plans for after the barbecue.

Angel grabbed me in a bear hug then shook hands with Toya and Gina. "I better make rounds. I'll be back, Trin."

"All right," I responded, attempting to show more attention to the droplets of moisture on my bottled water than to Angel.

Toya and Gina were talking to a couple of guys when I returned to my seat. I guess my presence was like kryptonite because the guys soon left.

"Sorry, y'all," I said. "I didn't know I'd send them away."

"Girl, please. That just means they can't handle strong women," Gina joked.

We talked for a while and several guys were brave enough to venture to our group and introduce themselves, but inevitably, they all left. It was just as well, though. We were so caught up in our chitchat about men and childhood memories that there was little to distract us. I recalled my plan to stay an hour and leave. A quick glance at my watch showed that it was almost seven.

"You have somewhere to go?" Angel seemed to appear from nowhere.

Well, until that moment, there had been little to distract us, and by "us," I meant "me."

"Actually, yes," I said.

He stroked his goatee. "Let me holla at you for a minute."

What is he up to?

"Okay," I said and leaned back in the chair until I realized that he wanted to talk in private.

"Oh." I turned to Toya and Gina. "I'll be right back."

Toya looked perplexed. For a moment, I thought she would follow me. Gina curled her lip and rolled her eyes as if to say, "Yeah, right."

I walked with Angel to the front porch, where we sat on the swing. He lived at his parents' first house, and his father had installed the swing when he and Angel's mom were newlyweds. A breeze came through and I reveled in it for a brief moment. I looked at Angel and waited for him to say whatever it was he had to say.

"So, what's up, Angel?"

"Nothin', Trin. I just haven't talked to you in a while."

"It hasn't been that long," I said as if I believed my words.

"You know that's a lie."

"Don't call me a liar, Angel."

"All I'm saying is I don't understand why you don't call me."

Maybe it is because sweeping up the pieces of my face after Johnny's card party became a long and difficult process.

"I don't want to have this same argument about who should call. If you wanted to talk to me, you should have picked up the phone," I said.

"You made it seem like you weren't interested," he snapped.

I looked him in the eyes and for the first time in a long time, I saw what looked like sincerity.

"If I didn't know you, I just might think you missed me."

"Good thing you know me," he said. When we finished laughing Angel said, "Maybe I do."

"Maybe you do what?" I asked looking at my nails.

"Miss you."

I had forgotten how sexy his lips were. It was odd hearing those words exit his mouth.

"Hmm," I shook my head and looked away. I expected a smart reply or another dumb argument. Instead, he turned my face toward him and leaned in.

Uh oh.

He kissed me, and I shouldn't have kissed him back. I should have played hard to get, but I hadn't locked lips with anyone since the last time I'd kissed him. I'd almost forgotten how to kiss... almost. He squeezed my knee and gently bit my lip. My heart began to race.

Chill out, Trin. You're not in high school anymore. You can handle this.

He moaned as we kissed and though it was a bit odd, I was enjoying the moment.

"Yo, Angel!"

We pulled away from each other like horny teenagers who'd been caught by their parents. Ramona was standing on the sidewalk only yards from us.

That bitch!

"Hey, Ramona," Angel said.

I sat there dumbfounded. She had done it again.

Ramona approached us, smiling.

It's official—she's the devil.

"Oh, hey, Trinity. I didn't realize that was you."

"I didn't realize that was you?" Does she think I won't snatch that ponytail out of her head?

"I haven't seen you in a while," she went on.

Yes, since you caught me in your web and tried to wrap me up in Angel's sexual escapades.

My eyes passed from her head to her toes and back up again. A spare tire pushed against the bottom of a yellow V-neck top. The top met a pair of white shorts that exposed her meaty knees. I sat forward and clasped my hands. "Yeah, I've missed you at spin class."

Ramona did not respond to my remark, but looked at Angel. "So what's up?" She popped a piece of gum.

"Enjoyin' the day," Angel said.

I tried to act as if her presence did not bother me.

"So what's going on in the back?" she asked.

Angel huffed under his breath. "Why don't you go back there and see?"

"Oh, I feel you, player." She winked and walked off.

"Why does she treat me like I'm your flavor of the week?" I asked, revealing my irritation.

"She's just... being herself." Angel looked toward the street.

I thought it was best to avoid giving the situation any more of my attention. "Well, I guess I should be going." I stood up and dabbed the edges of my mouth.

He followed and touched my face. "I wanted to talk to you some more. Can you come in for a minute?"

"No, I have to go. They're waiting on me, anyway."

He grabbed me in a hug and kissed me on the cheek.

"I hope you call me later. I really want to talk to you. Maybe I can come see you tonight when you get back."

I gave him a "we'll see" look, but I didn't respond. Angel walked me to the backyard where Ramona was hamming it up with some of his friends. Gina was cornered by some guy and Toya was finishing up another plate of food. Toya looked up at me with a curious look on her face. I motioned her toward me and we got Gina, then said our goodbyes. I couldn't get to the driveway before Toya was asking me what happened.

"Let's just say that she-devil has a knack for timing."

Toya's mouth dropped. "Girl, cut it out."

"I saw her prance in wearing her daughter's top," Gina said. "Come to think of it, I thought I heard the sound of hooves clicking on the ground!"

"Right!" I said, through my own laughter. "So, I told Angel we had to leave because we have other plans. I don't want to be a liar. We *do* look cute... and it's still early."

"Hell, I'm in," Gina said.

"We could go downtown to the festival," Toya said.

Gina looked at her in disgust. "With all those chil'ren? I don't think so."

"I don't know why you're acting like you have a better idea. You don't even hang out unless you're mad at Kenny. All it takes is Kenny banging your back out and you won't come around again for another couple of months," Toya responded.

"Toya!" I blurted out. "I can't believe you said that!" She rolled her eyes at my reprimand.

"Don't be mad at me because you can't keep a man!" Gina snapped back at Toya, who then raised her hand as if she were about to praise the Lord. But we all knew that praises were not about to cross her lips.

"What? As dysfunctional as you and Kenny are, I know you aren't saying *you* can keep a man." Toya huffed. "Keep some dick maybe, at least some of the time."

"You can't even get dick in the door. Don't hate!" Gina barked.

"Look!" I shook my right arm and pointed to Toya's black Chevy Malibu. "Both of you, get in the car." I walked over to the passenger side as the alarm chirped and Toya unlocked the doors. "As much as some folks in the neighborhood might enjoy your street performance, I am not as appreciative!" We all plopped it into our seats simultaneously.

"I swear you act like kids." I looked from Toya to Gina; Toya's bottom lip poked out; Gina stared out of the window. "Show some class. Some apologies need to float around in this car."

Gina scooted forward and touched Toya's shoulder. "I'm sorry for what I said. I know you could get dick in the door and keep it there if you wanted."

Toya laughed. "It's okay. I apologize for what I said about Kenny... and your back." They both broke into laughter and I joined in.

"I have an idea," I said, happy with the outcome of their spat. "Let's go down to Baker's. I think they have a jazz set at eight."

They looked at each other. "Okay," they said in unison.

We went to the lounge and talked over appetizers.

I was home by ten. There was plenty of time to call Angel and find out what he wanted to talk about. Who was I fooling? He didn't want to talk. He wanted to finish what we started. Not that I would let it happen... would I? Of course I wouldn't.

I'm celibate, remember.

If I ever had a weakness in men, it was Angel. He was the only man I had been stupid for, whether it was waiting by the phone or canceling plans with friends when he popped up out of the blue. After that incident last year, I decided to quit Angel cold turkey, but when the barbecue came around, I had to satisfy my curiosity. And I had satisfied it... at least I was pretty sure I had.

I decided not to call him. Instead, I'd make him think I was still hanging out, being pursued by the man of my dreams. I would make him think I was doing anything other than sitting here alone thinking about him. I had to do something to get him off my mind, so it was to the movie archives for me.

Let's see. Godfather? *Too violent.* Cooley High? *Sad ending.* Office Space? *Perfect. A cult classic with no requirement to think.*

I popped in the DVD, turned up the air, and nestled into the couch with a blanket. I couldn't resist my next action—I picked up the phone and checked for a dial tone—you know, in case of emergency.

Chapter Seven

The rest of the weekend passed with exceptional speed and I found myself fully engaged in another work week. I was working on strategy and budget details outlined in the marketing plan I'd developed for my newest and largest account. My boss wanted to see the entire plan by the end of the week, so I was under pressure to come up with some creative ideas that would make us stand out to the client and help me stand out to the boss.

A knock interrupted my brainstorming.

"Come in," I said while typing on the computer.

"Excuse me, Trinity. Do you have a moment?"

My project coordinator was standing in the door clutching a note pad. Her long red hair was pulled into a bun, away from her alabaster skin. She wore a navy suit with matching shoes—flats. An unassuming white blouse seemed restricted by the suit jacket, which was a full size too large. The shoulders of the jacket extended inches beyond her own and its sleeves reached for her knuckles. Her ensemble aged her far beyond her twenty-two years.

"Sure. I'm just finishing up a marketing plan," I told her.

"Jeff wants to see you. He'd like for you to help him interview a candidate for the account executive position. He's in his office now," she said.

Jeff was the account supervisor of our department and I reported directly to him as the senior account manager. He had been in his position for only two months, but was adamant about involving me and his other senior account managers in his own role.

"Well, he didn't give me much notice, did he?"

She shrugged her shoulders and grinned timidly.

"Okay. Thanks, Beth. Please let him know I'll be there in just a minute."

Beth nodded and walked out. I grabbed a note pad and a pen, then reached into my desk to pull my makeup bag from my purse. Glancing at my reflection in my compact mirror, I dabbed a bit of powder on my nose and forehead before lining my lips and following with a nude lipstick and a gloss for shine. I always made sure that I had makeup at the office in case I was pulled into a meeting. After running my hands through my hair, I slipped my shoes back onto my feet. I didn't know what I was walking into, so I wanted to be presentable.

Jeff's office was two floors above mine, so I took the stairs instead of waiting for the perpetually slow elevators. His door was ajar. I knocked and pushed it in slightly, then announced myself.

"Hi, Trinity! Come on in. I'd like you to meet one of our account executive candidates." Jeff's two high-backed guest chairs allowed me to see only the back of the candidate's head. It was a brother—I could tell that much. A black man in this company was a rarity outside of the mailroom. I walked around to greet him and began to extend my hand as the candidate rose from the chair.

"Trinity Porter, this is Tony Parsons," Jeff said.

On instinct I snatched back my hand. Realizing what I had done, I swept my hair behind my ear then re-extended my hand. I was certain he flinched when I offered my hand again. He cleared his throat, then we shook with one quick motion. I wanted to douse my hand in bleach. My heart was in my throat, but I managed to say, "Nice to meet you."

"Likewise," he responded in a prepubescent voice. His bottom lip quivered as he tried to smile. I sat in the guest chair next to Tony before my knees could buckle and wondered if I could discreetly move my chair away from Tony without anyone noticing.

"Trinity is our department's senior account executive," Jeff said while nodding at me. "Tony just relocated from Washington, D.C. and was telling me about his prior experience when you came in. Here is his résumé."

At that moment, I was thankful that Jeff knew little about my personal life. He had no clue that Tony and I had gone to school together. I glanced over the résumé but saw little more than random words assembled on a sheet of paper. Jeff prattled on but I heard little over the sound of my heart beating, and I was sure they could see the pulsations through my suit. My thoughts began to consume me.

He majored in psychology. Why would he even be interviewing at a marketing agency? And why did he have to pick this one?

I thought his mom said he was only home for a few months. Why would he be looking for a permanent job? Shouldn't he be preparing to go back to D.C.?

Did I make a pact with the devil years ago that I couldn't remember making? Could God just have a twisted sense of humor?

"So, let's get started," Jeff said. "Why don't you tell us what type of contributions you believe you can make to this company?"

"Yes, please do." I blurted out the sarcastic comment without thinking.

Jeff looked bewildered, but let out a nervous laugh. "And Trinity. Please feel free to jump in. I'd like your input, too."

I smiled and nodded then turned my attention to the paper on my lap, embarrassed by my incautious outburst.

Tony began to answer Jeff's question. Though I was paying more attention to my own thoughts than to his answer, his nervousness was apparent in the sound of his voice. It cracked, and his response was splattered with umms. It was only then that it hit me. I had the upper hand. I just had to determine how to take advantage of it and figure out how to return my risen heart to my chest cavity.

"What would you define as the most challenging situation you faced on your last job?" Jeff asked.

"That's an interesting question," Tony said. It seemed he was trying to buy time, but then something happened. "Well, I'd have to say the biggest challenge I faced occurred when my supervisor left the company while we were in the middle of a pressing project. His boss was just concerned with getting the project done on time, so he rolled my supervisor's responsibilities down to the team. As the marketing assistant, I was left to organize the remaining members of the team. Some were resentful because they were asked to perform tasks that were outside of their job descriptions. I had to get them to realize we were all part of fixing the problem, even though we didn't create it. When they realized it was a team effort, everyone came together and made it happen, on time and within budget."

Oh, come on. You're so full of it!

"So it sounds like you had a good rapport with your colleagues," Jeff said.

"I think it's important to have a strong rapport with coworkers because you never know when you're going to need people," Tony said. I don't believe in burning bridges."

I put my mouth in the bend of my elbow and let out a muffled "bullshit!" which I masked as a sneeze.

"Bless you," Jeff said with a smile.

"Thank you!" I smiled back at him then cut my eyes at Tony who was on to me. Under the circumstances, there was nothing he could do about it.

There was a knock on the door. "Mr. Heiliger?"

"Yes?"

Jeff's secretary, Linda, opened the door. "Excuse me," she said, addressing us all. She turned her attention to Jeff. "Matthew McPherson is in a meeting in the second floor conference room. He'd like to borrow you for a few minutes. They have an urgent question about the Brown & Adams account."

Oh my goodness. This is not what I need. Lord, I can't handle this right now. Please don't let this happen.

"Sure, I'll be there in a second," he told her. "Trinity, can you continue conducting the interview? I'll be back as soon as I can."

Noooooooooo!

Before I could respond, Jeff popped out of his seat, tapped me twice on the shoulder as he passed, and walked out the door. He closed the door behind him.

I sat in my chair and shook my head in disbelief.

"Trinity. We meet again. Last time I saw you, you didn't even give me a chance to speak."

I didn't respond. I didn't look at him. I simply tapped my pen on my notebook and uncrossed my legs hoping that planting both feet on the floor would stop my left leg from shaking.

"Say something, Trinity." Tony shifted his weight in the chair. "This situation is pretty awkward."

It was if I had been launched into another universe—one where karma did not appear to work in my favor. I turned to him and looked into his eyes until my stare penetrated his being.

"What the fuck are you doing here?" I asked.

"Woe. You never used to curse at Howard. What's that about?" He sat back in the chair, pushing out his pecs as if he were sitting on a throne.

"Why are you here, Tony?" I placed my notepad and pen on Jeff's desk and sat back, crossing my arms.

"I think that's pretty obvious by now."

"Yeah, I almost didn't recognize you—wearing a suit, and all."

"Cute, Trin."

By this time, I was looking out the window behind Jeff's desk. "Don't call me 'Trin.' We're not friends."

"I know that, and I've been trying to figure out why for the last six years," he said.

I sat up in my chair and redirected my attention to Tony. "'Trying to figure out why?'"

"Yeah. Why do you hate me, Trinity? Listen, whatever happened back then was a mistake. But that's the past. Can't we move on?"

I put my hands on the armrests of my chair.

"'Whatever happened was a mistake?' Can you clarify? What was the *mistake*?"

Tony sighed. "The whole thing."

"*What* whole thing?" I pushed myself to my feet and looked down at him. "Can you even say it?"

He sat there silently.

I sat down again and leaned my head against the back of the chair. "Thank you for confirming that I did the right thing when I saw you in Fridays. You *are* a coward."

"If I'm the coward, why can't you tell me why you're still mad? That was a long time ago. Let it go."

"Let it go? What should I let go? The fact that one night I woke up with you on top of me and inside of me? Or that one perverted act constituted the end of my virginity? Or maybe it's the fact that I got pregnant from it? Wait, could it be that you disappeared and changed your number after I told you I was pregnant?"

"Trinity, do you have to do this now? Here?"

"You're right, Tony. We shouldn't do this here. Maybe it would be better to discuss it in a courtroom. The statute of limitations is seven years... and it's only been six."

"Trinity, please calm down. Your sarcasm is unnecessary and you're making me uncomfortable."

"Sarcasm? Who's being sarcastic? And uncomfortable? Shut the help up, Tony. You don't know what uncomfortable is. If you want to know, why don't you ask me about what it felt like when that doctor shoved cold metal rods inside of me then vacuumed out a fetus before finishing the job by scraping my uterus?"

"Trinity, please. I'm sorry you feel this way, but you're acting like I raped you, and I just don't see it that way. Nothing happened that night that you didn't want to happen. Maybe you should chalk it up to a life lesson, a mistake that we—"

"There was no *we* to that action, Tony. Stop saying 'we.' *You* did that to me." I couldn't believe his blatant disregard for the truth. What happened that night was as clear to me today as it was six years ago.

I woke from a peaceful sleep to the sensation that I could not breathe. Tony's two-hundred-ten-pound body was crushing me as I lay on his bed. I looked around, confused as to how I'd gotten from the couch where we were watching television to the bedroom. Gasping, I clenched my fists in fear as his lips pressed

against my cheek, neck and chest with quick, hard motions. He slid his right hand down to my panties, moved them to one side and began to stroke me. I squirmed, trying to avoid his touch and whispered, "Stop. Please stop."

"Shhhhhh." Tony smiled, put his hand over my mouth, and returned to fondling me. I fidgeted, trying in vain to wiggle to the edge of the bed. It was then that I realized he was naked, as he rubbed himself on my leg, leaving behind a moist trail.

I used every ounce of strength in my forearms to push him away from me, but I buckled under his weight. "Stop! Stop!" I yelled. Only muffled noises passed through the palm of his hand, which he pressed harder to my mouth. I felt his erection on my inner thigh, and bashed my fists wildly into his head and back, continuing to yell into his clammy palm. He rubbed the saliva on his hand into the pores of my face. Without responding to my attack, he thrust himself inside of me. I threw my hands back and screamed in pain, as Tony released a pleasurable sigh. Both of our backs arched as he pounded himself inside me and I begged him to stop with words he ignored.

"Shhhhhh, it's okay" he whispered as if he were comforting a newborn baby. I drew back my fists,

preparing to bash his head in hopes of startling him enough to stop for a split second—a split second I could use to escape. Before I could land the blow, Tony grabbed my wrists and pinned them above my head with only one hand. He never even removed his other hand from my mouth.

Helpless, I stopped fighting. I lay there and closed my eyes, waiting for it to stop. I tried not to listen to the noises he made; I tried to hear only the things that I knew were good, like my grandmother's singing; the voice of the football game announcer as he yelled Bashaye's name after a touchdown; the joy on my parents' faces when we opened the envelope confirming I'd received a scholarship to Howard. I tried not to feel the pain that shot through my body or the blood from my throbbing vagina trickle down my thighs. But I could not tune out his words when he'd gotten what he wanted. "See," he said. "I knew you'd like it, once you let your guard down."

Now I faced Tony one-on-one. I stood up and pulled a letter opener from the organizer on Jeff's desk.

I twirled it in my right hand, feeling the smooth texture of the green marble handle.

I leaned backward on the desk, standing directly in front of Tony. "*We* did not make a mistake. My only mistake was trusting you. The only difference in our 'mistakes' is the fact that I'm still paying for mine."

He looked at me as if I were deranged and sat back, trying to create more physical distance between us.

"I'll tell you what, Tony. If you really want to know what it's like to be uncomfortable, you accept this job. I'll do my best to make sure your life is the least comfortable it could possibly be, at least during business hours."

I twirled the letter opener, watching beads of sweat form around his hairline. A lump passed in his throat and he looked around the room like a rat stuck in a maze.

"What's wrong, Tony? Are you still feeling uncomfortable?"

He tried to dismiss me with his body language. "Trinity, you're being real—"

I drew my arm upward and slammed the letter opener right between his legs. Like a balloon, the chair popped at the incision. Tony shrieked and began breathing heavily when he realized I had not disturbed his man-hood. I had always been a good shot, and I wasn't try-ing to hurt him. The last thing I wanted was to lose my job—for him. If there was one rule I learned in dealing with men, it was that a woman should always make a man think she is just a bit touched in the head. It keeps men on their toes.

I walked behind Jeff's desk to get a good view of Tony.

"One more thing...." I planted my hands on the desk, allowing my arms to form a perfect V, and leaned in toward Tony who was still trying to catch his breath. He clutched the armrests and panted faintly. I pointed to the letter opener and said, "Put that back before you leave."

Tony looked at me with words in his eyes that never met his lips. I smiled at him, gathered my things and walked out, pulling the door shut.

"Linda, when Jeff gets back, would you please tell him I finished the interview?"

"Sure, Trinity."

"Thanks!" I started to leave the area when I caught myself. "By the way..." Linda looked up.

"The candidate would prefer to see himself out."

"Okay," she responded. I smiled and walked away.

I made a pit stop at the bathroom where I ran cold water over my hands before dabbing my forehead and neck. I held my hands in front of me. They were shaking. I looked at my grandmother's ring and twisted it between the thumb and forefinger of my left hand before taking two deep breaths and releasing them slowly.

Ma Lo, please help me to calm my spirit.

I wondered what was going through Tony's mind—other than the thought that I had lost my own mind. But it was time to regroup. I had things to do.

Chapter Eight

I t was almost lunchtime when I got back to my desk. I had decided to finish my project before taking my break. Oftentimes I ended up eating at my desk, but today I was going to meet Malik for lunch. We had been friends since the ninth grade at Cass Tech where we had a class together in the Marketing/Distributive Education curriculum.

Physically, I was attracted to him back then. He had sunkissed skin and was a basketball player who stood six foot, four inches tall at fourteen years old. At that time, I had developed the habit of forming platonic relationship with guys based on my ability to make them laugh and their ability to return the favor. It wasn't long before I became "one of the guys" to Malik rather than a puppy-love interest. Soon I valued our relationship as a pure friendship. And that was a good thing, because with his charismatic nature, Malik was a bonafide player then, and I thought he would be until the day he died.

We didn't talk on a regular basis. When he dropped off the face of the earth, it usually meant that he'd met a new woman who thought she was his girlfriend. He would resurface when the sex got old.

Still, we had such a strong bond that our friendship would never let us stay mad for long about our hiatuses. After I forgot to return his phone call on the night that Caroline did her thing with Lil Mike, Malik called me back and fussed me out, then invited me to lunch on his day off. I was looking forward to it because I hadn't talked to him in a while. Plus, I found myself at the point of absolute boredom when it came to looking at the same four walls of my office.

"Trinity?"

"Yes?" I said before looking up. Jeff was standing in the door.

"Sorry I didn't make it back before you finished the interview. How did it go?"

"Well, I think Mr. Parsons is ambitious, but I'm not sure his qualifications are in line with the responsibilities of the position," I told him.

"Really? How so?"

"I was looking for him to demonstrate more project management and budget management experience," I said. "His experience in those areas seems little more than minimal. To be honest," I added, "if you go with Mr. Parsons, I believe a good deal of training may be required, which may be hard to come by, considering the present workload." I grinned and gave him the most sincere look I could muster.

I watched Jeff digest my comments. He always rubbed his chin when in thought. Normally I would have fought tooth and nail to get a qualified black man into the company, but this was *so* not one of those times.

"Hmm." Jeff broke the silence. "I appreciate your input, Trinity. I'll keep your comments in mind."

"Okay, great!" I replied with a smile.

He turned to leave. "Oh," Jeff said stopping in mid step. "Would you mind sitting in on additional interviews, should we get more applications?"

"I'd be happy to," I said.

Jeff nodded and walked out of my office, pulling the door behind him. I sighed heavily, leaned back in my chair and glanced at the small, pale blue soapstone plaque that sat next to my computer monitor. I ran my index and middle fingers across the inscription: "I will never leave you nor forsake you. (Hebrews 13:5)."

I had received the plaque as a gift from my dean of pledges at my graduation ceremony. She pledged two years prior to me and had "Delta Sigma Theta Sorority, Inc., Alpha Chapter" engraved in the middle of the plaque. On the left, she had engraved the number six, which was the line number we shared. The number bonded us, as we were both the sixth-tallest people on each of our respective pledge lines and it was tradition for sorority sisters who pledged before the current line to "adopt" the pledgee who shared their number. On the right, both of our pledge years were engraved.

A sense of guilt entered my psyche. It was guilt for failing to keep in touch with Deena Nelson as frequently as I used to. More important, it was guilt for forgetting to reference and live the Scripture. For the last year, it had blended into the arrangement of my office. I remember my excitement in moving it into my office so I could have a constant reminder of my Alpha Chapter sisterhood and God's promise. Now the plaque was a mere fixture, not a reminder. I rubbed my fingers together and watched a thin layer of dust absorb into the oil of my fingers.

I had gone back to my marketing plan for only a few minutes when the phone rang. I answered with my professional introduction including the company name, my name and my title. Our caller ID did not recognize external callers, so I never knew if I was preparing to speak to a client or my mom. This time, Malik's voice came through the receiver.

"You must be runnin' things over there at Keemer and Dewitt," he said.

"I'm just trying to keep my job," I laughed.

"I hear you. Are we still on for lunch?"

I glanced at my watch. "Of course. Are you picking me up?"

"For you, yes. How does Caribbean Tastes sound?"

"Perfect," I said. "Can you be here in half an hour? I'm getting hungry."

"No problem. I'll see you soon," Malik said before we hung up.

Caribbean Tastes was a family-owned upscale bistro. Though I hadn't been to the eastern Caribbean, a Detroit Free Press food critic raved that the ambiance made her feel as if she had stepped right into Jamaica or Trinidad without setting foot on a plane. After reading the article and realizing my next vacation was months away at best, I had tried the restaurant out and enjoyed it. This would be my fourth visit in three months.

When we got to Caribbean Tastes, we stood in the waiting area of the modest-sized restaurant. There were two small benches. Only one was occupied. Malik and I sat on the empty bench and continued the conversation we'd started in the car. Caribbean music played. Pictures, all having to do with the Caribbean, lined the bright yellow walls. In the waiting area, a large picture of Marcus Garvey hung behind the register. His eyes seemed to peer at everyone entering the door.

"All I know is that if I'm ever out with you and one of your fatal attractions mistakes me for one of your harlots, it won't be pretty," I told him.

"Harlots? Really, Trin?"

I shrugged my shoulders.

"You know I wouldn't let anyone disrespect you, Trin."

I grinned at Malik. "Mmm hmm. I also know that you haven't been able to stop any of your stalkers from hiding in bushes or keying your car."

"That's ancient history. Why'd you blow the dust off of that one?"

"Hey, it happened. I'm just speaking the truth." I patted his arm.

"Get off me," he said as if he had an attitude.

"Don't be nasty."

"You know nothing about me getting nasty, Trin. But I can show—"

I slammed my hand on the arm of the bench.

"Okay, why'd you have to take it there?" I said slightly disgusted.

"I may be your boy, but I'm still a man."

"And that would be your fatal flaw," I muttered.

Surprisingly, the wait for a table was brief. The hostess walked us to a table for two in the center of the restaurant. There were only tables, no booths, in the restaurant. Patrons often complained about the limited seating arrangements, but the inconvenience had not been enough to keep people away from the restaurant.

Malik pulled out my chair, and I scooted up to the glass table that sat atop a column shaped like a palm tree. A young man in a black and white uniform made brief eye contact and cracked a shy smile before pouring our water and placing a small plate of lemons on the table. I took one of the lemons and squeezed its juices into my hands, rubbing it into my skin. I squeezed a second lemon into my water and twisted it onto the brim of my glass before taking a few, soothing sips. "Mmm." I spoke my thoughts out loud. "This water is good."

"So how's your day going?" Malik asked.

"Oh, don't ask," I said and rolled my eyes.

"What's wrong? Is the Man getting to you?"

I chuckled. "Not exactly." I paused and took a deep breath at the thought of the story of the day. "Tony Parsons interviewed for a position today. I had to sit in on it."

"Yeah right," he said, unconvinced.

"No, seriously." I took a long sip of my water.

Before he could ask another question, the waitress appeared, ready to take our orders.

"Could you give us a second?" Malik asked. The waitress didn't speak, but pursed her lips and turned around slowly to walk away.

"Real nice, Malik. I already told you I was hungry. Why'd you tell her to come back? We'll be sitting here until dinner time before she comes back."

"You don't know what you want anyway," he said authoritatively.

He was right. I hadn't even opened the menu, but I knew everything that was on it. I looked over the lunch specials.

"So, uh, I know you don't think I'm going to forget what you said about Tony." He leaned forward and scooted up to the table, as if trying not to miss any details. "What happened?"

I sighed and prepared to tell the story with intentions of revealing everything *but* the whole story.

"I got called into an interview. It turned out that Tony was the applicant for the job. We both acted like we didn't know each other. When my boss got called into another meeting, he asked me to take over. So I told Tony that it would behoove him not to pursue the position any further, and I walked out."

Malik's eyes widened. "What?" He looked puzzled, then sat back in his chair and folded his arms. "I never liked his punk ass anyway."

I stirred the ice water with my straw to divert attention away from the fact that I'd left out major components of the story.

"Do you think he'll get the position?"

"I advised my boss against it," I said without looking up from the circular pattern that had formed in my water.

"You advised him?" he asked.

I continued to stare at the circles in my water. "It's up to him, but he doesn't like making decisions, so I tried to... steer him in the right direction."

"Man, Detroit is too small," Malik said.

"Yeah." I looked up and grinned, realizing my antisocial behavior.

"I thought Tony studied sociology," Malik said.

"Psychology."

"Whatever. I just know it had nothing to do with marketing."

"Well, I guess folks are just trying to get jobs wherever they can," I said.

"You never told me what happened with you two," he pried.

"I know."

"You always clam up when his name comes up."

"I just don't like to talk about people who are no longer applicable in my life."

Malik laughed. "Why do you get so corporate when someone gets under your skin?"

"What do you mean?"

He mocked me, "'I don't like to talk about people who are no longer applicable in my life... I advised my boss against it.'"

"Cute, Malik." I grinned and laughed *at* myself *to* myself.

"Are you ready to order?" The waitress had reappeared, seemingly out of thin air.

We placed our orders and she brought us bread. By this time, my stomach was growling with anticipation of food. The bread was piping hot. Steam rose from a piece as I buttered it. I savored its coconut flavorings as I swallowed.

"Is he the reason you're so cold toward men?"

"What?" I asked defensively. Malik had caught me off guard.

"You don't give men the time of day... no matter how they approach you. Is Tony the reason why?" He hadn't touched his bread. It seemed he was only interested in watching me.

"Come on now, Malik. I'm not cold."

"Woman, please. You're the Ice Queen!"

"I am not." I dismissed his accusation with little recognition.

"When's the last time you had a date?"

"None of your business," I said ripping another piece of bread and putting it in my mouth. I slid the bread basket toward him. "Here, have some."

The distraction wasn't enough to dissuade him from pursuing the topic. "You probably can't even remember. A woman as fine as you can't remember the last time she had a date. Hmm."

I remembered. It was early October of last year when Shawna convinced me to go out with a lame named Charles who worked at her job. I figured that since he shared a name with my father, I'd at least give him a chance. We met for dinner, and he told me to order whatever I wanted. I ordered a modest meal—chicken alfredo and ice water. Ice water! My meal cost thirteen dollars. When he got the bill, the cheap blockhead said, "Let's go Dutch on this one." I excused myself—to go to the bathroom, of course. Then I walked right out of the restaurant and drove myself home.

"Why does my dating history concern you, Malik?"

"I don't want you to be 'out there' Trinity, but damn, put your foot in the water."

I grinned at him with restraint for the callous words that sat on the tip of my tongue.

"Malik, I'm not like you. I can't use people like pieces of a chess game, then throw them out. Forgive me if I don't see people as disposable."

Oops... the words just slipped out!

"Disposable?" He was miffed. His eyes shrank under his eyebrows.

"Yes, disposable." I took another sip of water. "That's why you've got so many psychos chasing you."

"I have never led a woman to think I wanted more than I do. I always put my cards on the table."

"So why do you think you keep getting the same type of women?" Before he could answer, I followed with,

"They say you attract those who mirror what's in your own soul."

"And I see you sitting across from me right now, just like you have been for the last ten, twelve years. So what's that say about you?"

His rebuttal left me without a response. I sat back and shook my head, wondering how he could compare me to the targets of his sexual exploits. The waitress brought my chicken roti and Malik's curried goat. As we ate, I pondered Malik's last comment. We chitchatted through the meal, but his words were chipping away at me. I was almost finished with my meal when I couldn't stand it anymore.

"What did you mean by that—about me sitting across from you and mirroring your soul?"

"You're the one who brought it up. You know what it meant," he replied and picked up the last piece of bread from the basket.

He didn't even ask me if I wanted the last piece.

"You've hung around me since we were in diapers."

"Okay, it hasn't been that long," I said.

"Can I just get my point across?"

I nodded to give him the green light.

"You've hung around me for a while. In a way, I've attracted you all this time."

"Don't flatter yourself." I rolled my eyes.

"Well, let's flip it. What does your hanging around me say about your soul?"

I pulled the last couple of ounces of water through my straw. "I imagine it says that there are those of us who see some good in everyone... even someone with a shallow, empty soul." I stared at him before revealing a wide smile.

"That hurt," he said.

"Mmm," I said, unconvinced.

"You know, it's funny that you supposedly see so much of my empty soul, but you never show anyone your soul."

I sat upright, defensively. "Really?"

"Yeah." Malik dug deeper. "Trin, I know you think I'm not capable of loving because of my... lifestyle, but I do have a heart. I also have no problem letting people I care about know it."

I found myself listening attentively.

"I remember when *you* used to be loving and affectionate toward your friends. Something's changed in your soul, Trin. I can see it in your eyes."

"It's called life, Malik."

"Trin, life's not easy, but it doesn't have to harden you."

I looked at him as if he had no clue, but he had struck a nerve.

"I don't know what it is that has changed you, but you'll never get over it or through it by ignoring it."

I smiled. "You should have been a shrink."

"And you should have been my first," Malik said.

"What?" As soon as he started to soften my heart, he poured ice cubes all around it.

"Well, you should have. Maybe things would have turned out differently... for both of us."

"Oh, shut up, Malik."

He leaned over and grabbed both sides of my face then kissed my forehead.

"You know I love ya, girl," he teased.

"Watch the hair," I said, fixing my layers.

Chapter Nine

O n the night of the incident with Tony, I waited in the bathroom until I was sure he was asleep. I crept back into the bedroom, where he was spread across the bed as if he had been fatally shot in the back. His snoring made it clear that he was very much alive.

I stepped into my jogging pants, which were in a ball on the side of the bed, and glanced at him one more time. I needed personal confirmation that he was asleep, and unable or unwilling to follow me. In the living room, my purse—the only observer of the television's flashing screen—was positioned in the corner of the couch. With purse in hand, I stepped into my shoes, which I'd left on the mat. I opened the door to his apartment, careful not to make any noise. Tony's sneering snore rang out from the bedroom and made me jump as I closed the door and sprinted to the parking lot.

Three-and-a-half weeks later, I was doing my best to pretend it never happened. I was going to classes, working on the planning committee for my sorority's annual fashion show and preparing for my future. Simultaneously, I was wearing hats that leaned toward incognito, and giving no attention to the fact that if I were to slip into my favorite jeans one more time, they just might get up and walk to campus on their own. I was fighting for control, attempting to hold on to the life that had been mine just weeks earlier.

It was not until the daytime phone calls stopped, the classes were over, the air was still, and darkness covered the D.C. sky like a flannel blanket that reality crept into my consciousness. I was not the same person I was last month, and I wasn't sure how long I could continue to pretend to be her. I found myself praying at night that God would let me wake up and forget it ever happened, but every morning I still had memories of that night. Every morning was like confirmation that just as my prayers did not bring back Bashaye, my prayers weren't going to bring back my former self.

My constant activity was starting to wear on me physically. I had contracted some sort of virus that had me clinging to the toilet bowl before classes, comforted only by the cold, ceramic floor that cooled my feet. I ate chicken broth and a slice of wheat bread a couple of times a day—the only meal I could keep down. It had become a staple when I got sick to my stomach as a child. Three days into this routine, I was grateful for not having any Friday classes because it meant I could lie in bed and finally slow down.

After a predictable trip to hug my favorite porcelain friend, I began brushing my teeth when I heard a knock at the door. I continued brushing, knowing that I wasn't expecting anyone. The knock came again, this time with more might. Rap, rap, rap, rap! I rinsed a clean washcloth with cold water and wiped it across my mouth and face.

"Okay, okay," I said, significantly shy of the volume level required to let the person on the other side of the door know I was coming. The peephole revealed my line sister, Katrina, my "front"—she was number five and I was number six on my line. She leaned in toward the peephole, raising her right eyebrow before she stepped back once again. She gained about three inches in height, drawing breath from the deepest part of her small body. I knew what was coming next so I unlocked the door and pulled it open as swiftly as I could, but I was too late.

"Trin-i-tee!" she yelled as I stood in front of her.

Wisps of my hair blew back from the 130 decibels that shot out of her body.

"Really, Katrina? Some of my neighbors are still asleep."

She breezed past me. "Well, they need to get up. The sun is out!" Katrina dropped her purse and her jacket on the couch and began smoothing her shirt, which hung perfectly on her ample chest. Sometimes I wondered how gravity did not pull her to the floor. Boobs were the only thing that made her frame look post-pubescent. "What took you so long to answer the door? You had me standing out there like a stalker."

Her short pencil curls were freshly laid. She wisped the bang, pulling it toward her brow. I was still at the door, leaning on it with the weight of my back, as if staving off any more visitors.

"Well?" She turned her attention to me.

I stared back at her, wishing I had a remote control to lower her volume. "I've been in the bathroom... puking."

Her lip curled upward and she shifted her weight to the left before stepping toward me and touching my forehead and then pressing on my throat with her thumbs, index and middle fingers.

"You just can't help it, Nurse Wilson, can you?"

"Open your mouth." Katrina squeezed my jaw, forcing me to open my mouth, and tilted back my head. She peered down my throat before releasing me from her grip.

"Are you done violating me?"

"How long have you been sick?" she asked without answering my question.

"A few days," I said and walked over to the couch where I let my legs give out underneath me.

"Hmm. I knew you looked a little raggedy yesterday."

"Thanks. Nice of you to notice," I said, letting my head fall on top of the couch.

"Have you been to the doctor?"

"No, it's just a virus." I put my hand on my head. "I just need to rest... and drink a lot of juice."

"Come on. We're going to urgent care." Katrina picked up her purse and looked at me impatiently.

"I'll go to urgent care if I don't feel better tomorrow."

"Umm, no. Alpha Chapter takes care of Alpha Chapter... and you look like shit. Come on. Listen to this nursing student."

I got up from the couch and headed toward my room. "You can go to urgent care. I'm going to bed."

Katrina grabbed my hand and pulled me back.

"Come on, Trin. Just tell me where your purse and jacket are."

Thirty minutes later, Katrina and I sat in a waiting room with four other people whose enthusiasm for being there matched my own. After completing the clinic's health paperwork, I stared at the television inattentively, daydreaming about being in my bed. Katrina thumbed through a Life & Style *magazine on the table, and began making what seemed to be timed comments about the stories approximately every two minutes.*

I stopped daydreaming and started focusing on the activities of the waiting room. Each time the nurse called a patient back to an exam room, another patient seemed to enter the office and head to the sign-in sheet. I had watched the door that separated the waiting room and the rest of the office open and close three times. Each time, a repugnant odor wafted into the waiting room.

I turned to Katrina and muttered under my breath. "I don't know what they are brewing back there, but it smells like coffee-soaked feet."

"Coffee-soaked feet?" The other patients looked up from their magazines and the television, distracted by Katrina's voice.

"Why are you so loud?" I whispered, attempting to put some authority into my tone.

"Now, Trin. You know I'm not known for a quiet tone."

I smiled at her and she winked before turning the page in her magazine.

"Trinity Porter?" A stubby nurse was standing in the doorway. I glanced at Katrina who grabbed her purse and began to stand up.

I touched her hand. "I'm a big girl. I'm fine."

Reluctantly, she retreated into the chair. "Fine, but come get me if you need me!"

I grinned and grabbed my purse, following the nurse down a narrow hallway with pale green walls and fluorescent ceiling lights. Nurses wearing white scrubs weaved in and out between patient rooms, the hallway and the nurse's station. It all seemed to be the perfect setting for a movie—but not your average drama or comedy; this scene was more fitting for a thriller about a successful businessman whose sanity was suddenly being questioned.

The nurse stopped in front of a black scale that stood nearly as tall as I did. "Ms. Porter, let's get your weight." I placed my purse in a nearby chair and removed my jacket, dropping it on top of my purse, and stepped onto the black square at the base of the scale. The digital display seemed to go berserk. Red numbers ran through what I imagined was some sort of processor inside the scale.

If I were overweight, I would really hate this part.

It stopped on 128—five pounds lighter than I registered a few months earlier during my annual physical.

The nurse wrote what I assumed was my weight on my chart before turning to me. "I'm going to place you in a room now."

She led me back toward the front of the office, and we passed the nurse's station where a woman was drawing blood from a patient. Based on the expression of the 20-something man in the chair, the nurse did not have a gentle hand.

"You can have a seat in here."

I turned back to the nurse who was assisting me, as she held the door open to a room. A stool was to my left and the reclining patient chair was directly in front of me, draped with white tissue paper—visible crinkles absent. She closed the door behind us, and I placed my belongings on a hook on the back of the door before disrupting the crispness of the new sheet of paper on the chair. The nurse sat on the stool, inched toward me and began reading the paperwork I'd filled out in the waiting room. "What are your symptoms?" she inquired without looking up from the chart.

"Nausea, vomiting, dizziness…. Typical virus symptoms. It may be food poisoning." I rubbed my right temple. "I had Chinese food a couple of days ago. I got sick right after that."

She stood up and pulled a thermometer off the wall. It looked more like an archaic contraption. The thermometer was about the size of my first cell phone. The nurse gripped it tightly in her pudgy hand. She pulled out a slim, metal rod from the top of the thermometer and inserted it into a plastic covering before punching several buttons on it. "Open up. Let's get your temperature," she said, barely waiting for me to open my mouth before she slipped the thermometer under my tongue. When it beeped twice, the nurse pulled it out as if it held a bomb that was preparing to detonate. She jotted something on her notes before taking my blood pressure. The nurse ripped the band from my arm, flinging it back in its place on the wall, and noted the results.

"When was your last period?" she asked.

Why is she asking about my period?

"October."

"October what?"

My period was so irregular that I had stopped recording the dates. Instead, I got used to carrying around tampons in every purse I owned. I knew I could expect my period every 24 to 34 days, but with finals looming, I had lost count of my period's recent appearance.

"I can't remember the date."

The nurse was silent. Her only response was to look at me with a perplexed expression.

I felt a need to elaborate. "I've always been irregular."

The nurse scribbled something in her notes and looked at me for just a little bit longer than the average eye contact exchange. I broke the stare, switch-

ing my attention to the glass jar on the sink counter that held about 75 tongue compressors. They looked like fat Popsicle sticks. I cleared my throat, hoping she wouldn't use one of the tongue compressors on me. I knew it would trigger the gag reflex.

"Okay. The doctor will be in to see you shortly." She flashed a grin and walked out of the door, pulling it behind her.

That was awkward. How long is this going to take?

I hated waiting in examination rooms. You spent all of your time flipping through brainless magazines that were covered in unseen germs, glancing at the door every time a voice seemed to near, only to be disappointed when the voice continued to travel beyond your room. Then after glancing at your watch, you repeated the cycle, stopping only to play with the nostril/ear laser gadget or the stethoscope.

At page 36 of People, the door opened and a middle-aged man with rectangular glasses and a receding hairline entered the room holding my chart.

"Hello, Trinity. I'm Dr. Nida." He had an Ethiopian accent.

"Hi, Dr. Nida."

"So you're experiencing dizziness and nausea."

"And vomiting," I added. "I've been taking Pepto. If you could just give me something a little stronger, I'm sure I'll be okay."

"Well, I just want to make sure it's not something other than a viral issue."

Like what? The plague? Oh, God. Does he think I have the plague?

For a moment, hypochondria set in. Before I could comprehend his reply, he picked up the phone on the wall and called for a nurse. "Maryann, please bring me a specimen cup."

She was at the door within seconds, specimen cup in hand. She left as quickly as she'd arrived.

"Doctor, what is that for?" I asked, pointing to the cup.

"I'd like to get a urine specimen from you."

"What do you think you'll find in my pee?"

An upward curvature in his mouth led me to believe that he chuckled on the inside, but he maintained his professionalism. "We're going to do a pregnancy test. It's standard procedure with your symptoms."

I sat straight up and swung my feet so that I could face the doctor. "Pregnancy test? I'm not pregnant!"

"Are you sexually active?" His eyes judged me.

"No!" I dangled my legs below the table, wishing I could just drop them to the floor and run out of the room.

"Ms. Porter, are you a virgin?"

None of your business!

I opened my mouth, but no words came out. The truth was, I didn't know how to answer his question. I hadn't had a sexual experience out of my own volition, but still, I'd lost my virginity.

"Well," he said, holding the cup out to me, "let's just do this test to be sure. There are towelettes in the bathroom. Be sure to use one before you collect the specimen. The instructions for collecting the specimen are right on the cup. When you're finished, place the specimen in the silver window in the bathroom, and I'll meet you back in this room."

I was extremely confused, but still at a loss for words. A moment ago, I thought the doctor feared I had the Ebola virus, SARS or malaria. Now he thought there was a kid growing inside me.

The doctor continued to rattle off instructions. "Now, the bathroom is at the end of the hall. Like I said, I'll meet you back in this room when you're done." *He gave me a sympathetic grin and walked out.*

I felt like I had been recruited as part of some degrading experiment. I wondered if the clinic was running pregnancy statistics on all of the college students so they could send them to the government as part of some slutty-girl list.

"I'm not a slut," I said aloud. "Does he think I'm a slut?"

I wanted to track the doctor down and give him a piece of my mind for making such an ungrounded assumption, but I figured I'd show him instead. The sooner I could prove I wasn't pregnant, the sooner I could get a prescription and climb into my bed. I took the cup and walked down the hall, stopping before a silver door with a blue restroom sign. Inside the bathroom, I put my purse on the hook and took a quick glance around. There was a toilet, a sink, a mirror and a small silver window on one of the walls. Above the toilet was a ledge with a bowl of what appeared to be hand wipes, but there was no barbecue in this bathroom, so I knew they were meant for use on a more personal part of the body than my hands. I dropped my pants and reached for one of the wipes, disposing of it and its packet when I finished.

I came in for a frickin virus, and the doctor thinks I'm pregnant? Wait 'til I tell Katrina about how her clinic cohorts treated me.

I read the instructions on the cup. "Start to urinate into the toilet. While continuing to urinate, place cup under stream of urine and fill to 1/2 or 3/4 full. Finish urinating in toilet. Use lid to seal urine cup tightly. Return specimen to nurse."

I followed the instructions and opened the silver window with some expectation of seeing someone on the other side asking, "What's the password?" I gathered myself, washed my hands—attempting to scrub the embarrassment from them—and returned to the examination room.

The room seemed different. It was as if it were watching me, talking about me. The light buzzed over my head—a sound I had not heard the first time I sat in the room. The faucet seemed to have acquired a slow, sporadic drip that continued despite my efforts to fiddle with the handle.

With a rapid double knock at the door, Dr. Nida entered the room. He sat in the stool with my chart in his hand.

"So, can I get my prescription now? Do you need to do any more tests?"

"Ms. Porter, your pregnancy test came back positive."

"My what came back what?" I asked.

"You're pregnant."

"There must be some sort of mistake."

"Well, our tests are more than 99 percent accurate and your hormone levels indicate a pregnancy."

I stared past the doctor and through the door, imagining what I would have been doing if I hadn't let Katrina talk me into walking into that office.

"Ms. Porter?"

"Yes?" My voice was only a whisper, and I was too humiliated to look him in the eye.

"We do counsel on options. I don't know what your situation is with your significant other, but—"

I found my voice again. "There is no significant other."

"Okay," he paused. "I'm here to let you know that there are options. I can discuss them all with you."

"I should go. Excuse me," I said, getting up from the chair and attempting to get my belongings from the back of the door.

He stood up and tried to stop me from leaving. "Ms. Porter. I know this is difficult news, but—"

"No, Doctor." I gestured for him to stop speaking. "I'm sorry, but you don't know."

For a moment, there was silence.

"I apologize, but I have to go. I'll consider what you told me and can call back for another appointment, but I have to go."

He stepped away from the door and made one last attempt to stop me. "Ms. Porter?"

I glanced at him quickly before grabbing my purse and my jacket. "Thank you, Doctor," I said before walking out of the room.

I gave the nurse at the checkout counter a credit card for my copay and tried to concoct a quick story to tell Katrina. When I returned to the waiting area, she sat straight up. "Well?" she asked.

"Virus. I got some medication samples... I just need to rest."

"Okay, sweetie." She rubbed my back, and I wanted to fall into her arms crying. Instead, I just said, "Thanks for bringing me."

"That's what I'm here for!"

We walked outside to the car.

"So what kind of virus did the doctor say you have?"'

"Just something that's going around."

I hated lying to her, but I was ashamed.

"Well, we have been seeing people in the clinic with symptoms like yours. Usually, they give an antibiotic and advise them to drink plenty of fluids and get rest. You should be fine in the next few days."

"I'm sure you're right," I said. "A few days." I wished everything would go back to normal in a few days, but I knew there was no possibility of that.

That night, I lay on my bed without even bothering to pull back the comforter or change into pajamas. I pressed my hands to my stomach, which showed no outward signs of life. I stared at the ceiling, searching my heart for an answer. The doctor's words ran through my head. "There are options. I can discuss them all with you."

The sun rose, and I found myself still staring at the ceiling, my eyes dry and irritated. I'd forfeited my chance to sleep and prayed through the night, asking God to make the situation go away. Instead of prepar-

ing myself for attending Chapel on campus, as I usually did on Sundays, I got in the shower and prepared to visit Tony. I didn't know who else to talk to. Since he was the reason I was facing this dilemma, I wanted to see him in person. I put on a jogging suit and ran a brush through my tangled hair, pulling it into a ponytail before slipping out of the door.

It was cool outside, and I'd left without putting on a jacket. The temperature gauge in my car read 49 degrees. I rubbed my arms, wishing I'd worn a jacket, but I knew that if I went back into my apartment, I would lose the courage to talk to Tony. The sun seemed to be fighting the clouds, but it was in a losing battle. Each time it peeked through, a thick cloud bullied it, shutting the city out from feeling its warmth.

Ten minutes later, I was at Tony's apartment. It was 7:45. I sat in the car for 20 minutes, burning gas and running the heat, debating whether I would make that walk up the sidewalk and to his doorstep. Finally, I opened the car door and was soon standing in front of his nondescript door. I took a deep breath and rang the bell. A wind blew past, whipping right through my jogging suit. I held myself, trying to shake off the cold. There was no answer, so this time I knocked. I began to rock from left to right, trying to keep warm. I knocked one more time before the door whipped open, and Tony was standing there squinting.

"Damn. What is it, Trinity?"

"I, I need to talk to you." I squeezed my arms tighter and glanced at the ground before catching his eye.

"Now?" He rolled his eyes in annoyance.

"Yes."

He opened the door and I walked in, stopping in the foyer, where the tile met the carpet. Tony closed the door behind me and sat on the couch.

"Do you want to sit down?" he asked, looking at me as I stood in the middle of the floor.

"No," I replied.

"What's up? Why are you here? And so early?"

I tried to gather the right things to say, but all that came out was, "I'm... pregnant."

Tony's expression changed. "Pregnant?"

I nodded my head and Tony sat forward, chuckling, letting his hands dangle over his knees.

"Nice, Trin. Why are you telling me?"

"What?" I was baffled. Did he think there was a possibility I was pregnant by someone else?

"I said, why are you telling me?" he repeated himself.

I uncrossed my arms and lifted my hands. *"Because I clearly didn't do this by myself."*

"So, get rid of it." He pushed off from the couch and went into the kitchen. I heard him pour a bowl of a cereal and milk, which he brought back to the living room.

"That's all you have to say? Get rid of it?"

"What do you want me to say?" he asked while picking up the television remote and turning to ESPN. *"Do you want to keep it or something?"*

"I, I don't know." I could barely be heard over the television.

"You don't know? Well, let me help you, Trinity. Picture it. Graduation. You walking down the stage to get your diploma," he paused to count on his fingers. He continued, *"... seven month pregnant. Perfect! With all you worked for, you'll end up as nothing more than another single mom."*

He laughed again, shoveling the cereal into his mouth and focusing on the television.

He slammed the bowl onto the table and it spun around in a circle like a top before coming to rest.

"Hold on." Tony walked down the hallway that led to the bedrooms and returned a minute later. "Here." He held out his hand, expecting me to do the same. When I did, he pressed a wad of crumpled money into my hand. "That should take care of it." He walked back to the couch, picked up his cereal and began to carry on as if I weren't there.

I stood in the doorway with my hand still extended, holding the money.

"How long you gonna stand there, Trinity?" he asked without giving me the decency of eye contact.

A tear fell down my face and I shoved my hand in my pocket. I felt like I'd been thrown away. I walked out of the door without my dignity, without my pride.

Three weeks later, I was still praying and still waking up sick every day. I was waiting on God to "make it go away," but He hadn't. So I decided to make it go away myself. I scheduled an abortion. Trinity Joi Porter, the same girl who scolded her high school confidant for having one, the same one who wrote a high

school paper on all of the reasons that abortion was wrong, the same girl who swore that if she ever got pregnant, she'd do the right thing, had not. What she had done was become a hypocrite.

Chapter Ten

June was here and the flowers were in full bloom all around the city. Convertible tops were dropped, families were planning vacations, and my life was business as usual. I was able to enjoy the season during those precious moments when I wasn't in the office. My job was going well, but unfortunately, Shawna was not as happy on her job. A paralegal, she had just been transferred to another department and her new boss seemed to find any opportunity to criticize her work.

After graduating from Cass together, Shawna went to Howard with me, but she only stayed for a year. Technically, she'd gotten to sophomore year, but shortly after getting housing she found out that something happened with her financial aid paperwork. It could have been fixed with a little effort, but her mom told her to come back home. Shawna's mom had gone to nursing school at Wayne State University and had no appreciation for the black college experience. She couldn't understand why her daughter was heartbroken over having to leave Howard. Shawna ended up working full time to pay for her tuition while she went to school at Wayne State part time. Eight years later, she was still trying to get her degree. She was studying law, and for now, she was stuck in the paralegal world until she finished school in another year.

She wanted me to go downtown to Flood's with her so she could let off some steam and the two of us could catch up. We hadn't seen each other in a couple of weeks. We sat at the bar, where I brought her up to speed on Angel's party and gave her my edited version of the Tony interview. We had moved on to talking about the pains of corporate life when a friendly, female bartender with wispy, short hair appeared.

"Good. I'm ready for a drink," Shawna said.

"Excuse me. This is from the gentleman across the bar."

The bartender put a glass of wine in front of me and walked away.

What was this—a scene from a bad movie?

"Uh uh. You don't even drink and you get strangers sending you wine?" Shawna said.

I looked across the bar and saw a somewhat handsome man grinning back at me. He raised his head in acknowledgement and gripped a cognac glass. A huge diamond ring wrapped his pinky like a venomous snake. The head of the snake sparkled like the North Star. I nodded in a gesture of thanks.

"Girl, don't waste that wine. I'll drink it," Shawna said.

I pushed the glass to her. "Knock yourself out."

We chatted and people watched—which was entertainment alone.

"I'll be back, Shawna." I headed for the bathroom.

I entered a stall, and when I came out, there were four women vying for a spot in the mirror.

"Excuse me," I said trying to get to the sink. I just wanted a little sanitation.

The door creaked open and another woman slipped into the bathroom.

"It's too crowded in here for me!" a voice said as I washed my hands. I looked up to see that the woman who had just entered was standing next to me, smiling. She was tall and thin and wore a long weave that stopped just above her behind.

"I'm with you on that," I responded while rinsing my hands.

"You know," the woman continued, "that guy who sent you a drink at the bar is my man."

"Oh." I turned off the water with the back of my wrist and faced her. "Well, I don't know your man, and I don't want him."

She laughed. "You didn't even touch your drink. Are you more of a mixed drink connoisseur?"

"No, actually." I wasn't sure of what to say, so I pulled a towel from the holder and began drying my hands.

"Listen, I'm not confronting you. I just thought you should know that he thinks you're very attractive."

Where the hell was this going?

I stood there, dumbfounded.

"You are beautiful, I must admit."

"Thank... you?" I tried to reply but it turned into a question. I was wondering if I should draw back my fist and let one land where it would. To ease some of my discomfort, I looked toward the mirror and acted like I was fixing my hair, but ended up misplacing pieces in order to straighten them.

"Where do you work?" she asked.

I was taken aback by her inquiry but simply replied, "Not far from here."

"Oh! I'm in the New Center Area and my man has an office in the Penobscot Building. Maybe the three of us could meet for lunch or even get together for dinner."

My face twisted. I could not bring my lips to form any words. There were other people in the bathroom, but their conversations seemed to keep them from noticing ours. I wanted to say, "Does anyone hear this?"

Finally, in my confusion, I managed to say, "What?"

"I'm so sorry, I didn't even introduce myself. I'm Maya." She extended her hand, but I didn't want to touch it.

Reluctantly, I extended mine and said, "Joi." Joi was my middle name. I didn't want this chick to be able to identify me by my first name. "Look, Maya, I'm a little confused right now." I crossed my arms, hoping she'd pick up on my desire to maintain a decent distance between us.

"I don't want to make you uneasy. I just want to keep my man happy. He's a good man and he's good to me. He's just got some unconventional thoughts about relationships."

Uh, yeah.

I tried to talk but all of my words seemed to transfer to involuntary physical reactions. My eye started twitching, and I was sure she could see it.

"Okay, it was nice meeting you, but this isn't something I want to be involved in."

I tried to turn toward the door but she stepped closer, touched my wrist with one hand, and reached into her purse with the other. She pulled out a card and slipped it into the front pocket of my purse.

"Listen, just think about it. We're good people. Call me anytime if you change your mind about lunch."

Before I could react, she moved her hand to my shoulder then leaned in close to my ear to say, "Just think about it."

She left just as cool and collected as she had entered, leaving nothing but a faint aroma of the Bath and Body Works Coconut Vanilla lotion that drifted from her skin. I, on the other hand was flushed, sweaty and overcome with anxiety. I ran my hands under some cold water and shook them off before turning to the door to leave the bathroom. I wondered if anyone could tell I had been violated.

Some guy was hitting on Shawna, but she was hardly paying attention to him.

"Hey," I said, taking my seat.

"Did you fall in?" she asked.

"No, just got caught up talking to some chick."

"Well, your boy across the bar left you this." She handed me a business card. Apparently he owned a mortgage company.

A white collar freak, huh? Worst kind.

He'd written his cell phone number and the words "call anytime" on the back. I glanced at Shawna's glass. It was half full. She lifted it toward her mouth, but I grabbed it from her grip, tilted it back, and swallowed as much as I could in several gulps. I placed the glass on the counter, my taste buds tingling. Shawna's mouth dropped. Before she could respond, I plunked both business cards in the glass and tapped her on the hand. "Let's go."

We moved through the crowd and out of the door. My body was warm. I raced toward the car while she babbled inquiries in my ear. I never answered.

"I'm not going out with you anymore," she finally said.

"Actually, that might be in your best interest," I told her.

"Trinity, I love you, but you're starting to scare me. What is really going on with you?"

I stopped where I was and looked her in the eye, buzzing from the three ounces of wine I'd consumed. In the most serious of voices, I said, "You wouldn't believe me if I told you."

Then, without warning, I belched right in her face. We laughed, but only I couldn't stop. I threw my hands to the sky and yelled, "Why is this my life?"

"Girl, come on. I see why you don't drink. You could never be this dramatic," she teased.

My cell phone rang as we approached my car.

"Booty call?" Shawna asked. "Oh, they must not know they're wasting their time."

I gave her a mean look as I unlocked the car. I handed her my keys and headed toward the passenger door.

"Here. That half glass of wine had no effect on you." I removed the phone from my purse, and answered it, even though I didn't recognize the phone number.

"Hey, girl!" A deep voice responded on the other end. I could hear music in the background.

"Who is that?" Shawna whispered.

It was Malik. "What's up, Malik? Where are you?"

"I'm at the crib. Had to change the number yesterday, baby." He laughed. "Who are you with?"

"Shawna," I answered.

"Oh, Lord."

I wanted to tell him not to act like that, but I couldn't because Shawna was hanging onto my every word.

"Well," he continued. "I don't know what you two are doing, but I have some people over, and I want you to come by. Since your girl is with you, I guess that invitation is open to her, too," he chuckled.

"All right. Let me see what Shawna wants to do. She's driving."

"Well, I better see you soon."

"You still have the same address or did you move because ol' girl was stalking you?"

"Don't play, Trin."

"All right. Later, Malik," I said before hanging up.

"Shawna, do you want to go to Malik's get-together?"

Her eyes lit up. "You pulled me out of Floods like there was a fire. Yeah, I wanna go! I've still got energy to burn."

"I bet you do," I said and gave her a sly grin that she tried to ignore.

Shawna had had a crush on Malik since she met him at my eighteenth birthday party, but much like the response I received from him in the ninth grade, Malik didn't take Shawna seriously. It wasn't because she was one of the boys; it was because she was too aggressive for him.

Malik lived in a beautiful, brown brick Georgian home in Indian Village, which was just a few miles from downtown. Only three streets made up the neighborhood, and Malik lived on Iroquois. Most of the homes were built in the early 1900s by Detroit's most famous architects. Indian Village had once been home to some of the most prominent people in the city, including Edsel Ford. What I found most alluring about the area was that each home was different. Some homes even had carriage houses where people used to store their horse carriages and many were as big as modern homes.

After the 1967 riots, crime increased, and the surrounding neighborhoods were a far cry from the well-preserved gem known as Indian Village. Still, as a financial planner who dabbled in real estate, Malik knew he couldn't pass on the opportunity to live in the historic district.

Malik had purchased his home two years before from an elderly woman who had lived in the house for thirty-five years until her philanthropist husband died and the upkeep became too much for her. The house required some work, but Malik saw its potential and the price was right, considering the seller's situation. He bought the house and began restoring what became the only woman he'd ever been true to.

I parked across from Malik's house where a number of cars already lined the quiet street. Shawna primped in the car visor mirror, touching up her lipstick and combing her hair before we went in. She tugged on her shirt, causing me to realize that her top exaggerated the term "fitted."

"Girl, come on here," I said, getting out of the car.

Malik answered the door. His dimples held up both sides of his radiant smile. He was dressed in a cream colored V-neck shirt and a pair of loose-fitting dark jeans. The light from the fixture that hung from the vaulted ceiling gleamed on his bald head. He hugged us heartily before taking our jackets.

Hip-hop blared from the surround-sound speakers placed strategically around the house. Our heels clicked first on the Pewabic tile in the foyer and then on the wooden floors that lay across the rest of the house. I spoke to a group of girls who were crammed into the smallest couch, failing miserably to look comfortable. Malik's brother, Ali, and three other guys were playing Spades at the dining room table. I didn't want to interrupt their game, so I rubbed Ali on the shoulder as I passed by to give him an unspoken acknowledgement, but his boys looked up at me like, "Who are you?" Their response caused Ali to turn around.

"Lookin' good, girl," he said, grabbing my arm over his shoulder. He kissed my hand. "Get some food in the kitchen. Drinks are in the basement."

I never knew why their mother gave them Muslim names. They were Christian—well, at least they were

Christian in theory. Not to mention their last name was Jenkins.

Ali and Malik Jenkins. What was she thinking?

We walked into the kitchen. Some girl was making spaghetti and garlic bread. Another was making a tossed salad. I looked at Malik and rolled my eyes. He glanced at me quickly as if to say, "Don't say a word."

"Bobby and Tim are downstairs." He interrupted our telepathic conversation with actual words. Shawna and I followed him to the basement. About ten guys were there and only half as many women. A movie was playing, but the volume was very low. Speakers were run from the living room to the basement, so the music was just as loud downstairs as it was upstairs. Watching people trying to talk over the music was like watching a silent movie with no subtitles.

Bobby and Tim were attempting to start conversations with two girls, apparent friends, who were paying the guys no attention. As soon as Bobby and Tim turned to say something to each other, the girls went upstairs.

"I see not much has changed. You still have *no* game."

"Trin!" they yelled. They hugged me in the flirtatiously desperate way guys do when they're attracted to women but know they haven't got a chance. Bobby and Tim had been friends with Malik since elementary school. When I started hanging out with Malik, they sort of came with the package. I introduced them to Shawna and watched their eyes light up as they sized her up without an ounce of discretion.

"Don't even think about it," I said before they could come up with an uninspired pickup line. "I'll catch up with you later," I told them and motioned for Shawna to follow me to the couch. Malik headed back upstairs to turn down the music a bit. Shawna and I talked while I watched Bobby and Tim make goo-goo eyes at her.

"Will they ever grow up? They still act like they're in puberty."

"Why, because they're attracted to *me*?" Shawna asked with annoyance in her voice.

"Chill out, Shawna. If you're flattered because the Wonder Twins like you, then cool. Have fun with it, I guess."

"Now you're wrong, because one of the Wonder Twins was a girl," Shawna said.

"And your point is?" I retorted through our laughs.

"Trinity, come here for a minute," Malik yelled from the top of the stairs. A guy was checking out Shawna from the other side of the room, and he was kind of cute. I figured she'd be all right for a couple of minutes.

"I'll be right back."

Shawna nodded and went to the wet bar where she poured a glass of white zinfandel. Malik was waiting for me at the top of the stairs. He grabbed my hand and pulled me up the last step and into the kitchen, where the girl who was cooking the spaghetti cut her eyes at me. "Hello," I said to her in my friendliest voice, as if I were a restaurant greeter. I wasn't surprised that she didn't speak back but only tended to her spaghetti.

I turned to Malik. "She better not try to slash my tires."

"She's nobody," he said and led me up the staircase. He pulled me into one of the four bedrooms, flicked the light switch, then closed the door. Malik sat me down on the bed and plopped down about a foot away from me. The ceiling fan ticked by slowly, causing just enough of a breeze to cool my face. He squinted as he looked in my eyes. At that moment I wished I had some mouthwash. I didn't want him to smell the wine on my breath, so I looked to the artwork on the opposite wall and my gaze drifted to the floor. "The house is really coming along." I cleared my throat. "It's got so much charm. Did you refinish the floors by yourself?"

"Why are you suddenly so interested in my floors?"

"I'm just admiring them." I looked in every direction but Malik's. "Take it as a compliment."

"Well," Malik said, changing the subject. "I just wanted to kick it with you for a minute."

He cupped my right hand inside both of his, and I faced him for the first time since entering the room.

What was he doing?

"Trinity, I've watched you grow up—"

"Watched me grow up? How about you stop sounding like one of my uncles," I blurted out.

"You know what I mean. I've watched you become a woman, and—"

"Okay, I'm going to the bathroom, now. You're going to make me vomit."

I felt as awkward as I did when I had the sex talk with my parents.

When a man and a woman love each other...

"Would you please stop cutting me off?" Malik asked.

I was used to reacting to Malik's shenanigans, but this time I could see he was perturbed. "Listening," I said.

"You've got your shit together. Two degrees, a good job, your own place, good credit, no kids, you're gorgeous..."

"Thanks. Now, where are you going with this?"

"I just don't understand why you haven't found a good man."

How was I supposed to answer that? It was true that I hadn't known a good man since Diori and, let my mother tell it, I messed that up worse than Lot's wife when she turned back to look at Sodom. But I hadn't been looking for a man, so what was this "find-a-good-man" business?

"I mean, you deserve to be with someone who makes you happy."

"I make me happy, Malik."

"Cut all that women's lib shit. I know you can take care of yourself. I'm talking about someone who can bring you the kind of love and support you can't give yourself. God created man *and* woman for a reason."

"You should know. You're doing quite well with your goal of conquering all the women under His creation," I said, trying to divert his attention from me.

"Why do you have a problem talking about this?" He didn't dignify my comment.

I sat quietly, pondering his question before answering. "I guess having a man isn't that important to me," I responded.

His expression was smug. He said nothing, but his thoughts spoke to me. I heard him say that I should give a guy—the right guy—a chance; that I can be intimidating; that I might be missing a blessing. His eyes sparkled under the light with each pass of the fan. Then he put his hand at the back of my neck and kissed me on the forehead.

"I just know you deserve more." He stroked my hair, and I smiled at his words. I knew what he was trying to say, but I don't think he understood that his "more" was not necessarily my "better."

"Thank you, Malik." I hugged him. "Well, I better go check on Shawna," I said before standing up.

He knew I was trying to get out of an uncomfortable situation.

"Come with me." I grabbed his hand and pulled him down the stairs, into the basement. Shawna and the guy who'd been eyeing her from across the room were talking, so I made my way toward Bobby and Tim. Apparently they had worked the room to no avail because they were talking to each other and drinking beer on the couch. Malik and I sat down next to them, and we all talked for only a moment before Shawna was standing in front of me.

"Hey! What's up?" I asked. Her attention was not on me, but on Malik. I followed up with another question. "Why'd you leave your new friend?"

"Oh, he'll be all right," Shawna answered and turned around to squeeze her well-endowed hips between me and Malik.

"I really like your home, Malik," she said.

"Thanks," he said, trying to show her appropriate, yet brief courtesy. I watched him wiggle to his left to get some breathing room. Bobby and Tim were to my right and burst into laughter, but Shawna wasn't fazed by it. I nudged Bobby with my elbow to shut them up.

I leaned into Shawna's right ear and whispered, "Why don't you just give him your panties?"

"What?" she asked emphatically.

"Stop throwing yourself at him. If you really like him, give him a chance to approach you. Don't just plop your goods in his lap."

"Oh," Shawna raised her voice. "Is that how you've managed to keep him hooked for all these years?"

"Excuse me?" My voice got trapped between a whisper and a yell as I tried to maintain some degree of discretion.

"No need to play dumb. You're his challenge, Trinity. The one he can't have. Hell, you're the one no one can have. He'll just be in love with you forever. Unrequited love is a bitch."

I sat back and crossed my arms. "You sound crazy."

"You haven't figured it out in all of these years, and I'm the one who's crazy?"

She was getting under my skin. "Don't start with me, Shawna."

She rolled her eyes and sucked her body from between ours, losing her balance as she walked toward the bar.

Malik scooted toward me. "What's up with your girl?"

"She's fine." I crossed my legs and sat back on the couch, grateful for some space.

"Yeah, well, she should relax. I'll put her ass out."

"Be quiet, Malik. She means no harm."

He stood up and went upstairs, muttering something under his breath. I chuckled, but hoped he hadn't heard what Shawna said.

Shawna returned with a cup in her hand.

"Shawna, need I remind you—you're driving?"

"You *need* to do whatever the hell you think is best."

"Right now, whoopin' your ass is crossing my mind."

She looked at me, rolled her eyes then smacked her lips.

"You can sit here and roll your eyes until Jesus comes back, or you can tell me what the problem is," I said.

Shawna was silent, but I could see that she was processing something. She sighed then said, "I just wish he would look at me the way he looks at you."

"What?" I was puzzled by her words.

"Malik—he looks at you like he adores you."

"Shawna, you've clearly had one too many." I glanced at my watch.

"I'm serious. No one has ever looked at me the way he looks at you. And you don't even see it. It sounds stupid, but sometimes I wish I were you... just for a moment."

I was baffled by her admission. I convinced myself that it was the alcohol talking. "Shawna, being me for a moment would get you nowhere with Malik. There is nothing romantic about our relationship."

"No shit, but maybe it should be." She sipped her wine.

I let her words marinate for a moment while the wine in her glass trickled away.

"I should drive," I finally said.

"It's your world," she said and handed me my keys.

"I think it's time to call it a night."

Shawna nodded in agreement. I said goodnight to Bobby and Tim, then went upstairs with Shawna in tow. Malik was in the living room. I hugged him to say goodnight then nudged him to give Shawna a hug. He did, then leaned toward my ear.

"Remember what I told you in the bedroom," he whispered.

I nodded, then Shawna and I headed out. I drove us back to my condo where I insisted she spend the night in the guest room. We exchanged few words beyond "goodnight."

I slipped into my room and turned on the overhead light. A glance across the room showed that everything was in its place. My royal purple duvet cover lay neatly on the bed with two goldish-brown pillows, which matched the beading that traveled the length of the cover. Kitty-corner to the bed was my terracotta accent chair, which I bought at a garage sale in a ritzy Birmingham neighborhood. The seller had bought it for her home, but soon determined it "clashed" with her décor. Directly in front of the bed was the twenty-seven-inch television which never failed to deliver the latest tragedies and celebrity breakup news. A pair of mauve BCBG stilettos stood outside my closet, positioned as if they walked out on their own. I bent down to pick them up and put them back on the first shelf in the walk-in closet. Since I was already in the closet, I slipped off the shoes I was wearing. The leather wedge-heeled sandals offered less style than the stilettos, but provided much more comfort.

I pulled the cover back on the bed and sat on its edge. To my right was an end table, holding a lamp and two pictures. One was of me and Bashaye, but it was the other picture that drew me. I picked it up and studied it. My grandmother posed alone, grinning as if she knew something the photographer did not. Ma Lo looked to be in her early forties when the picture was taken, which would have been well before I was born. Her long hair, already silver-streaked, was pulled into a neat, inconspicuous bun. Her chocolate skin glowed, and its smooth richness was noticeable, even in a photograph. I wondered what she was thinking when she posed for the picture; wondered how she felt that day; wondered if she knew she wouldn't be alive in just twenty years.

I put the picture down and lay on my back with my legs bent. I inhaled and exhaled slowly. The scent of a ripe pink grapefruit lingered in the air from the candle I'd lit earlier in the day. Closing my eyes, I began to twist Ma Lo's ring on my finger. It was so simple, so delicate, so worthless to anyone but my family. I pulled it off and looked inside of the ring to read the fading inscription.

L & T Love Honor Cherish

My mom would often tell the story of how Papa Theo not only wanted to buy my grandmother a ring, he wanted to get it engraved. But as a musician—a trumpet player—he couldn't afford to pay for it. My grandparents lived in Black Bottom, a black community on the near east side of Detroit that had been just a memory for decades. Papa Theo played gigs at a couple of the clubs in the neighborhood. After every show, he put aside money to pay for my grandmother's ring, the engraving and his own wedding band until finally, he had saved up enough. I was mystified by the significance of the humble piece of metal I held between my fingertips.

I sat up and the ring slipped from my grip, falling to the floor. It lodged between a strand in the carpet and the end table. I reached for it once more and was distracted by a Bible on the end table shelf. It was covered by folders and a stack of thank you notes. I plucked it from its position and turned on the lamp that sat behind the pictures on the end table. The once-white bonded leather was riddled with wrinkles like those on the face of an elderly person. The gold lettering had faded, but the imprint reading "TRINITY JOI POR-TER" remained in the bottom right corner.

I opened the Bible, realizing I hadn't done so in years. Tattered and aged, the Bible was no longer pre-sentable. I traded it in years ago for one that I found more appropriate for public view. Since then, I'd been through one more. I ran my fingers over the dedica-tion page and read it out loud. "Presented to: Trinity Joi. By: Ma Lo. Date: June 27, 1993." Below the date, my grandmother had written a message. "Before I formed you in the womb I knew you, before you were born I set you apart; I appointed you as a prophet to the nations.—Jeremiah 1:5"

Of all the passages in the Bible, I wondered why my grandmother had chosen that passage to write on the dedication page. I turned to the passage and read it for myself. "Before I formed you in the womb I knew you, before you were born I set you apart; I appointed you as a prophet to the nations." I knew my grandmother was trying to tell me something about myself; some-thing about life. I pondered it for a while, but fell asleep before I had my answer.

In the morning I awoke wearing the same clothes I had on when Shawna and I went out. The light bulb in the lamp next to me was hot from being on for hours and the Bible was on the pillow next to me.

I can't believe I fell asleep like this.

I remembered that my grandmother's ring was still on the floor, so I picked it up and walked over to my dresser, placing it in my jewelry box. Slipping the bathroom, I brushed my teeth then stepped into the shower to wash away the previous night. I spread coconut body butter on myself and threw on a T-shirt and a pair of shorts to fix breakfast. I began cooking an omelet with turkey, onions, green pepper and cheddar cheese. It was a quarter to ten, and I thought Shawna was still asleep, but she came into the kitchen with her purse on her shoulder. "Morning," she said.

"Good morning," I said, barely taking my eyes off on my omelet. "Would you like half? It's big enough for both of us."

"No thanks. I need to take my niece to the mall."

She sat at the table with her hands on her head. Her usually well-kept hair was unfettered by a comb, brush, or even a few fingers.

I flipped the omelet and headed to the fridge, pulling out the orange juice. I poured two glasses and handed one to her. "Drink this, at least."

She took a few sips and stared out of the window as I continued to fix my omelet.

"I said some things I didn't mean last night," she said.

"I know. Don't worry about it."

I pressed the spatula onto the omelet to make sure it was done.

She downed the rest of the juice then put the glass in the sink.

I turned off the burner and reached for a plate. "Maybe you had a point last night. Sometimes I don't see things that are clear to others. I apologize. I know what I said hurt you. But you're my girl. I don't want you looking silly."

Shawna grinned timidly—a reaction that did not fit her personality. She rarely set aside her pride.

I sat down at the table with my plate.

"Let me get out of here so you can eat." She popped up as quickly as I had sat down.

"I told you there's enough for two," I insisted.

"No. I gotta shower and get dressed." She fidgeted with her purse strap and moved toward the front door.

I smiled to let her know it was okay.

"I'll call you this evening?" She seemed to be asking permission.

"I'll be here." I wanted her to know that I was there for her whether or not she wanted to talk about what happened at Malik's party.

She smiled and opened the door.

"Talk to you tonight," she said looking as if she weren't quite sure what else to say.

"Okay, Sweetie." I closed the door behind her.

Chapter Eleven

The next day was Friends and Family day, and even the rain didn't keep people away. While you could usually expect a full house, the church was especially crowded, and there were quite a few faces that I did not recognize among the many familiar smiles. We sang the Hymn of Praise: "I Will Trust in the Lord." When I sat down, I lifted my purse and Bible and inched toward the woman to my right to make room for others who were entering the sanctuary. A heavy-set woman with a little girl, who was about Autumn's age, sat to my left. People were entering on both sides of the sanctuary, filling it like ants in a hill seeking shelter at the start of a storm.

I listened to the announcements and glanced over the program. On the cover was a full-color picture of Reverend Smiley and his wife. The forty-something couple stood side-by-side on the steps of the church, his shoulder just inches above hers. He wore a basic black suit and round-rimmed glasses that accentuated his defined cheekbones and broad nose. She was clad in a conservative yellow suit, with a skirt that hung to her calves. At about five-foot nine inches tall, Reverend Smiley's slim stature was no indication of the fullness that abounded in his spirit. I thumbed through the pages of the program. One of the ads was for after-school tutors.

I should volunteer. It's been a while since I tutored. It will be fun.

When I looked up from the program, I quickly forgot about any volunteer efforts. It felt like someone turned up my internal thermostat, as if I were a victim of perimenopause. My program slipped through my moist fingers and I scrambled to recover it, nearly bumping heads with the woman next to me as she reached for it, too. I smiled at her graciously, while wondering just how this Negro had found his way back to Michigan, into my workplace and now into my church. Tony was getting ready to park his behind just two pews in front of me, and what's this? He was holding the hand of a young woman.

Lord, I don't think I can handle this right now. Please don't do this to me.

They sat down and all I could do was hope that Tony would not turn around—not once through the entire service. Wishful thinking did pay off sometimes.

Brother Thomas Oliver read the announcements. When he finished, I knew it could only mean one thing—the recognition of visitors was near. Reverend Smiley approached the pulpit, gave a brief history of Friends and Family day at Ray of Light and welcomed all of the visitors. Then he asked them to stand.

The congregation looked around and offered smiles to all of the friendly faces that came to worship at Ray of Light. Tony and his mystery lady stood with the rest of the visitors. As they rose to their feet, I looked behind me and to each side—everywhere but in front of me to avoid the possibility of him turning around and spotting me. After the ushers passed out registration cards and the visitors sat down, I wondered if my anonymity had been compromised. I figured that if it had, the last thing Tony would do was acknowledge me.

Sister Donna James stood at the lectern and prepared to read the Scriptures, which would come from Mark 11: 25-26 and Matthew 18:21-22. I found the passages and followed along.

"And the Word says," Sister Donna James began, "'And whenever you stand praying, if you have anything against anyone, forgive him, that your Father in heaven may also forgive you your trespasses. But if you do not forgive, neither will your Father in Heaven forgive your trespasses.'"

She turned to Matthew, then read, "'Then Peter came to Him and said, 'Lord, how often shall my brother sin against me, and I forgive him? Up to seven times?' Jesus said to him, 'I do not say to you, up to seven times, but up to seventy times seven.'"

"Amen!" a woman exclaimed from the front of the church.

My heart was heavy as I tried to fathom how I would be able to forgive Tony seventy times seven. The number may as well have been infinite. I had so much hatred for him in my heart. I peered at the back of his head and, for a moment, wondered if I had an undiscovered power to penetrate bodily flesh with my X-ray vision and melt the neurons of his brain. I quickly determined that if I did have that ability, it would be of the devil and not of the Lord, so I let the thought pass.

The children's choir was belting out "Oh, How I Love Jesus." I tried to concentrate on them in their cute little burgundy robes, but I was hopelessly distracted. My eyes drifted to the young woman sitting next to Tony. She was attractive... tall, slender, shapely. All I could see was her profile, but it was clear to me that she was younger. Her shoulder-length, streaked hair was due for a hot oil treatment, but she was cute, nonetheless. I watched them exchange words and brief gestures. He raised his left arm and placed it behind her, as if he were doing the age-old "movie theater stretch." He gently stroked her shoulder and she leaned in to absorb his affection. I wondered if she knew what kind of person she was nuzzling up to. I knew I had to stop watching them and focus on the service.

My line of sight drifted back to the pulpit where Reverend Smiley now stood. He offered a prayer before his sermon, took a couple sips of water and sifted through several papers on the stand before him—presumably his sermon notes. He raised his head, rolling his shoulders backward. I could see his bosom was full of fire. It was evident in his eyes. I was not sure what to expect, but I had a feeling that this would be a sermon that I would not soon forget.

Reverend Smiley reiterated the text from the scripture reading. He paused, took another swig of water, then asked, "What type of baggage are you carrying?"

Some people looked perplexed, some cracked a smile and others stared back at him blankly.

"You may wrap it in Gucci, Louis Vuitton, Dooney and Bourke or even a plastic bag, but when you unwrap it, it's still baggage," Reverend Smiley continued. "What's in your bags?" He stepped away from the pulpit and made his way to the center aisle, peering into the faces of apprehensive recipients.

"What's in your bag?" he asked one woman who sat at the end of a pew. His smile reassured her that his intent was not to single her out.

He moved on to a man who sat several rows behind her.

"How about yours?"

The man chuckled as the animated reverend made a silly face, and muttered, "What's he talking about? I don't have any bags." Reverend Smiley searched his surroundings as if he were looking for actual bags.

"As you may have guessed, I'm not talking about physical luggage but emotional luggage that everyone in this sanctuary carries with him or her every day." The congregation had an overall stillness to it that was broken only by a rumble or two of chatter.

"Don't get quiet," the reverend insisted.

"What is it?" he asked searching the faces of the intimidated congregation. "An old boyfriend or girlfriend? The memories of a school bully? How about that thing your spouse did ten years ago that you *still* bring up during an argument? Hmm?" He smiled as the congregation burst into laughter.

"Y'all know what I'm talking about!" He looked at an older man who seemed particularly tickled by his words. "Don't you?" he asked the man. The gentleman nodded his head vigorously as the woman next to him, presumably his wife, patted him on the back as if to say, "Don't embarrass me!"

"Think about all of those things that you just haven't let go of. The prank your high school nemesis played on you in eleventh grade; the heartache your first crush caused when she denied your advances; the coworker who didn't acknowledge you at the grocery store; the boss who didn't give you the raise you deserved; the bank that didn't grant you the loan; the relative who never paid you back; the man who cut you off on your way to work!"

He paused and extended his arm from the left side of his body to the right, as if wiping the whole congregation. "What's your baggage?"

Reverend Smiley went into a mocking voice. "Well, why should I talk to her? She stole my boyfriend in the seventh grade."

He returned to his normal voice. "You're thirty eight years old! You are married with three children! Why are you holding on to that? Instead of letting go, you want to keep that in your bag and even pass it on to your children. Your daughter goes to school with that woman's daughter, so you teach her to despise the daughter, just as you despised the mother."

"Woo!" a woman exclaimed from the front pew.

"Someone knows what I'm talking about." He returned to the pulpit and sipped his water. "You worked so hard for that raise and you didn't get it. Your boss was wrong. Dead wrong! So you walk around sabotaging projects—even your own. Why should you give your all to some idiot who can't recognize what he has in you?"

"Uh oh!" a man yelled from somewhere behind me.

"I'm not suggesting that you do nothing when you've been wronged. By all means—confront the situation." He took a moment to analyze his statement. "Now wait. Don't take what I just said and run. 'Well, Reverend Smiley said it was okay to cuss him out!'"

I laughed out loud at his point of clarification, because I knew it was going through someone's mind.

"What I am saying is this: It's okay to confront people by letting them know how their actions made you feel. It's not okay to do it with spite, and I know this is not an easy thing to do.

"We are emotional creatures. We get angry! We want to knock a head off once or twice, or if we have children—especially teenagers—thrice." After the laughter died off he continued. "You can't cuss someone out and walk away saying 'in the name of Jesus!' But you can approach confrontation with tact and honesty."

Some affirming phrases burst through the stillness of the worshippers.

"I hope you are so quiet because you are allowing what I'm saying to penetrate. I hope you aren't quiet because you're not willing to entertain the idea of what I'm presenting." He paused, staring into a sea of faces that stared back at him. "There's one thing I left out, though. Once you make your confrontation, you've got to let it go." He lowered a fist to his waist and dramatically spread his fingers.

"All right!" a woman to my left shouted. The entire pew turned to look at her. She stood to her feet, flailing her arms before sitting down and rocking silently.

"Letting go implies that you offer forgiveness. It means that your heart is big enough to release an unforgiving spirit. You can't tell someone you forgive their wrongs then bring them up every time they make you angry."

The reaction from the congregation was mixed, but it was evident he was speaking directly to the hearts of many who were within earshot.

"Do you know why you can't go on thinking this way?" he asked. "Consider this. Think of all the times you've gotten on your knees and gone to the Lord. What if He came back to you and said, 'You know what, I'll let you off, but this is going on your permanent record'? A lot of us would be in big trouble!

"Jeremiah 31:35 says of those who know the Lord, 'For I will forgive their iniquity and their sin I will remember no more.'" He looked around the sanctuary as if he were trying to enter our minds and hearts to ensure our spiritual understanding. "No more. 'I will... remember no more.' If we work to be like Christ, how can we as Christians expect forgiveness from the Lord if we refuse to forgive our brothers and sisters in Christ?"

My eyes dropped much like those of a shamed child who was grappling with guilt.

"Brothers and sisters, we must learn to let go. I know the thought seems unreasonable, uncomfortable, absolutely foreign, but how ridiculous is it to continue to walk around with all of that old, dusty baggage? How can you ever expect to get where you're going if you've got that to weigh you down?

"God doesn't want us to experience that burden. 'Cast your burdens on the Lord, and He shall sustain you; He shall never permit the righteous to be moved.' Psalm 55:22. Give your burdens to Him. Turn over all your bags to Him and He will take care of them. It's as simple as that.

"So why are you resisting? What are you afraid of? Moving out of your comfort zone?" He patted his head with a handkerchief and gulped down more water. "If you go with God, He will never leave you. Maybe you're saying, 'Rev, I know the Lord won't leave me, but this... this is small stuff. The Lord has bigger concerns. I can handle this one.' Well, I'll tell you this much. He does not want to see you walking around all broken down, weighed down with bags that you should not be carrying.

"And let me shed a different light on things. All of those things you are carrying that are full of spite, hatred, jealousy and envy take a lot of energy to per-petuate. You see, when you carry those bags, hour after hour, month after month, year after year, decade after decade, they harbor energy. And you feed that energy. You are the fuel. When your body can no longer host that energy, it begins to break down, as would any other machine. You get sick. Headaches, colds, the flu, cancer. How can you expect to fight these things when you yourself are feeding them by offering your energy to negative things in your life?

"And for what? Do you think that ex-girlfriend, that married man, that boss, that stranger is sitting up at night worrying about you? Do you?" Laughter reverberated throughout the sanctuary, but Reverend Smiley was quick to remind us of the seriousness of the matter.

"Of course they aren't. So don't give them that energy. Give it back to yourself. Love yourself enough to drop the bags. Trust God enough to cast them away and never look back. They'll be history if you are only willing to let go." After a final sip of his water, he returned the glass to the stand and spread his arms, palms toward the sky. "In the name of Jesus. The doors of the church are open."

The congregation praised God with adoration and clapping as people approached the altar. I heard applause from those with a better view, as they watched people preparing to make life-changing choices. Sister Donna James instructed the congregation to be seated, allowing those who had gone to the altar to be seen. I counted them.

Four, six, ei—I don't believe this. Noooooo! This can't be happening!

Tony and the young woman were standing at the altar awaiting the opportunity to speak. The nurturer passed the microphone to the first person, who would pass it down until everyone had the opportunity to say a few words. The congregation clapped after each testimony. I clapped, too, but I heard nothing anyone had to say. I was merely awaiting the moment when Tony would take the mike. Only one more person separated me from that moment. A long-winded, middle-aged gentleman talked about his struggle with prostate cancer and said something about his daughter bringing him to Ray of Light.

Come on, come on. Speed it up, Uncle Leroy. We've got other folks to get to.

Finally, he passed the microphone to Tony who was smiling ear to ear.

"My name is Tony Parsons." He turned to the young woman, who was to his right. "And this is my fiancée, Veronique Gibson."

Fiancée? She's like twelve?

My hands sweated as I held my knees and did all I could do not to yell out, "The jig is up! Okay, okay, where are the cameras?"

"I grew up here in Detroit, went to Howard University in D.C. and stayed out there for a couple of years after graduating."

Yeah, and it only took you six years as a full-time student to get a bachelor's degree.

"I took a leave from my job in D.C. to come home and spend time with my family. Veronique is a family friend who I knew was supposed to be my wife, so I proposed."

Family friend, huh? Were you her babysitter?

"We're getting married next spring. Detroit is home, and I'm coming home. I quit my job in D.C. and just got a new one here in the city." Tony switched his weight from one foot to the other. "We, uhh, really want a church home. This is the first time we've visited Ray of Light, but it only took once for us to see that this is where we belong."

The sanctuary exploded with applause. "Amen!" the nurturer said as Tony's fiancée took the microphone.

"As Tony mentioned, I'm Veronique. We are so excited to be here. I thank you for welcoming us into your church home." She handed the microphone back to the nurturer.

"We are so grateful to see young people who want to work for Christ through their union," the nurturer said, before inviting all of the new members to pray.

Tony, who I was so sure I'd forgotten, was turning up in every part of my world. I had left the part of me that knew him in D.C. and all was well with that arrangement. So why was he shaking up everything I'd worked hard to build? And what was this newfound desire to be a Christian? As many churches as there were in Detroit, why did it have to be my church? He never even went to chapel at Howard.

The rest of the service was a blur. My thoughts were consumed by the message and its application to my life. I thought about the bags I was still carrying around and I realized that the essence of Tony Parsons was in one of those bags. I had been carrying him around with me since the day he raped me.

I had packed up and moved away, but it was with that bag in hand. It was almost as if I had him tucked away in a zippered section of a suitcase long enough to forget he ever existed at least until the moment I packed for another trip and unzipped that pocket. Unknowingly, I unpacked the memories I'd buried in my subconscious when I saw him in Fridays. I tried to pack him away again that night, but an arm emerged from the bag when I ran into his mother at the grocery store. Out fell one of his husky legs the day he interviewed at my job. Those fated encounters brought old wounds to the surface and added weight to the bag.

It was only now I recognized that the memories of Tony had ruptured my soul. The fact that he made my blood boil made it clear to me that I had given ownership of part of my spirit to a man who had lost no sleep over me. All I ever really wanted was for him to acknowledge his wrongs and to apologize. Chances were that I would never get that apology.

So where did that leave me now? There must be a reason that life had placed him back in my path. I believed the sermon hit that reason on the head. It was time that I somehow found the strength to forgive him. But how would I do this when he hadn't even recognized that what he did was wrong? Though I lacked confidence, something told me that it would be okay. I did not know what putting down that bag would do to change my life, but I was finally ready to find out.

After brief conversations with several members, I headed outside with lunch plans on the brain. Glancing at the ground, I saw no signs of the rain that was falling as I entered service. It was as if God split the clouds and pushed them beyond the state lines. The sky was so vibrant it reminded me of a landscape painting that jumped right off the canvas and into reality. Lavender hydrangea lined the front of the church, and all of the season's flowers would be in full bloom for the church's Fourth of July celebration. I could almost touch the beauty of that summer day, and for a moment, I tried to imagine what could possibly make the view any more mesmerizing. I relished the privilege of witnessing God's blessings in seasonal cycles.

I was so engrossed in my thoughts that I had arrived at my car before I knew it. Autopilot often kicked in for me when it came to finding my car. I think I was born with a carrier pigeon's instincts; I rarely got lost, even when driving in unknown territory. What I neglected to do was to take my keys out of my purse before I got to the car. Naturally, the keys had wiggled their way to the bottom of my purse. I fought to get to the source of the rattle that echoed from the insides of my faithful Kate Spade handbag. Peppermints and loose change tried to distract me, and I just couldn't get my hands on the keys.

I lifted my purse to eye level and began to shake it like a gift—as if that would make the keys pop out of the purse and into my hands.

"Come onnnnn!" I said out loud, forgetting that opening your mouth, adjusting your lips and using your vocal cords produced sound. I lowered the purse again and resumed my apple bob when I was distracted by two pair of feet in my peripheral vision. The feet were quickly closing in on my personal space, which was narrowed considerably by the car to the left of mine. Finally, I got my hands on the keys and pulled them out. I tried to scoot toward my car door to allow both pair of feet to pass, but upon impact, I discovered that I was too close to the side mirror.

Ouuuch! I think I ruptured my spleen! You are such a klutz, Trinity!

"Excuse us," a woman's voice said. I looked toward her in acknowledgement, and at that moment I knew that I was really being tested. I stared into the face of Veronica... Vivica... whatever that little girl's name was who was engaged to Tony. He was right behind her. My eyes shifted from her to him and back again. It was obvious that until now, he had no idea that I was the idiot fumbling for my keys. His expression spoke volumes.

"If I had known it was you, I would have run the other way yelling, 'Psycho on church grounds!'" I imagined that's what he would have said, anyway.

I pushed three words from my gut in response to the girl with the name that began with 'V.' "No, excuse me." I smiled at both her and Tony.

His eyes were as big as saucers, like those of a cat trying to follow the path of a penlight. For a moment we all stared at each other. Her at me, because she was probably wondering why I wasn't getting in my car; me at her because I wanted to feed my curiosity about her; and he at me, probably because he wasn't sure if I'd castrate him.

"You... you two joined church today, right?"

Her eyes lit up. "Yes, we did!" She extended her hand and shook mine. "I'm Veronique."

Yeah, that's it... Veronique.

"Trinity. Nice to meet you," I said.

"This is my fiancé, Tony." She gleamed as she said, "fiancé."

"Yes... I remember," I said innocently and nodded my head to acknowledge him. I clasped my hands behind my back. He nodded and quickly turned his attention to Veronique.

"Come on, Nikki. We don't want to block up this area since people are trying to leave."

He pushed her along. His insincerity was conspicuous to me only. She turned around and said, "Nice meeting you, Trinity. We'll see you soon!"

I threw up my hand in a "what in the world just happened?" kind of wave before unlocking the car door. I practically jumped into the car and quickly pulled the door shut. It occurred to me that Veronique had no idea who I was. My name had not set off any light bulbs. While I was sure any living, breathing human being with a heart would have grappled with himself over a situation like ours, it was clear to me that the friendship we once had was one he did not value; my feelings were ones that he did not respect; that night was one he'd rather forget than face. Tony had no intentions of apologizing to me or expressing a desire to right his wrongs. He only wanted to move on with his life, yet I had allowed Tony to consume much of my own energy. And Tony was right... I needed to get over it.

Whether his words at church were sincere; whether I'd ever have to see his face again when I worshipped; whether he was a changed man—none of it seemed to matter in the grand scheme of things.

"Lean not toward your own understanding," I said and drove off, leaving Tony's baggage right there in the parking lot.

I felt good... but I was still hungry, so I called Malik from my cell phone.

"Meet me at Beans and Cornbread for lunch. I've got something to tell you."

Chapter Twelve

S everal weeks passed, and my mother and I were getting ready for Caroline's bridal shower on Saturday—an event that Caroline and my Aunt Georgia had been preparing for since the day Simon proposed. Now the shower was just days away—one month before the wedding date.

Mom, Lydia and I decided to drive, since Lydia had gotten a new SUV. We could have flown and arrived in less than an hour, but since we'd have to make the trip again just two weeks later with my father, Autumn and Aaron, we decided to save some money and hit the road. Our plan was to meet at my parents' house on Friday where Lydia would pick us up by three. I had packed the night before and loaded my car for the trip before I went to work. I went in early so I could slip out at 2:30. Lydia took the day off, and Dad was going to baby-sit the kids until Lydia's husband got off work early Saturday morning.

The plan was perfect. The execution was not. I got to my parent's house at 2:45. Mine was the only car in the driveway. When I got in the house, Mom was on the phone, making mad dashes between her bedroom and the kitchen where her bags were mounting like sand in an hour glass.

"Hey, baby!" she said scurrying toward me with the phone to her ear. She slowed down long enough to kiss me on the cheek.

The house was in unusual disarray. Chi-Chi pranced down the stairs to greet me. Pink ribbons were tied above her ears. Mom had just gotten her groomed. I petted Chi-Chi. "Hey, girl! When are you gonna tell Mommy you're a dog, not a person?"

She tilted her head as if she were trying to grasp the meaning of human speech.

I spoke as if I were talking to an infant. "I'm a dog. Come on girl, say: I-am-a-dog!"

Mom hung up the phone and began trying to straighten up the house. "Woo! Your auntie tried to talk my ear off! Lydia called, too. She's on her way."

"Okay, Ma." I watched her bounce around like a gnat. "Ma, why don't you finish getting ready. *I'll* clean up."

She paused long enough to smile. "Okay, Trinity. Thank you, baby!"

"No problem."

My mom had a habit of writing everything down on sticky notes. When I started straightening up, I realized that sticky notes were everywhere. I couldn't figure out what to do with them all—phone numbers, grocery lists, reminders. Some notes were attached to bills, others were attached to newspaper clippings. I tried to get a stacking system going, but it was no easy feat. After battling the sea of random sticky notes, I washed dishes and swept the floor.

"Triniteee..." I heard Mom call from the stairs. I followed her voice and looked up from the foot of the stairs. She stood at the top step.

"Thanks for helping me out. You know I've been trying to get ready for this all day. I'm so embarrassed that the house looks this way. Your father would flip if he were home."

I chuckled at her words. My father was hardly the type to flip at the sight of a messy house. He would clean it up himself, first. He was the most considerate man I knew.

A light bulb went off in my head. "Mom, if Dad is going to baby-sit the kids, why isn't he here?"

"Because like you, he knows Lydia's always late. He's at the Seven Mile restaurant, but he'll be here any minute."

She continued her scavenger hunt, looking for things to take on this brief expedition. Before I knew it, I had mopped the floor and vacuumed the living room. It was 3:30, and still no Lydia. I started up the stairs, listening to my mom sprint from room to room.

We crossed paths in the hallway. She was putting some serious mileage on the carpet between her bedroom and my old bedroom, which now served as Mom's extra closet and Chi-Chi's abode.

"Ma, did you say that Lydia was on her way when I got here?"

"She clicked in when I was on the phone with Georgia and said she was picking up the kids from school."

"Well, she must have switched them to another school system because we're only four miles from the school. I could have picked them up myself," I said.

My mother tried to comfort me. "Relax. She'll be here soon." She headed to her room and I followed, sitting on her bed. The perimeter of the room was lined with several pieces of luggage—some large and some small. Another suitcase and a makeup bag were on the bed.

"Mom, there is no excuse for this. She had the day off. We're going to be leaving right in the middle of rush hour *and* I snuck away from work just to sit here and wait for her." I looked at my mother. "Wait, why aren't you ready? And what's with all the bags?"

My mother packed the bags on her bed and raised her right hand, pressing it to the air. "Girl, don't start with me. You know I like to be prepared."

"For the war?" I asked.

"Look, Grouchy Greta. I don't want to hear it."

"All right, Ma. I'll leave you alone."

"Make yourself useful. Grab this bag and take it downstairs, sweetie."

It felt like I was carrying a body bag. My mother did not know how to pack. I added the cadaver pouch to her array of luggage and sat at the kitchen table trying not to be riled. My extended family had no concept of time. It wasn't even that they were always late. Sometimes they were inconveniently early—like anytime food was involved.

My father walked in as I thumbed through the latest issue of *Black Enterprise*. "Hey, baby!" he said, putting down his keys. He walked over and kissed me on the cheek. I gave him a big hug. My feelings were all over my face.

"Girl, I see you still haven't learned. Your cousin is only on time when dinner is being served." He patted me on the back.

"Yeah, I guess I should have known better."

"Well, that's okay. I admire your faith in family."

I grinned at him. My dad sat down next to me and we talked about the restaurants and my job for a while. He told me about some of the crazy employees he'd been dealing with. I told him about all of my overmedicated coworkers.

When Lydia finally got there, it turned into a virtual madhouse. She was trying to give my father instructions for the kids; my mom was searching every corner of the house for her lip liner; Chi-Chi was trailing behind her; and the kids were playing hide and seek. I was busy watching the clock. I sent Autumn and Aaron to the back yard and took the keys to Lydia's SUV so that I could load it. I popped the trunk and at one glance, all I could say was, "You've got to be kidding me."

Lydia had stuffed bags into the trunk like sardines. I leaned on the trunk door and raised my hand to my pounding forehead. "Lord, please give me strength."

I went back in the house and interrupted Lydia's instructions for my dad. "Lydia, which of the bags in the trunk are for the kids?"

"Oh, their bags are in the back seat," she said.

"So you're telling me that all of the bags in the trunk are for the trip?"

"Yes!" she said with a toothy smile.

"You *are* aware that there are three of us going on this trip?" I asked.

She looked puzzled. "What's wrong? Isn't there room for your stuff?"

I was unable to call any more words to my lips, so I stared at her, wondering what substance her brain was made of. Walking back outside with the largest bags in my mom's pile, I managed to rearrange and re-pack the suitcases. Darting between the house and the car, I finished loading all of our bags in the trunk and the back seat, leaving just enough room for the three of us. I returned to the house. "The truck's ready!" I yelled. "Let's go!"

After some last-minute mayhem, many kisses goodbye, Lydia fumbling over directions for Dad to take care of the kids, Mom giving Dad instructions on what container held which food for dinner, and Mom finalizing the checklist for Chi-Chi, we were on our way. You would have thought we were going on a true sabbatical. I sat in the back seat, accompanied by a stack of bags containing Mom's shoes and Lydia's makeup. I had become the eight year old of my past, who sat on the hump when there really wasn't enough room for her in the car. I whipped a book out of my bag and prepared to entertain myself through reading. Fortunately there was enough space between the front and back seats of the SUV to remove myself from their front-seat conversation and to avoid Lydia's prying questions about my boring personal life. No sooner had we gotten to the Southfield Freeway than we hit rush-hour traffic.

Why couldn't she have gotten her flighty behind to the house on time?

My cell phone rang, and I fished it out of my purse. I did not recognize the number and debated about answering it when my mother said, "Aren't you going to answer it, baby?"

I made eye contact with my mom. With a single nod, I affirmed that I would answer it.

"Hello?"

"What up, girl?"

I didn't recognize the voice. "Hi. Who is this?"

It was Jay, my promoter friend.

"Hey, Jay. What's going on?"

This guy didn't call me on a regular basis, so I figured he had the scoop on a weekend party that, clearly, I would not be attending.

"I'm having a cabaret tomorrow. I have tickets for you and your girls, if you want to come through."

"Oh, thanks for thinking of me, but I'll be in Chicago."

"Oh, yeah? You're getting away for the weekend?"

"Well, I'm going to a bridal shower."

"Oh, okay, sweetie. So, are you next?"

"Next for what?"

"To get married."

"No. Not even close," I laughed.

"So, who's getting married?"

"My cousin, Caroline."

"Caroline from the club?"

I had forgotten he'd met her. One night in town, and she'd managed to establish a nice little calling card for herself.

"Yo... has she, uh, been engaged long?"

"Yeah, it's been a while."

Jay's wheels were spinning. It was obvious he had seen her with Lil Mike.

"All right, all right," he said trying to sound like he was clueless.

I felt a need to change the subject. "Well, I appreciate you thinking of me. Let me know when you have another cabaret. I'll try to make it."

"Okay, sweetie. I'll be giving you a call soon... just to check on you."

"Okay, Jay."

"Be safe in the Chi. Have fun!"

"Thanks! Bye."

I have never understood why guys you don't know well call "to check on you." What if he called to check on me and I couldn't breathe? Was I supposed to utter directions to my house so he could come save me?

"Honey, are we keeping you from a date, going on this trip?"

I shook my head. *Here we go.* "No, Ma."

"Oh, you're seeing someone new, Trinity?" Lydia asked.

"No, I'm not." I drew out the last word, trying to maintain my cool.

I know they wanted more information, so I quickly opened my book and said, "This is the perfect time for me to finish reading this book."

They gave a few confirming words then surprisingly backed off. After we got through the traffic and construction, the trip was relatively smooth. I read, they talked. We stopped twice for bathroom breaks and snacks for the road.

We pulled up to the house to find five cars already in the driveway. Aunt Georgia met us at the door and attempted to hug all three of us at once. Uncle Jonathan came behind her and kissed each of us on the cheek before beginning to take our stockpile upstairs. I was surprised to find him home, with all of his frequent travels that no one talked about.

He was still strikingly handsome, standing about six-foot-one with a build that could be compared to a defensive back football player—a retired one. He carried about fifteen more pounds since the last time I'd seen him. His thinning hair dotted a bald spot forming on the crown of his head. Still, he was aging gracefully.

Voices erupted from nearly every room of the house as Aunt Georgia explained that Caroline and Simon had gone to a movie. I suspected that most of the relatives had come to support Caroline, but some had the primary purpose of getting some good, home-cooked food. Once we'd seen and hugged all of the relatives who were in the house, Aunt Georgia directed us to the kitchen. She and some of the other women in the family had prepared dinner—spinach salad, tri-tip, grilled salmon, macaroni and cheese and peach cobbler. The food was neatly arranged on an island centered perfectly in the room. Stainless steel appliances and granite countertops made the capacious kitchen seem as if it were a place to admire rather than a place to eat. Just one rumbling of my stomach reminded me that I was in a place where breaking bread was appropriate. I fixed a plate, sat at the kitchen table and ate, trying to resist the temptation to inhale it like a heathen. The food was the best I'd had in months.

Sustenance achieved, I was ready to face the many anecdotes about my childhood that my relatives had either recalled or concocted. For instance, there was Uncle Buddy—Mom and Aunt Georgia's second cousin. He swore that in 1982, Bashaye and I visited his house in Chicago and he took us to a Fourth of July fireworks show. Only, I didn't meet Uncle Buddy until 1989 when Lydia had her high school graduation party. I don't know who he was confusing me with, but I knew I was not the right relative. He was sweet, but he was nuttier than squirrel poo. I think it was due to his time in Vietnam.

It was only ten, but food coma had settled in. I went to the room that Mom and I were sharing to change my clothes. I was halfway undressed when the sound of commotion travelled throughout the home and was followed by Caroline's shrill voice. She and Simon had arrived.

Daggonit.

I took a second to decide if I'd say to-hell-with-it and see them in the morning or re-dress and go back downstairs. My first instinct was to climb into bed, but I knew Mom would knock the door down, telling me to get up so I could see Caroline and meet Simon. She still acted like I was six when she introduced me to people, thinking they'd make a good playmate.

I put my clothes back on and went downstairs to find that a crowd had gathered in the living room. Peeking through the cracks between the limbs that were attached to family members, I could see Caroline and Simon in the middle of a harmless mob. I made my way to what had become a greeting area. My mother and aunt were directing access to Caroline and Simon.

You've got to be kidding.

Caroline lit up when she saw me. "Trinity!" she shrieked before embracing me. She grabbed Simon's hand and introduced us. She looked so happy. He extended his hand and shook mine with nothing short of vigor.

Ah, young love. I hadn't been that happy about a young man since I was fifteen. That lost its luster when he called my house, asked for another girl then hung up on me when I called him on it.

"It's wonderful to finally meet you, Trinity!" Simon took my hand and kissed it.

I pulled my arm toward my body and let my hand dangle. "A gentleman!" The three of us laughed.

I couldn't help but be drawn to his teeth, curious as to whether they'd perpetuate or shatter the stereotype of English people having bad teeth. To my relief, Simon's teeth appeared to meet American standards.

"I've heard so much about you," I told him.

"All good, I hope," he said with a wink.

Turning up the charm, I see.

"Certainly."

Simon was tall—about six foot two—and slender. He had creamy skin and dark, slightly wavy hair that was long enough to tickle his earlobes. His face was void of hair, so much so that his smooth skin suggested he was younger than his age.

"So, are you two managing to keep your sanity with all of these crazy people around?"

"Oh, it's wonderful! Your family has been nothing but good to me and I'm just like a dog with nine tails!"

I took pause with his idiom and pulled back slightly. Caroline quickly read my expression.

"That just means he's really happy." She giggled and kissed him on the cheek.

"Yes. My apologies. I do tend to forget I'm in America."

"Oh, no. Don't apologize. It's a good learning experience for me." I smiled at them both and tried to block the inner voice that said, "Now they think you're just a Detroit girl who has never been anywhere."

They were so bubbly and happy that it was irritating, yet cute. After about ten minutes, Aunt Georgia pulled them toward the basement where most of the men had gathered, so I saw my opportunity to slip away and go back to the bedroom. To my surprise, my mother was already in the room, draped in her robe, which covered a long nightgown. She stood in front of the mirror, carefully placing rollers in her hair.

"Hey, baby!"

"Hi, Ma." I kissed her on the cheek and sat behind her on the bed. "I see we've got the same idea."

"I know you're not ready to go to bed, Trin! It's a Friday... and it's early."

"And I'm tired. I'd love to hang out with Uncle Buddy to hear more of his made-up stories, but—"

"Girl, be quiet. Don't talk that way about your family."

"Crazy is crazy," I said and glanced at her out of the corner of my eye. I think I was expecting some object—a roller, maybe—to come flying my way, but all I saw was my mother trying to hold back her laughter.

"Uh-huh," I said. "You know I'm right."

"That's your family, too," she said chuckling.

"Yeah, but there's more of their blood in you than me. Daddy's family is sane."

"You barely know Daddy's family. That does *not* make them sane."

"It does to me," I looked down with a smirk. "The less I know, the more I like them."

"You don't like my family?" She placed the last roller in her hand and turned around to face me. For a brief moment, I had to adjust to talking to her face to face rather than face to reflection.

"Mmm hmm." I looked her in the eye. "But they're crazy."

"Don't make me pop you."

"Ma, you're so violent!"

I stood up and pulled her into a big bear hug until she begged me to stop.

"I love you!" I kissed her on her forehead.

"Mmm hmm," she said. "Oh, your phone was ringing earlier and then it started beeping. I guess you have a message or something." She went back to the mirror and put on her satin bonnet.

"Okay. Thanks, Mom."

I went to the bathroom to wash my face, brush my teeth and wrap my hair. When I got back to the room, Mom was asleep. I grabbed my cell phone and listened to my voicemail. It was Malik making sure I got to Chicago safely.

I am not sure what possessed me to but I told Malik about the Tony thing over dinner a week earlier. Releasing my unforgiving spirit for Tony had allowed me to finally be able to talk about it—to a certain extent. I avoided key words like rape, pregnancy and abortion—they were too hard to say. But I was still able to tell Malik that my anger toward Tony was due to betrayal and that even though he joined my church, I was determined to move on with my life. I never got the impression that Malik was surprised by my story. He sat and listened without judgment. It reminded me of confessing to something I did as a kid and getting the "I-was-wondering-when-you-were-going-to-tell-me look" from my parents. Maybe that's why I decided to tell Malik—because he already knew.

I knelt at the end of the bed opposite my mother to say my prayers, tuning out the voices downstairs. As I rose, I realized that I hadn't said goodnight to anyone, which was—well, rude—but I quickly determined that amid the conversation and spirits, no one would really notice.

The next morning I awoke to the smell of breakfast— pancakes, eggs, sausage, ham and homemade biscuits. I was sure there was even more, but that's what my nose could distinguish. I went downstairs to see how I could help. As I set the table and made a fruit salad, people started appearing as if they'd walked right through the woodwork.

After breakfast and a clean-up process that any five-star restaurant would implement with pride, a mad dash ensued for the house's five bathrooms. Thankfully, I had beaten them to the showers. I didn't like using the shower after other people—even family. Men leave facial hair in the sink. Women leave unwrapped sanitary items in the trashcans. Children pee in the shower and leave dirt rings in the tub. I would rather get up early and only have to clean up after myself. Selfish, huh? Well, that was just the way I liked it.

After skipping up the stairs, I joined my mom in unpacking clothes. I should have taken the dress I was planning to wear to Caroline's shower out of my suitcase the night before, but with all of the hoopla, I'd completely forgotten. It was creased from the trip, no thanks to being crammed between Lydia and Ma's precious cargo. If there was one thing about my mom's chronic overpacking, it was that I knew she brought a steamer.

"Ma, may I use—"

"Here, baby." She set the steamer next to me without missing a beat.

"Wow, you're good."

"Motherhood makes me this way. I bet you're glad I'm ready for the war, now, huh?"

"I deserved that," I replied. "I'll eat my words."

Mom and I got dressed and waited in the kitchen for Lydia, Aunt Georgia and Caroline as they dressed. When the three emerged from the staircase, we all headed to Lydia's SUV and made our way to the bridal shower.

Chapter Thirteen

The bridal shower was in a banquet room on the grounds of Uncle Jonathan's country club. Fountains lining the plush yard spewed water as guests walked by. Caroline and Aunt Georgia had invited one hundred fifty people to the shower. Quite frankly, I thought it was ridiculous to invite that many people to a bridal shower for anyone short of celebrity. The guest list included wives of the country club members and Uncle Jonathan's business associates, Aunt Georgia's sorority sisters, several prominent lawyers and judges, Caroline's friends and us—the lowly family members.

None of the men in the family was invited to the shower, but several of them used the trip as an opportunity to bond while the women were away. My father declined the invitation because he didn't want to be away from the restaurants. Well, at least that's what he said. I believe his decision was rooted more in the desires to avoid being trapped in a car with three women for five hours and being surrounded by many more loud, cackling women at Aunt Georgia and Uncle Jonathan's house. Add in potty breaks for mom and Lydia—they say it's never the same after having children—and his patience would have been only a memory. He really was a smart man.

Inside the country club, guests poured into a banquet room with a dome ceiling and tables draped in ivory lace cloths. The seats were camouflaged by matching lace seat covers and swathed with honeysuckle organza bows. A band played as waiters served hors d'oeuvres and champagne, and people assembled at the tables.

I sucked my cheeks and lifted my hand limply before extending my pinky. "Trés chic!"

I returned to my normal nature. "Goodness. If this is the shower, what should we expect for the wedding?"

My mother tried to hush me with her eyes because Lydia was behind her.

"Oh, so what, Ma. She's thinking the *same* thing."

Lydia had eloped and never received a portion of the attention her sister was receiving. In actuality, she was probably thinking, "Why is my spoiled little sister, who has never had to lift a finger in her life, being treated like royalty? I didn't get a dime for my wedding and when it was over, I barely got an acknowledgement!"

Mom, Lydia and I sat at a table next to Aunt Georgia and the maid of honor, who was a cute bubbly blonde. A small, rectangular table was before us with a single chair. Tripods held blown-up pictures of Caroline and Simon on each side of the table. They appeared to be engagement announcement pictures, but I had never seen either one. Go figure.

Several small-framed young men with dark, short hair offered guests plated appetizers. There were mini crab cakes topped with chives, shrimp and avocado canapés, and eggplant and goat cheese mini tarts. I tried them all but returned for seconds on the crab cakes. Five large fruit and cheese arrangements lined a large S-shaped table near the entrance. Cheeses like cheddar, brie and dill Havarti checkered each platter between wedding-inspired pieces of fruit that were shaped like bells, dresses and cakes. I fixed a plate to share with my mother, selecting several types of cheese, strawberries, honeydew melon, and kiwi.

About twenty minutes after our arrival, the maid of honor approached a microphone-equipped podium. She welcomed everyone and asked us to take our seats before inviting us to pause for the blessing of the food, delivered by Reverend Anna Taylor, the pastor of Aunt Georgia's church.

We were served a large strawberry-melon-spinach salad for lunch, accompanied by piping hot, individually cupped dinner rolls. The strawberries, honey dew and cantaloupe were arranged on a bed of spinach and encircled with strategically placed pine nuts. It was clear that they were paying for the presentation, but this was also Caroline's idea of a meal. As much food as I'd eaten at breakfast, this menu was fine with me. Besides, I knew that the best was to come—cake!

There were too many people to do the usual shower games or open gifts. I thanked God for that. I loathed the pomp and circumstance of crossword puzzles filled with silly facts about the bride and groom, emptying the embarrassing contents of my purse and having a stranger take my belongings because I crossed my legs. Then there was the routine of oohing and ahhing over gifts that would surpass repetition by gift number thirteen.

Instead of making guests endure that painful ritual, Caroline's bridal party thought it best that we were allowed to mingle. Those with words of wisdom were asked to approach the podium to talk about making marriage work. Since I had no experience with marriage, I decided it would be best if I played observer. The podium perspectives turned into many walks down memory lane that began with, "I remember when Caroline was just two months old," or "I've watched Caroline grow into a beautiful woman." It became a monotonous process, but it was better than sitting through games and gifts.

A cameraman recorded everyone's sentiments. My mother started crying when it was her turn and began a chain reaction. Tissues flapped across the room like tiny truce flags, but I was not in need of one. I could not relate to their emotions.

Come on, people. This is a happy occasion. Laugh, already! Enough with the tears.

Still, I realized this was a nice way to record the thoughts of the guests and would become something for Caroline and Simon to look back on.

Many people offered what seemed to be great ways to keep the fire going—remember to date your spouse, reserve quality time every day, always talk it out, etcetera. I was actually beginning to enjoy the reflections—that is until Aunt Ginger, Mom and Aunt Georgia's adopted sister, stepped up to the podium. Ma Lo and Papa Theo adopted Aunt Ginger when she was a toddler. Aunt Ginger was the biological daughter of Aunt Eloise—Ma Lo's sister. When Aunt Eloise decided she could not handle raising a child, Ma Lo and Papa Theo raised Ginger as if she were their own.

Aunt Ginger was ten years younger than my mom and three years younger than Aunt Georgia. She was the black sheep of the family and had given my grandparents such a hard time. Everyone was sure that all of her acting out was a result of feeling unwanted, although my grandparents treated her like their own.

Ma Lo and Uncle Theo would often find Aunt Ginger staring out the window waiting for her mother to return. Aunt Eloise never came back. When Aunt Ginger was thirteen, she stopped waiting in that window. Aunt Eloise's boyfriend had killed her in a drunken rage. Having her baby sister taken away from her in violence crushed Ma Lo. No one was ever allowed to talk about it around my grandmother. The tragedy changed Aunt Ginger from an obedient, trusting child to a rebellious tyrant who began to indulge in sex, drugs and alcohol.

When Aunt Ginger grabbed the microphone, it was clear that she had become acquainted with one too many glasses of complimentary champagne. Trying to appear composed, she began with her memories of Caroline as a child, Caroline as a teenager, Caroline in college, blah, blah, blah. Her rambling sucked me right into the middle of a Charlie Brown episode. Her words were just noise. I watched my mom attempt to send Aunt Ginger messages through her eyes.

"Wrap it up, wrap it up! Don't make me come up there!" her eyes said. But Mom needed to work on her range because only I could hear her words. Finally, Mom tried to sit back and let Aunt Ginger finish. "Please God, don't let her embarrass us," was written all over her face. Then Aunt Ginger uttered words that rang in my head like church bells to Beelzebub on Sunday morning.

"Caroline," she said, "just remember this." I'm sure most guests were prepared for some touching remark that Caroline would be able to hold close to her heart. Instead what my smashed aunt said was much different. "When he says all those late nights are spent in the office, girl, he's lying like a rug. Hell, he may be lying on the rug... with his *secretary*! Don't believe me? Just ask your mama!"

She grabbed both sides of the podium and laughed hysterically. Her voice resonated throughout the room, causing the microphone to squeal with feedback. The entire room released a simultaneous gasp. I couldn't believe this was happening. My mother sprang to her feet. She pulled Aunt Ginger off the podium and escorted her out of the room. Her pace had a vengeance that I hadn't seen since I was nine years old and said "Damn!" in the church Easter play after forgetting my lines. As Mom carried Aunt Ginger away, I heard my aunt ask, "Was it something I said?" between hiccup-laced giggles.

Aunt Georgia's caramel skin was a shade of red. I turned to Caroline whose eyes were welling up with tears. I was so embarrassed for them. I didn't know what to do. Neither did anyone else. Just then, I realized the camera was still rolling.

Ohmygoshohmygoshohmygosh.

Giving only a split second of thought to what I would say, I approached the podium, grabbed the microphone and said, "Who knew my Aunt Ginger was such a believable actress?" I smiled and nodded, making eye contact with strangers at two tables in the front of the room, hoping my nods would be first hypnotic then reciprocated. Would anyone really think that Aunt Ginger had just put on a one-woman show? Fat chance.

"Well, in all seriousness, I want to say a word about my cousin, Caroline." After recalling some favorite moments I shared with Caroline in years past, I continued to try to lighten the mood by saying, "As a single woman, I obviously have no marital advice."

Wait... what's that noise? Oh, it's laughter. Thank you, Jesus!

I looked at Caroline as I prepared for my closing words. "But what I *can* offer is this: I once heard a pastor say, 'The moment you allow someone other than your spouse to become your best friend is the moment you remove Jesus from the center of your life together.' Caroline, don't part from Him and never take His role in your relationship for granted."

Caroline was staring back at me with widened eyes. I hoped that despite the fiasco that our socially- challenged aunt had created, Caroline would remember what I said.

I wasn't sure what placed that quote on my heart. It wasn't one that I had even realized was there. Still, I had faith that it would reach Caroline, despite the fact that religion wasn't a staple in her upbringing.

I walked back to my seat. Some people clapped; others sat among whispers about Aunt Ginger's outburst. Aunt Georgia reached over and squeezed my hand. She didn't even look at me, but I knew she was thanking me. I squeezed back to say "you're welcome." I glanced at the cameraman, knowing that Aunt Georgia would be demanding he edit it judiciously.

The band began playing and mingling followed. The wait staff served a scrumptious cake—a moist, white, double-tiered cake that had a layer of strawberry filling at its center. Each piece was adorned with white chocolate shavings and a fanned strawberry.

A crowd formed around Caroline. It was like watching a swarm of bees seeking honey. My mother still hadn't returned, which made me a little curious, but I decided to let her handle things. Aunt Georgia went on playing hostess. With Aunt Ginger gone, it almost appeared as if nothing had ever happened. Almost. Some of the guests twisted their torsos toward one another and began a hushed exchange of words and loaded glances. The distance that separated us prevented me from hearing their conversations. I could only imagine what they were saying.

"Who was that incredibly uncouth woman? Is she a relative?"

"Georgia must be devastated! Look at her acting as if everything is okay. The shame."

"That poor Caroline. She must be absolutely mortified!"

Say what they wanted, chances were, their husbands were cheating on them, too. All of the money I was looking at in that room didn't come without a price tag.

That night, Caroline invited Lydia and me to a bar with her and Simon. It was a hang-out spot for Northwestern students. I felt like I was too far removed from collegiate life to hang out in a college bar. Couple that with the fact that I didn't drink, and I might as well have been a dwarf trying to play center for the Detroit Pistons. But I would figure a way to adapt. I always did.

But if I felt out of place in the college-life scene, how would Lydia feel? If I were thirty three with two kids and a husband, I imagine that being in a college bar with my baby sister would make me feel a bit out of my element. We both sucked it up and went anyway. I did it because, well, what else was I going to do? And I wanted a chance to see Caroline and Simon together—away from family. I think Lydia did it because she desperately wanted to spend time with Caroline.

Carl's Corner was a bar and grill. They had a stage for live bands and pool tables in the back. We sat at a cozy circular table where we could all see and hear each other. Aunt Caroline and Mom had cooked again, so no one was very hungry. We ordered appetizers, and Caroline and Simon ordered beers, while Lydia and I ordered cranberry juice.

"You drink beer?" Lydia asked Caroline. She was obviously surprised.

"Yeah, big sis," Caroline teased before taking a sip out of the icy mug.

We engaged in some general conversation that was devoid of any references to the shower. Simon told us about his plans for becoming a chemical engineer and his experiences as an intern at a global research and development company. Caroline talked about her plans for... well, marriage. I shared some stories of my post-college experiences in corporate America. Meanwhile, I think Lydia was still trying to digest the fact that Caroline drank beer.

I was actually having a nice time. I watched Simon and saw the degree of adoration that he had for Caroline. He was so attentive. He wanted to make sure she was comfortable and had everything she wanted. Caroline had found someone who treated her like the royal brat she was. And the fact that he was from England—touché!

Lydia, whose relationship lacked romance, wanted a personal account from both Caroline and Simon of how they met and fell in love. Simon's eyes sparkled as he talked about seeing Caroline in a class where he was a teacher's assistant. Because of his position, he didn't feel right in approaching a student. He spent that time observing her and kept his desires to date her to himself. Once the class was over, he immediately asked her out. Things blossomed from there.

"I just knew she was meant to be my wife," Simon said, grabbing Caroline's left hand and outlining the perimeter of her engagement ring with his thumb.

"Awwwww," all three of us women said in unison. Caroline kissed Simon on the forehead. Lydia looked like she wished she could possess Caroline's body and become her. I sat there amazed at the fact that I honestly felt all warm and fuzzy... at least for a fleeting moment. Simon excused himself and went to the bathroom.

"Caroline, I am so happy for you," Lydia said. "It's so important to be with a man who truly loves you and connects with you, and I can tell that Simon is that man." She looked at me after making her statement.

"What?" I asked defensively.

Why the hell is she looking at me? See, Lydia, I was enjoying this and you had to go and treat me like the pathetic cousin who can't find a man.

"Nothing, I just hope that one day you'll find a man like that."

Hell, I hope you do, too.

"You know what," I responded, "if I decide to make a move like marriage, there will be no doubt that he will be a man who truly loves me and connects with me. But if that doesn't happen, I'll be sure to send my cats over to spend the weekends with you."

Caroline giggled uncontrollably and even Lydia cracked a smile. She leaned over and squeezed me. "Okay, I'll lay off, little cousin," she said.

Caroline's laughs stopped abruptly. "Oh my goodness," Caroline muttered, staring into a corner near the bathrooms. Lydia and I snapped around to see what she was looking at. Simon was talking to a guy, who I assumed went to Northwestern. He was holding a pool stick while chatting it up with Simon.

"Who is that?" I asked.

Caroline tried to downplay the situation. "No one, really. Just a guy I used to see."

"Oh," Lydia and I said as if we'd received a cue.

"You look a little perplexed," Lydia said.

"Oh," Caroline said with slight disappointment. "I just didn't know they knew each other."

"Oh?" Lydia's interest peaked.

I wasn't about to continue the cycle of oh's, so instead, I tried to offer some degree of solace. "Well, people meet, they date, they go their separate ways, and then they fall in love with other people... right?" I asked.

"Is that the order?" Caroline asked sarcastically. She took a gulp of her beer.

Lydia looked puzzled, but before she could inquire about Caroline's question, Caroline said, "Oh, no."

"Now what?" I asked.

"They're coming over here."

Instinctively, Lydia and I began to turn around.

"No, no! Don't look!" Caroline was panicking. I felt like we'd been spotted by a wild and hungry animal. I could hear the Crocodile Hunter whispering in his Australian accent, "No sudden moves or it will attack!"

"Just look relaxed," Caroline said taking another sip of her beer.

Lydia and I turned back around in our chairs. I swished my straw around in my juice then reached for a chicken finger. Lydia tried to look relaxed but sat up completely erect with her hands crossed. She looked as if she were battling hemorrhoids.

"Darling," Simon said to Caroline. "I'd like to introduce you and your family to Adam." Adam extended his hand to Caroline and shook it.

"Nice to meet you, Adam," she responded, shaking his hand forcefully. Her face was flushed. A strange silence fell over us. She needed an out so I extended my hand to Adam and introduced myself and Lydia.

Adam looked like a skater boy. He wore a retro T-shirt, a pair of worn out jeans, and Converse shoes. He had a rugged handsomeness that reminded me of Hugh Jackman—minus the muscles. Adam's attire and the visible stubble on his face let me know that he was one of those guys who did not put much into appearances, but I got the impression that his lack of effort had little impact on his popularity among young women.

Simon pulled up a chair for Adam right between himself and Caroline. I thought Caroline would pee herself. Simon seemed oblivious to the tension between his fiancée and Adam. Simon began to tell the story of how he knew Adam. They had lived across the hall from each other in the same apartment complex. With that revealed, I looked at Caroline.

Girl, what were you thinking?

She looked back as if to say, "I swear I didn't know."

Unless Adam was always going to her place, I just didn't understand how Caroline pulled off that indiscretion.

Simon went on to tell a story of Adam locking himself out of his apartment, Simon trying to jimmy the lock, and a neighbor calling the police because she thought they were burglars. I missed the details of the story because I was too busy noticing Adam's flirtatious body language, directed at Caroline, and his disregard for Simon's account. Caroline responded by keeping her eyes glued on Simon, who was still talking. Lydia was hanging on to Simon's every word, so I knew she hadn't noticed what was or was not going on between Caroline and Adam. Simon was just as unaware.

Adam excused himself, saying something about meeting a friend. "It was nice to meet you all." He paid particular attention to Caroline who was giving her undivided attention to her beer mug.

"Nice meeting you," I responded. Lydia reached out and shook his hand once more.

As Adam was on his way out, Simon popped up. "Adam!" he yelled before darting to catch up with him.

Lydia wasted no time trying to get more information from Caroline. "So I guess Adam decided not to tell Simon that he knew you."

"Biblically," I said under my breath.

Lydia looked at me as if she were trying to determine if I'd said what I said. I smiled innocently. She looked as if she was trying to convince herself that she heard otherwise. Caroline's concern was on her fiancé's conversation with her former booty call. She bit her finger and tried to read their body language.

"He wouldn't say anything, would he? It was just a casual, hook-up thing. Besides, that was over six months ago," Caroline said.

Six months ago? Okay, so you've been trickin' for a while. You're a nasty little thing, aren't you?

"If it was just a casual relationship, you probably don't have to be so paranoid," Lydia said.

Caroline and I both looked at each other. It was clear that Lydia's understanding of "casual" and "hook-up" had nothing to do with sex. She totally missed the fact that Caroline basically confessed to cheating on Simon through her "six-month" comment. Caroline opened her mouth to speak, but I shook my head and widened my eyes the way a mother would when watching her child reach for cookies before dinner. She closed her mouth and went back to her beer. It was probably best for us to let Lydia have her fantasy that Caroline was her virginal little sister, no matter how far from reality that may have been.

Simon returned to the table and put his arm around Caroline. She looked like the cat that swallowed the canary, but to Simon she could do no wrong. He began talking about the wedding and how excited he was. He and Caroline talked about all of the tiny details that were going to make their wedding perfect. It was as if we were listening to two future brides instead of a future bride and groom. Lydia offered her suggestions and I chimed in periodically, but the more they talked, the more my thoughts drifted. I wondered if there were more transgressions of the flesh for Caroline to commit. I wondered if Simon were as naive as he seemed or as committed as he seemed.

It was then that I realized the number of masks that people wore. People were willing to become chameleons in order to get what and who they wanted. It was clear to me that just as things weren't always what they seemed, things were often exactly what they seemed.

Chapter Fourteen

W e left the next morning. The drive home started off uncharacteristically quiet. Lydia, who rarely drove with music, popped in one of her husband's Smooth Jazz CDs. Mom flipped through a newspaper. I had finished my book on the way to Chicago and was not interested in trying to amuse myself with childhood car games.

I spy something yellow.

Besides, it wasn't as if the car games would be any fun by myself.

I figured that last night's revelations would be kept between me, Caroline, and Lydia, who I was pretty sure missed all of Caroline's disclosures.

What surprised me were the obvious attempts of my mom and Caroline to ignore what happened at the shower. It was as if no one wanted to acknowledge it except for me. I tried to take my mind off of the deafening silence by reading billboards and observing the scenery, but eventually, I became aware that I could not contain myself any longer.

"So, that was an unexpected turn of events at the shower," I said.

Lydia glanced in the rear view mirror. She raised an eyebrow as if she were confused— like she had no idea what I was talking about. My mother simply folded the newspaper first lengthwise and then widthwise and said, "The shower *was* lovely."

"Oh, yes," Lydia agreed.

Did I miss something? Were you both in the same room I was in, 'cause I sat next to two people who looked just like you.

I paused for a moment. "Yes, it was lovely, but I was referring to Aunt Ginger's outburst."

My mom reached into her purse and pulled out three peppermints. She handed one to Lydia, one to me, and unwrapped the other one for herself.

"Well, you know she's always been different."

Different? What the hell? Different is showing up at the bridal shower wearing a tank top, corduroy pants and stilettos. Different is not getting on the microphone drunk and putting Uncle Jonathan's business on Front Street. I think Mom is just trying to shut me up by giving me candy. That's what she used to do to

Bashaye and me when we became too "inquisitive" as children.

Lydia was silent. Mom hummed along with the CD. I played with the candy wrapper wondering if I missed a road sign that read, "You are now entering The Twilight Zone." I chuckled and sat in silence... for a second, anyway.

"Ohhh-kay. Mom, you were gone for quite a while with Aunt Ginger. I can't imagine I'd be able to find the right words to say to her."

Apparently, at that moment, my mother was the one who couldn't find the right words. She stared at her paper, saying nothing.

"Is Aunt Georgia okay?" I asked.

Finally, Mom responded with a dry, "I really don't think it's appropriate to discuss this at this time."

"I agree," Lydia said.

What?

I pondered Mom's reason for such a prudish response. "Would that be inappropriate as in Aunt Ginger's display, inappropriate as in Uncle Jonathan's wayward penis, or inappropriate as in wearing white after Labor Day?"

My mouth spit out the words before my brain processed them, or better yet, before I thought about how they would be interpreted. Lydia almost swerved across the white line on the freeway. My mom sat straight up and turned around to look at me. Fury was in her eyes.

Why did I say that?

"You have no idea what is going on in their marriage," Mom scolded.

"You're right. And while we're at it, how could I? No one ever talks about it. Ginger may have been wrong doing what she did, but she wasn't wrong about what she said." I looked at Lydia through the rear view mirror. "Lydia, she's your mother. Don't you care about how he's treating her?" There was silence. "Why does the whole family refuse to discuss it?"

My mom leaned back in her seat and folded her arms. I knew I had made her angry.

Lydia grasped the wheel like an old lady, refusing to look to the left or to the right. Suddenly the sound of the tires on the pavement, the buzzing of passing cars, and Kirk Whalum blowing away on his saxophone magnified as if we were in a surround sound theater.

I wouldn't let it go. "I just don't understand why everyone turns a blind eye to Uncle Jonathan's blatant cheating. I mean, has anyone ever taken the time to think about how his actions and the family's passiveness have influenced Caroline and her thoughts about marriage?"

"She knows right from wrong. That has nothing to do with her," Lydia snapped.

I must have had diarrhea of the mouth. I couldn't seem to stop.

"Nothing to do with her? Do you *really* believe that?" I asked with deep inquisition.

Lydia was quiet.

"It's not our business," my mother responded.

"But isn't it? We're family. Isn't family supposed to look out for family? I just don't understand," I said exasperated.

"No, you don't understand, Trinity. I would appreciate it if you left this alone. Now."

Contemplating the whole conversation, I felt relief for speaking my mind, regret for choosing the words I used, and dizziness from sitting in that blasted back seat. I wished I had one of those memory zappers like they had in the sci-fi movies. I'd zap both of them and they'd never know the conversation had occurred. Then I could tolerate the rest of the trip home.

"Sure, we can end it," I said and sat back in defeat.

My trip concluded with more sounds of tires contacting the pavement, more cars buzzing by, and more, well...

I spy something blue.

Who was I kidding? How would I endure four more hours of that? Maybe I'd just go to sleep since no one in the car was talking to me.

Lord, please don't send me to Hell for this.

When we pulled into the driveway, I began apologizing, admitting that I let my emotions lead the conversation. It was not my intent to hurt my mom's feelings or Lydia's. I guess the whole situation bothered me more than I ever realized. Like my mom, Lydia, and the rest of our family, I hoped that Caroline would be able to separate the dynamics of her parents' relationship from any relationship of her own. But her actions during her visit to Detroit, coupled with last night's incident at the bar, made it clear to me that that was not the case.

The three of us did the kiss-and-make-up thing, then went into the house, but I felt uncomfortable with the entire situation. I pulled out my mom's bags and my own as Lydia got the kids and their belongings. Gathering Autumn and Aaron's things was likely to be a task in itself. As history had it, once the kids got comfortable at my parents' house, they marked their territory by strewing their clothing and toys all around. Lydia and the kids soon headed home, and I was alone with Mom.

"Honey, when you asked if we thought about how Uncle Jonathan's cheating has affected Caroline, were you really talking about you?"

"What?" I couldn't figure out where she was coming from. My eyebrows rose and I heard my voice crack at an elevated volume. "Daddy's cheating on you?"

"Of course not, Trinity," she quickly assured me. "I meant your feelings about Uncle Jonathan."

"Oh." My confidence was renewed and my blood pressure lowered. "Uncle Jonathan's not my father. Besides, the only thing it has affected are my thoughts about him, not marriage."

"But why do you think Caroline is any different?"

Ah, now I get it.

I smiled at my mom. She made a good argument, but I maintained my stance.

"I see your point, but I think the situation with Caroline is different. She grew up watching that behavior day in and day out. It has a normalcy to her."

In my mind, there was no concern that Simon might do to Caroline what her father did to her mom. There was only her seemingly casual view of marriage. Of course, I could have been very wrong. Maybe in her brain she had separated the engagement period from the actual marriage. Aren't there some people who can do that and go on to lead happily married lives?

Maybe so, but I had a hard time believing Caroline would be one of those people. I figured that time would tell. Maybe I should have just taken my mom's motto: "It's not our business." I would just be tight-lipped as our whole family went to Hell in a hand basket because no one had enough guts to stand up and say what was right from wrong. What if I did end up like the rest of them, smiling away, in a robotic, false sense of happiness as my ethical standards rotted away? Somehow, I didn't think that was my destiny.

Chapter Fifteen

More than a week had passed since the trip to Chicago. I had been following my usual routine at work, but I easily drifted into thoughts about family and friends that kept me fighting to stay in the same mental stratosphere as those who surrounded me.

From the moment I walked out of the huge glass doors of the main entrance at Keemer and Dewitt on Friday afternoon, I knew I had to spend some time alone. I fell asleep before I could even consider eating an adequate dinner or wrapping up my hair. Fourteen hours later, I awoke, late for my hair appointment and with hunger pains. I called Laila to reschedule for another day. As much as I valued keeping up appearances, I knew this was not the day to fight the way I felt on the inside. I was drained, physically and emotionally. I just wasn't sure why.

I lay back in bed, my right arm across my forehead, and stared at the ceiling. The eggshell-colored paint bored me, but I wondered what color would have entranced me in a room that had become almost purely functional. I realized how mechanically I lived my life. I ate in the kitchen, watched television and read in the living room, combed my hair in the bathroom, and dressed in the bedroom. Until now, I had never really noticed how bland I found the color of the walls in my bedroom.

My stomach rumbled. I raised my listless body from the bed and went into the bathroom. One glance in the mirror compelled me to wonder why I cancelled my hair appointment.

Oh well. What's done is done.

I tried to fix my bed head by running a brush through my hair, but it was going to take more than a brush to make this mess presentable.

I'll handle this hair later.

I decided to make myself feel a little better by fixing breakfast—a real breakfast. It had been weeks since I'd broken the routine of fixing anything other than cereal, turkey bacon or toast. I often washed down some combination of "the usual" with a glass of orange juice and headed out the door. On rushed days, I was lucky to grab a granola bar and call it breakfast, despite the disappointing effect that ritual left on my insatiable appetite.

In the kitchen, I pulled out a couple of eggs, flour, baking powder, sugar, milk, butter and cinnamon. I wanted some homemade waffles. Ma Lo had made sure I knew how to cook from the time I was old enough to wash dishes without breaking them. But she would have been disappointed with the frequency of my cooking escapades. I went to the pantry and pulled out two potatoes then grabbed my peeler from the silverware drawer. I could just taste the hash browns. I returned to the refrigerator and pulled out an onion for the potatoes and a package of turkey links, then I grabbed my seasonings from the spice rack.

I'm so glad I made it to the grocery store the other day.

Everything was on the countertop, waiting to be turned into a delectable meal. Before I began, I slipped into the living room and popped in a couple of old Tribe Called Quest CDs to get me going as I cooked. I put them on random, cranked up the volume and bopped to "Award Tour" as I went back to the kitchen. I made so much food that there would be plenty left over to repeat the meal before church the next day. I ate at the kitchen table, allowing Phife and Q-Tip to serenade me with their hip-hop rhymes over beats by Ali Shaheed Muhammad. In my humble opinion, their talent was still unparalleled by any of the cats in the business today.

I was somewhere between the lyrics to "Butter" and a bite of hash browns when I heard the doorbell ring. On instinct, I gave myself a once-over. My red Mickey Mouse pajamas were dusted with flour and my yellow "house socks" were worn at the toes. On my left foot, I saw my big toe, painted a deep berry color, peeking through the thinning threads. I dropped my fork and tried to rub the sleep from my eyes.

The doorbell rang again. Although I was in my own home, I panicked, knowing that not only was someone making an unexpected visit, but also I looked a hot mess! I drank some more of my orange juice in attempts to further mask any traces of morning breath, as I had not yet brushed my teeth. If it hadn't been for the music blaring in my home, I would not have answered the door. It may have just been my neighbor, Ms. Fleming, asking me to turn it down. She was a retired school teacher in her late sixties. I didn't think she'd give much thought to my appearance.

I looked through the peep hole and found it was not Ms. Fleming. I flipped around, pressing my back to the door with my arms outspread.

"Crap!"

The doorbell rang for a third time, and I spun back around, dusting off my PJs. I cracked open the door to reveal my eyes, nose and fingers. "Hey." I tried to hide my braless upper body behind the door.

"Why are you hiding?" Malik made his way past me and walked right into the living room.

"Well, come on in," I said, a bit surprised at his gall.

He sat on the couch and turned around to see me. I was still near the door, standing with my arms crossed in front of me.

"What's that on your face?" he asked.

I didn't think he'd be able to see eye crust from where he stood, so I lifted my hand to my face and tried to do a quick swipe that covered the entire left side of my face.

"It's on the right," he said and walked over to me.

I stepped back, not wanting him to see my eye crust or smell my breath.

He wiped my face. "Flour? *You* cooked? Ooh, it smells good in here."

I tried not to notice the look on his face as his attention moved from the aroma back to me.

"Damn, girl. What happened to your hair?" He laughed and ran his hand across the top of my head like I was a lap dog.

I pulled away again. "I missed my appointment," I said walking toward the table. I still didn't want to speak directly in his face. "Are you hungry?" I asked as I took my plate into the kitchen.

"You know I never turn down free food!" He took a seat at the table.

I fixed him a plate and began to clean up the kitchen, still unaware as to what blew him in my direction.

"I see you went into the archives with this one," he said referring to the music that was still trumpeting from the stereo.

"Yep. It's classic."

I loaded the dishwasher, wiped the counter with the dishcloth and swept the floor. Flour, potato skins and pieces of diced onion that blended into the cream colored floor became visible in the blue dust pan. I washed my hands and opened my snack drawer, grabbing a pack of gum I'd stashed there a couple of weeks ago and ripping it open. Popping a piece in my mouth made me a little more comfortable in returning to the dining room.

"So." I turned down the music and sat in a chair across from Malik, pulling my knees to my chest. "What brings you my way?"

"You haven't returned my calls." He barely looked up from his plate as he spoke.

"I know. I haven't returned anyone's calls. It's been that kind of week."

"Yeah, well, you'll mess around and lose good friends that way."

"I took a play from your book. You haven't lost *me* yet."

He looked up and grinned, acknowledging the hypocrisy. "So, you gave your girl Shawna my number."

"I did what?" I asked.

Malik repeated himself, assuredly.

I moved my head with each syllable. "Umm, no. I didn't."

"Has anyone told you your sarcasm gets tiring?"

"What's your point?"

Malik returned to the previous topic. "She called me. You didn't give her my number?"

"She what?"

He nodded his head and tipped back his glass of orange juice.

"Why do you think I gave her your number, especially the way you act when she's around? I'm not going to set her up to be disappointed like that."

"Okay, you didn't give it to her. Anyway, she called and apologized for the way she acted."

"She did?" I wondered why she'd call him without telling me and what moved her to do it. "I can't believe she did that." I realized that she must have gotten Malik's number from my cell phone on the night I wouldn't let her drive home. "She just called to apologize?"

"Well, I don't know. But we ended up talking about more than that."

"Malik, please don't play with that girl like that. You know she's been head over heels for you and would jump off the Ambassador Bridge if you'd only ask her to."

"You know, I now see there's more to her than I once thought."

"What do you mean?" I asked.

"She's very insightful. She made me realize something that I'd really already known."

"If you already knew it, what was there to realize?"

"Your tone is not cute," he said. "Can we sit on the couch?"

All of my defenses went up. "Oh, you want to watch TV?"

"No, I want to talk."

I kept thinking of my unbathed body, the bra that was in my drawer instead of surrounding my bosom and the Mickey Mouse pajamas that until now were for my eyes only. "Aren't we... talking now?" I asked, desperate to avoid close contact.

He got up from the table and pulled me toward the couch. With a tug of my granny's afghan, which lay on the back of the couch, I covered my frontal area. I backed my body into the end of the couch, separating him from my unproven yet very possible funk.

"What's wrong?" he asked.

"Just a little chilly." I flashed a smile.

He scooted closer. I dug my feet into the couch, trying to draw my knees closer to my body.

Malik sat forward, then folded his hands and stared at them. A pensive look came across his face. I knew this wasn't a regular visit.

"My turn. What's wrong?" I asked.

I realized that his deep dimples were pronounced, even when he wasn't smiling. He took one of my hands and began to rub his fingers across mine. By the third stroke, my nerves had me so edgy that the afghan, which was keeping me warm according to my lie, was adding fuel to the fire in my body. I knew this could not have been good for the concern I already held about my current state of hygiene. I also knew that I couldn't remove the afghan. If I did, my bosom would have only been covered by Mickey's ears. That would not work for a woman who refused to buy a bathing suit without support, even though I was only a B cup.

"Breakfast was good."

I nodded my head in thanks, waiting for him to say whatever was on his mind. He continued to rub my hand. My comfort level dropped to the depths of hell.

"Okay, look. You know I've never had a problem with a loss of words." He looked me in the eyes. "This is more difficult than I thought it would be."

I was sure he was trying to see if I was paying attention, so I gave him some affirmation. "It's cool. Take your time."

Take your time?

I sounded like a saint of the church, reassuring the sinner prior to his testimony.

"Well, I've realized something recently." He paused, contemplating his next words. "Trinity, you know I've been with a lot of women. Most times I just wanted to see how far I could get. I considered the consequences only after the damage was done."

His hand was starting to sweat. I wasn't sure if it was a reaction to my body temperature or a reflection of his own nervousness. Malik let go of my hand and rubbed his thighs.

"You've been my best friend, and I cherish our relationship," he continued. "I thank you for that. Thank you for being my friend when I disappear and show up later. I appreciate that you've never left, and I appreciate that you are always honest with me, even when I need to be checked."

We both chuckled at his last remark.

"That's what friends do," I said.

"I know," he said looking into my eyes, briefly before looking at the floor. "I just realize that in all the dates I've had, all the meaningless sex, all of my conquests... I'd never be happy because that wasn't what I wanted; it wasn't what I needed."

I felt as if my saliva ducts were in overdrive. I wondered if he could hear me swallowing. Surely the movement in my esophagus was evident to the naked eye.

Malik grabbed my hand again and maneuvered so his torso faced mine. "Trinity, you're my best friend. You've been everything to me in that regard. All these years I've watched you and you've always been just who you are now. You've been an example—not just to people watching you in your family, on the block or at church—you've been an example to me." His face showed a foreign vulnerability.

"I'm no example, Malik."

"But, you are. And I want more than to be your friend, Trin. I want... I need to be with you."

Oh, sweet God. I'm getting dizzy.

"C-come again?" His words repeated in my head. "Umm, Malik, if this is another joke about getting in my pants, it's not funny."

"I know I've joked with you about this in the past, and that was because I had feelings for you then. I just didn't know how to interpret my feelings. And I wasn't ready to. I was still trying to see what was out there. But now I know. Nothing.

"Aside from my mom, you're the *only* woman who ever gave a damn about me; who ever took the time to know Malik; who ever cared about my dreams more than my money. Do you know that? Do you know that every time I hear your voice on the phone, see your name on the caller ID, watch you walk into a room...."

I sat there looking as lost as I had in my college statistics class.

"I don't understand." I had to push the words through my lips.

"I *do* understand, now," he said. Malik stood up and pulled me up, too. My neck was cocked back, as I stared up at him.

"Trin, I know this sounds corny, but you're everything I've asked for. You've always been right here in front of me, and now I finally see you and have the courage to pursue you."

My thoughts were rapid, but my words were slow to form.

He ran his hand over my hair, gently this time. "Say something."

I had been standing there with my mouth open. I was flabbergasted.

"I, I'm here in my floured PJs." I looked down at the stains that hadn't come off with a futile attempt to pat them away. "I'm unshowered." I touched my hair. "I'm unkempt. And my best friend is telling me that he wants to be with me. Forgive me; the words just aren't coming together. It's... almost like I'm waiting to wake up."

Malik took a step back and raised his shoulders, slightly. "Oh, so this is like a bad dream?"

"No." I knew the words hadn't come out right. "It's surreal more than anything." My knees felt as if they would buckle. I sat back on the couch and rested my chin on my right hand.

Malik began speaking again. "Look, I don't want to make you uncomfortable. I just don't want either of us to miss this opportunity. Trin, if I had been smart back then, Tony would have *never* had the opportunity to hurt you."

"Don't do this." I signaled for him to stop.

"I read him from *day one*. I could have convinced you that he wasn't interested in friendship. I could have been on the phone with you that night, so there would have been no need for you to be there in the first place. I could have been on a plane to see you, just like your roommate's man was there to see her. I could have—"

Irritated that he had stirred those memories, I shook my head. "But you didn't. And it's not your fault, Malik. What happened, happened for a reason—some reason I haven't yet figured out." I paced the floor. "But there's nothing anybody can do about that now. Not you or anyone else. Just... leave it alone!"

He placed his hands on my shoulders. "It shouldn't have happened," he persisted. "When you told me about it, I knew I should have been there. While I can't change the past, I want to be there for you in the future."

He wrapped his arms around me, and I felt my eyes well up.

My voice cracked. "You will not make me cry." I tried to push away from his grip and he only held me tighter. "Don't make me regret what I told you."

He released his grip and stepped back to look into my eyes. He held onto my biceps with his large, yet unthreatening hands.

"Please, I don't want you to feel that way. I just want to protect you."

I managed to free myself from his hold and pointed my index finger toward his head. "Don't you understand? You can't protect me; Bashaye couldn't protect me. All I have is me!"

"If all you have is you, what am I doing here?"

"Wasting your time," I said and plopped onto the couch. I pulled the afghan to my chest, gripping it like it was my lifeline.

"You don't mean that." Malik sat at my side.

"Malik, I don't think I'm right for you."

"Why, because you think I'm intimidated by the wall you've put up? That doesn't intimidate me. I love that you're different than the girls I've dated. You're what I want in my wife."

I tilted my head and felt frustration move through my body as my facial muscles contorted. "But I'm not so sure you're what I want in my husband."

His expression revealed that he thought my words were lined with audacity rather than earnestness, but he spoke only with his eyes. I had to explain what I meant. I spoke slowly and clearly, so that I would not speak out of haste.

"There are so many things I love about you and that I want in my husband—if I go that marriage route. You are handsome, intelligent, strong; you're also financially responsible, respectful, articulate. We have fun together. I can have a conversation with you without worrying about what to say next."

I looked at Malik to see if his expression had changed. He was grinning at me, humbly, so I continued. "We have the same sense of humor. You're the type of man who could finish my sentences. We like each other's family members and they like us. Those are all things I want in my relationship with my mate." I hesitated looking for my next words. "Still, there are so many things I need to sort out with myself before I can even entertain the idea of sharing myself with someone else. I'm not marriage-minded right now. Until a few minutes ago, I really didn't think you were either."

"Well, every man gets to a point where he realizes it's time to stop playing games." He hung his head but quickly pulled it up. "Trin, you said you don't know if

I'm what you want in a husband. What is it about me that doesn't make me marriage material?"

I dreaded the thought of that answer. I had never thought of Malik in that way, so I wasn't even sure how to respond. I only knew what was in my head, so I closed my eyes and began to speak.

"A husband offers everything I have with you: friendship, support, honor, respect. He's funny, goofy, not too corny, though. He knows how to make me laugh and how to defuse me even when I'm angry. He knows how to make me comfortable in any kind of situation. He senses when he upsets me, goes out of his way to make it better and loves me enough not to do it again. He always comes to my defense and supports my ideas, even if he doesn't agree with them. He knows my heart, my fears, my desires without me having to say a word.

"But he's even more. He accepts me in my brokenness and encourages me on a closer walk with God. He nurtures his soul and mine, so that our time together will not end on this side of creation. He feeds my soul, loving me as Christ loved the church. He is virtuous and brings out the virtue in me. He is there to complement me, not complete me because I am already whole. He is there to show me and others that love still exists as God meant for it to be."

I took a deep breath and opened my eyes. Malik was looking at me with childlike adoration. He put his arm around me and pulled me close, kissing me on the forehead.

"I wish I could be all those things to you. I'd do anything to be that guy."

I nodded my head. Malik would be "that guy" if he could, but we both knew that he wasn't the man I wanted for a husband.

"I love you, Trinity."

"I know."

"And for the record, you haven't only got yourself. You just pissed on me and called it rain, and I'm still here. I'll always be here as long as God gives me breath. And speaking of God, I'm not church folk, but I know that as long as you believe in Him, He'll always walk with you. You'll never be alone, Trin."

"You're right." I knew he was telling the truth. I was embarrassed that I'd even spoken that way. Too many times I felt like I was walking on my own, and it took an angel in disguise to show me my error.

Malik hugged me and I hugged him back, no longer concerned about my bralessness or my body odor. I knew that Malik was a true friend who would always be in my corner. He pulled back. "You know, Shawna was right. You are something to envy."

"Be careful of the words you choose. Envy is a dangerous thing, especially when you only see what people want you to see."

Malik left after asking to attend church with me when I got back from Caroline's wedding. I told him he had an open invitation. After he left, I showered and got dressed, then picked up the phone and called Shawna.

"Are you mad at me?" she asked, without saying hello.

"No."

"I'm sorry. I just wanted to fix things. I got his number from your phone. I was just planning to apologize, but we started talking about you, and I just want you to be happy."

"So do I, Shawna, but it's not your job to make me happy. It's just your job to be my friend."

"But you deserve to be together."

"We deserve to be with the right person at the right time. Malik and I talked. We both realized that our relationship is good the way it is."

"But you—"

"Everything is not for everyone to understand. Just know that I love you and I love Malik, but things are not going to be the way you'd like for them to be."

Her disappointment saturated the silence.

"But I'm grateful that you love me enough to not only make things right, but to try to make something happen with me and Malik," I said.

"Okay." Her voice was like that of a small child who had realized she wouldn't get her way.

"It's in God's hands. He'll make sure things work out the way they should if we just allow him to have His way."

"I guess you're right."

"There are a whole lot of things I don't understand, Shawna. But I understand that if we allow Him to move in our lives, He will. I'm trying to learn to allow Him to do that in my life."

"Well, that's easier said than done."

"I know. It's been a constant struggle for me—learning to be still, giving up on my way of doing things."

Shawna was quiet.

"All I'm saying is that if we let God be God, we won't have to worry about figuring things out on our own. He will have already done it for us."

"So basically, you don't want me to pry in your love life."

I laughed. "Well, basically, yeah. But I want you to trust that God will take care of it."

"Well, I was just trying to give you a head start."

"I know, and I love you for it," I said. "But let's just see what happens. If worse comes to worst, we'll buy houses next to each other and become old cat women, feared by all little kids in the neighborhood."

"Great, I can't wait for that," Shawna said with sarcasm.

"As long as we're friends, I'm cool with it."

"That's the first thing you've said during this conversation that I truly understand," Shawna said.

We ended the call and I headed outside, not for a jog, but for a walk. This time I not only saw the beautiful homes of the University District neighborhood, but I also heard the heartbeat of the community. I listened to barking dogs secured behind backyard fences; watched new parents load car seats into their SUVs; followed the paths of squirrels that chased one another around the yards; watched an elderly man rake leaves while two small boys took turns jumping in a large pile in the center of the yard. I took everything in, slowly and surely.

Chapter Sixteen

Days later, Lydia and the kids met me and my parents at the airport. We were on our way to Caroline's long-awaited wedding. The trip to the departure gate was a journey in itself. Autumn and Aaron trailed behind Lydia and my mother, arguing about how the arm of Autumn's baby doll, Jenna, ended up detached during the car ride. Autumn said Aaron stepped on the doll; he said Autumn sat on it.

Despite the fact that Lydia had performed emergency surgery on Jenna to reattach her arm with a couple of safety pins, an argument continued on the way to the gate. Aaron's frustration with his sister's accusations was apparent. His cheeks darkened to the shade of the red bell pepper that decorated the salad I'd eaten earlier. It made his freckles seem to pop right off his face. Aaron balled his fists as if he were holding candle sticks, and emphatically pushed his hands toward the floor. He proclaimed his innocence while he stomped along.

Autumn trotted in front of him with her head held toward the ceiling. "I don't care what you say. I know what you did to Jenna," she kept repeating as if she were a police officer interrogating a suspect. She pulled the doll closer to her chest. Jenna's previously amputated arm bounced with the force of each step in Autumn's forty-seven-pound body. Autumn's stride was an imitation of her mother's short strides and tendency to meander. Lydia was at least twenty feet ahead of her children and was paying them no attention, nor was she aware of the strangers she almost ran into on her crooked path. Since my father and I were behind the kids, I guess Lydia figured one of us would handle the disagreement.

I thought of the cartoons I watched as a child and I knew it was doubtful that a lid would form at the crown of Aaron's head, allowing his anger to vent in the form of steam. Growing concerned that he might huff himself to death, I tugged at his wrist and passed him a peppermint. It was just a piece of candy, but for a kid who was nearly four, it held the power to divert his attention from Autumn just long enough for us to get to the gate without any more bickering. It had obviously worked for my mom for many years.

"Good thinking, Trinee," my dad said, patting me on the back.

When we got to the gate, Mom was already busy directing us to designated seats in the waiting area. Forty minutes later, we boarded the plane without incident. An hour after that, we touched down and were retrieving our suitcases at baggage claim.

Uncle Jonathan had a corporate limousine pick us up from the airport. The driver was holding a sign that read "Porter." It was the one time I had been in the position to walk over to a driver and say, "We're the Porter party." After hearing my words, I wondered if it sounded like I was confirming a dinner reservation or reciting part of a limerick, but I decided that it was still a simple but gratifying experience. Gratifying, that is, until embarrassment kicked in as I watched the driver attempt to fit all of the bags in the trunk. He looked at my father and offered to call another limo.

I watched the driver develop a twitch at the left side of his mouth as he awaited my father's reply. It entranced me so that for a moment, I was unaware of my father's motioning me to get in the limo where Mom, Lydia and the kids were already waiting.

"No, that won't be necessary," my dad told the driver as he took a mental inventory of the bags that sat on the curb. "We can hold the ones that won't fit."

While he didn't say so, it was clear that my dad thought that needing two ten-passenger limos to transport six people—two of them kids—to the same location, was nothing short of asinine. I took a seat and began a game of hot potato. The driver handed the stray bags to Dad; Dad handed them to me; and I passed them down the line. In the end, I still got stuck with a bag. What should have been an enjoyable limo ride to Aunt Georgia and Uncle Jonathan's house turned into a balancing act for my dad, Lydia and me. As we did our best to keep the luggage from flying into anyone, I wondered if I'd ever get to take a family trip without having someone else's bag on my lap.

When we arrived at the house, things were more chaotic than they were before the shower. The wedding was only a day away. Family, friends and hired help filled the home. Everyone was working on something. I watched centerpieces, decorative bows and wedding favors dance in the arms of and above the heads of the workers as they traveled between the hallways and the rooms of the lower level of the house. As I observed this fascinating sight, the queen of the colony emerged from a bedroom and appeared at the top of the stairs. She made her way to a blissful sister, a nonchalant brother-in-law, an excited daughter, two hyperactive grandchildren and a niece who was bemused by it all.

"Ooooh!" she screamed and ran into the arms of my mother who was rubbing her hands in anticipation of embracing her sister and sharing her joy. When they met, they began jumping like two small children on Christmas morning. My mother took Aunt Georgia's hands in her own. Both were dripping with pride.

"Oh, girl, I'm so happy for you!" My mother's smile revealed every tooth and crown.

Aunt Georgia nodded her head and fought to hold back the tears. She opened her mouth to speak, but Mom jumped in before my aunt could form a sentence, phrase or even one simple word.

"I can't wait until this is me," Mom gloated. "I just hope it happens before I'm too old to know what's going on!" She broke into laughter before grabbing me in a bear hug and kissing my forehead. I did not reciprocate her affection. Instead I mimicked a dead fish, allowing her to toss me around in her grasp. I couldn't even bring myself to smile or laugh it off. The only bodily response I had was twisting my mouth in the same way I did when acid rushed up my esophagus after eating chili fries.

Maybe if I tell her I'm a lesbian, she'll just stop with the marriage jokes altogether.

Almost immediately after the thought entered my mind, I realized that would not have been the route for me... not even when playing a cruel joke on my dear mother.

"Here, baby. Let me take your bags to your room," Uncle Jonathan said as he picked up my suitcase and one of Lydia's and headed upstairs. I wasn't even sure where he had come from. He completed the move so quickly, I didn't have a chance to tell him that only one of the bags belonged to me.

"Hey, Charles," he yelled down the steps. "Meet me in the basement. The Crew is already down there."

His "crew" was at all the family functions my aunt and uncle hosted and consisted of three of Uncle Jonathan's college friends from his days at the University of Chicago. They were all in the law program in the seventies when black folks weren't in abundance on campus. They nicknamed themselves "The Crew" back then, and continued to hold on to the name, as well as the persona. I wasn't sure if it was a touching example of bonding or just a pathetic outlet for middle-aged men to congregate and perpetrate like they were still young men.

I headed up the stairs and peered over the rail to watch Dad walk toward the basement steps. Though he rarely said much, it was clear that my father was content to be out of the company of three women and two children. I knew that it was only Mom who kept him from checking them into a hotel. She insisted they stay at the house because there was no way she'd pass on helping Lydia to get the kids ready for their parts in the wedding. Autumn was the flower girl and Aaron was the ring bearer.

Mom fancied herself an unofficial wedding planner—unofficial because no one had actually hired her as such. She just offered her services, whether folks asked for them or not. Interestingly enough, no one ever turned her down. I think it may have been due to intimidation rather than the desire to have her assistance.

Caroline was at her final fitting for the wedding gown and Simon was at the airport seeing that his own family arrived intact. In just a couple of hours, I'd get to see how these two families would come together. The rehearsal dinner was at six. I had two and a half hours to imagine what the dinner would actually be like. I was curious about Simon's family—whether his parents had good teeth like his, and how they really felt about him marrying Caroline. Caroline was from "good stock." She was beautiful and charismatic. But underneath it all, she was still a black girl. The desire to know how they felt about that was curiously irresistible.

The wedding party was rehearsing at a historic Catholic church on the north side of Chicago. Though my aunt went to a non-denominational church, Uncle Jonathan was raised Catholic. Despite the fact that he hadn't attended church in years, he somehow convinced the church, which was known for its aesthetics, to allow Caroline and Simon to marry there. I really wasn't sure if they had to convert to be married there or if, once again, money talked.

Nearby, family and out-of-town guests were gathering at a posh seafood restaurant on the water. Mom and Lydia had taken the kids to the rehearsal, but Dad and I decided to stay at Uncle Jonathan and Aunt Georgia's house. We would ride to the restaurant with Uncle Jimmy—Mom's first cousin who had made a career out of bachelorhood. I always considered him my uncle rather than my cousin because he was the same age as my mom.

I climbed into the front seat of Uncle Jimmy's black Cadillac Escalade that sat on twenty-two-inch rims. His license plate read "ONLYJ," and his windows were tinted. His SUV was upstaged only by his outward appearance. My uncle was decked out in a teal suit with matching gators.

It wasn't the color of the suit or the matching gators that got to me. My uncle lived on the south side of Chicago—not a far stretch in fashion sense from the east side of Detroit. There were others who shared his flair for clothes, even though I was not a fan. What got to me was the gold rope chain with an oversized cross that stopped in the middle of his pot belly.

My uncle, bless his heart, looked like a wannabee rapper from the eighties. I wondered if he had either forgotten his age or gotten confused with the Julian calendar. Perhaps he thought that when he drove the Escalade, it would turn into a time machine that would cause women would see him as a younger man rather than an older man trying to recapture his youth. Unfortunately, the latter was all I saw when I looked at him. I was willing to bet that's what other women saw, too.

Uncle Jimmy turned over the engine and a Lil Wayne song blared through his speakers.

"Uncle Jimmy. What are you doing listening to this?"

His raspy voice came through loud and clear. "Aww, sweet pea. Your uncle knows what time it is!"

What time it is? I must be taking a ride with Kurtis Blow, the "Father of Rap."

I heard a faint chuckle from my dad travel from the back seat to the front seat. I hoped he was amused because he thought my uncle looked as stupid as I thought he did. I just knew he couldn't entertain the thought of adopting my uncle's real or imagined lifestyle. If the thought even crossed my dad's mind, I would commit him without hesitation.

After some idle conversation, we arrived at the restaurant. As Uncle Jimmy made the turn into the restaurant driveway, I grinned at the marquee which read, "Congratulations, Caroline and Simon!" in gold lights.

When we pulled up to the valet, my door opened before Uncle Jimmy could put the Escalade in park. I inched my way toward the attendant, who effortlessly pulled me out of the commodious seat and toward the ground, which seemed feet away—a far cry from the vehicle-to-ground distance of my Acura.

Two glass doors with brass handles opened inward as we approached. It wasn't until we reached the entrance that I realized they were being held by two employees. A pleasant greeter stood ahead and directed us to round a corner.

We stepped into what appeared to be another realm. Purple paint, the shade of royal garments, extended from the top to the bottom of the walls and white marble lined every inch of the floor. The ceiling was a collection of individual murals with themes from each season spreading from the center to one of the four corners. The winter theme drew my eye. The trees had lost their leaves and looked like they'd been plucked from the ground, dipped in water, then returned to their resting place. A perfect coat of ice wrapped the branches. The evergreens were only glazed with the ice, but the weight on the tips of the trees caused them to lean to one side or the other. With closer examination, I saw that a small deer seemed to peek out at me through the trees, watching me as I observed its environment.

"Right this way!" A twenty-something woman with olive skin and Hispanic features met us, picking up where the greeter left off. Her long dark hair was restrained in a ponytail that swayed as she turned around to lead the way to the dining area. "Sit anywhere you'd like." She smiled and offered a slight bob of her head, as if asking permission to be excused.

We obliged and faced about fifteen round tables that awaited guests. Nearly half of the tables were full. We chose one near a wall with ceiling-to-floor windows, where we looked over Lake Michigan and watched the passing boats.

My father pulled out a chair for me and my uncle pushed it in. It was a rarity for me to observe a double team of chivalry outside of an Audrey Hepburn-era movie. The men of my generation seemed to be done with the ways of the men who came before them.

Our table, like the others, was decorated with a floral centerpiece that appeared to have birthed the thin, ivory candles protruding from the center of the arrangement. Chrysanthemums and dahlias filled crystal vases detailed with gold. The flowers were shades of red, orange and melon. Cream-colored roses were strategically placed between the mums and dahlias. The place settings included china charge plates and crystal glasses. Both were Waterford. I didn't own anything Waterford, but my mother's long-term relationship with the brand had taught me to recognize it when I saw it.

I tried to disguise my astonishment and spoke to a couple who'd followed us and sat at our table. But my mind was not on them. I was wondering if the restaurant had a collection of Waterford china and crystal which they'd rented to the tune of Uncle Jonathan's platinum card, or if Aunt Georgia had negotiated her way into allowing her to provide the table settings. As outlandish as the second option sounded, nothing was to be put past my aunt. She had single-handedly organized parties for two hundred of her "closest friends," so she probably had place settings for all the people who were attending the rehearsal dinner.

The lights were dim and the candles glowed, creating a romantic ambiance as a pianist played classical music on a beautiful, black Baldwin piano. My uncle excused himself to go to the bar. I tried to shield myself from a breeze by rubbing my hands over my forearms. Looking toward the ceiling, I found an air vent forcing the power of the Antarctic onto our table. The slinky, calf-length black dress I wore that night met my curves, but it wasn't tight. It found a comfortable place between classy and sexy, but even with elbow-length sleeves, it did little to keep me warm.

"Cold, baby?" My dad had begun to remove his suit jacket, but I reassured him I was okay. I was cold, but not cold enough to interfere with the look of my outfit by covering it with an oversized, square-shouldered jacket.

"It's okay, Daddy. I'll just ask the waitress for some tea."

Before I could flag down our waitress, Dad had found one and ordered my tea, even though she was not assigned to our table. In all of his quiet ways, my daddy knew how to take care of his family, and I adored him for it. He just wanted people to be happy.

My uncle returned with a mahogany-colored drink in his hand just as my tea arrived. We made small talk with some of the guests and enjoyed hors d'oeuvres, which included shrimp and vegetable pot stickers, crab quiche and a delectable lobster wrap.

The wedding coordinator, a pear-shaped white woman in a snug taupe suit and stilettos that seemed to shiver under her weight, approached the podium. Her streaked hair hit her neckline and flipped on the ends rather whimsically.

"Good evening, everyone." She flashed a bonded smile. "We are so pleased you could make it to Caroline and Simon's rehearsal dinner." The guests clapped.

"The wedding party has arrived," she continued. "We graciously ask you to take your seats."

The coordinator grinned out of what seemed to be courtesy rather than genuineness. She made her way to the photographer, who was preparing to take pictures of the party as they entered the dining area. Everyone entered, with Caroline and Simon in the lead, hand in hand. My aunt and uncle, the bridesmaids, grooms-men, my mom, Lydia and the kids followed.

Aaron caught a glimpse of my dad. "Auntie Charles!" He waved as if he were on stage at a school concert and had spotted his parents in a crowd, just as he took his place on the bleachers. He tried to dart over to my father, but Lydia snatched his small body and plopped him in a chair at their table. The room filled with laugh-ter and I saw a gleam in Dad's eye.

Mom and Lydia made their way to the seats we saved them. Two waitresses placed bread baskets on our table near crystal butter dishes that held wedding-bell-shaped butter slices. Each dish was strategically placed on opposite ends of the table. My uncle imme-diately reached for the nearest bread basket and pulled out a steaming sesame seed roll. He had barely placed it on his plate when he began reaching over another guest for one of the butter dishes.

Politely, the man to his right tried to stop my bar-baric uncle. "Allow me," the man said as he passed the butter dish to Uncle Jimmy.

"Aww, thank ya," he said as he held the dish in one hand, a knife in the other, and proceeded to pop the roll open with his thumb. He stuck the knife in the middle and spread the butter onto the bread. Perhaps knowing more bread was in his future, he managed to scrape three more bell shapes from the dish and slap them square on his bread plate. He then returned the knife to the butter plate, crumbs and all. I wondered if he forgot that nine other people, four of whom were strangers, sat at our table.

I tried not to watch, as halfway into my first piece of bread, he was reaching for his third piece. I wasn't the only one to notice his affection for carbohydrates.

"I'll have your waitress bring more rolls," a young pimple-faced man said as he refilled our water glasses.

My dad snickered at the water attendant's passive-aggressive politeness. Uncle Jimmy was inattentive to any of us, yet enthralled by what remained of the sesame seed roll.

When everyone was well into the salads, I took a few minutes to speak to the wedding party. Autumn and Aaron were telling me about how one of the bridesmaids tripped walking down the aisle during rehearsal. I tried to end their laughter by telling them they weren't being nice because she could have hurt herself, but it only made them resort to a lengthy rationalization of their behavior.

Finally, I found a way to end their bantering. "Wow. You've got so much to tell me, but I've got to sit down so we can all finish our food." I knew that leaving was the only way to get them to stop talking about the bridesmaid, who was surely within earshot.

Autumn used her fingers to pick up a leaf from her salad, held it above her head and lowered it into her mouth.

I glanced at Lydia who was mouthing, "Use your fork!" from across the room.

Autumn looked at me and exposed her missing front tooth through a devilish smile. She picked up her fork and used it to finish eating her salad. I tried to contain my laughter and returned to the table just as our meals were served. Our choices were broiled lobster tail, Atlantic salmon or a vegetarian meal. I chose the lobster tail. It was accompanied by asparagus and smashed potatoes.

After dinner, Caroline and Simon walked to the podium. They thanked their families and friends for their support and talked about how excited they were to have everyone there to join them. Simon called up his parents and Caroline called hers. All four surrounded

Caroline and Simon at the podium. His mother stood there, adoringly and rather reserved. His father grinned, periodically adjusting the brown, plastic framed glasses that continued to slip on the bridge of his nose. Both were dressed conservatively; she in a navy, long sleeved, ankle-length dress with functional matching pumps; he in a basic black suit, white shirt with a black tie and black loafers. If not for his meek demeanor, one might have mistaken him for a member of the wait staff.

In contrast, Aunt Georgia stood in a silk, cantaloupe-colored suit with a single-button closure and a skirt that met her knees. The simple richness of the suit was stunning alone and adorned only by a silk flower on the collar. Uncle Jonathan wore a chocolate-colored suit with one of his trademark monogrammed shirts—this one cream-colored, with faint stripes that were nearly invisible. His multicolored tie had the same shade of melon as my aunt's suit. The cufflinks sparkled as much as the five-karat diamond on Aunt Georgia's wedding finger.

"Mum, Dad," Simon said as he turned to his parents, mindful not to move away from the microphone. "You are the reason I am who I am today. You led by example. I know that all of your hard work had a purpose. But you showed me your unconditional love by giving up your dreams to make mine come true. You've always supported me. Even when I wanted to go to America to study engineering, you supported me and found a way to help me enroll at Northwestern and get me on an airplane to Chicago. When I wanted to quit, you encouraged me to continue. Sometimes I got discouraged, but I could hear your voices telling me to keep going, even when you weren't on the phone." His parents chuckled and his father reached out to squeeze his mother's hand.

"And then," he turned to Caroline. "Then I met Caroline." He took a deep breath. "It was only a matter of time before I knew that I was there for more than becoming an engineer." He turned to my aunt and uncle. "It only took one conversation to fall in love with your daughter." My uncle rubbed my aunt's shoulder. She raised her hand to her mouth, trying not to become emotional. "Caroline had a glow that I saw from the first day I met her while tutoring engineering students. Not only was she beautiful, but I soon discovered she was so full of life." He pressed his hand to his chest. "And I am very grateful to you for allowing me and my family to become part of your family."

Simon turned back to Caroline and kissed her hand. The guests applauded. Simon motioned for Caroline

to take the podium. Her voice cracked as she began to
speak. She was shaking. "Umm...." She tried to regain
her composure and Simon kissed her on the cheek.
"What can I say?" She giggled nervously. "How could
anyone *not* marry this man?" There was laughter.
"Simon has been so good to me. He came when I wasn't
expecting it and saw in me what I didn't see in myself.
And I thank him." She twisted like she was on a turn-
table and faced his parents. "And I thank *you* for giving
me such a wonderful fiancé who I know will make a
wonderful husband!"

No one on stage went without a hug from each person who stood before us. The guests were still clapping when Caroline and Simon stepped back from
the podium, leaving their parents there. Both couples
looked back and forth at the other, providing offerings
of politeness. "You go first. No, really, you go first,"
their expressions said. Finally my aunt and uncle won.
They stepped back and Simon's parents leaned into the
podium.

Simon's mom took the lead and began to speak, her
accent much heavier than her son's. "Wow. I must say
my husband and I are much less eloquent than our son.
We also talk less." Everyone laughed again, as if on cue
at an awards dinner. "Simon is our youngest son and

my baby. When he told us of Caroline, we thought he was in love. When he came home to visit us in the summer, we *knew* he was in love—actually we were sure of it after we got the phone bill." Simon blushed at the revelation and Caroline bubbled over with delight. "But we couldn't be happier," she said and nodded to her husband to say his piece.

He stepped forward, pushing his glasses to the bridge of his nose. "This is my—and my wife's—first time in the States. I want you to know we are so appreciative of your hospitality and your kindness," he said addressing my aunt and uncle and then the guests. When he turned to the guests and opened his mouth once again, I saw that Simon was blessed not to inherit his father's teeth.

It looks like there was a train wreck in his mouth! What color is that, anyway?

If I was going to get through the rest of his speech, I would have to focus my attention on something else, so I stared at the condensation on the glass in front of me. Simon's dad continued, "I am confident that Simon will be just fine with his family away from home. Thank you for being more than we could have imagined or asked for."

❧

It was nearly one in the morning. All of the day's festivities had faded into the darkness. Everyone at my aunt and uncle's house was asleep, except for me. I was not sleepy, so I slipped downstairs into the movie theater of the house to watch a movie on their wall-sized screen. The theater was intimate—ten black, leather rocking chairs and red-wine colored walls. I settled into a chair in the middle of the room and wrapped myself in an afghan that lay on the seat. Ma Lo had knit this afghan, just as she'd made the one I had at home. I snuggled in deep, hoping to connect with a distant memory of her.

Uncle Jonathan had catalogued all of his movies in an online database and transferred it to display on the screen. I was flipping through the movie titles when I realized one thing was missing—popcorn.

To the kitchen.

To my surprise, Caroline sat at the table with an open pint of Ben & Jerry's and a tablespoon in the grip of her right hand.

"Did I wake you?" I asked.

"No. I just couldn't sleep and got tired of staring at the ceiling."

"Pre-wedding jitters?" I tried to comfort her.

"Hmm, kind of. I guess." She maneuvered the spoon to break up the hardened ice cream.

I read the carton: Cinnamon Buns.

"Want some?" She raised the spoon to her mouth, holding it like a small child just learning to use silverware. She took a chunk from the spoon. A portion the size of a BB remained on it.

"I love that flavor, but no thanks. I just came up for some popcorn." I wondered if she really thought I'd be interested in sharing the ice cream after watching her eat out of the pint. Would she have used her own spoon to serve me? I hadn't been into sharing food like ice cream or popsicles as a child, and I wasn't going to start now.

"It's in the pantry. Third shelf."

"Thanks." I located a personal-sized bag of sweet and salty popcorn and put it in the microwave. Caroline continued to indulge in the ice cream, holding the spoon like a sucker and biting away at mounds of cinnamon bun dough. I sat down across from her, and she seemed to have forgotten I was there. I watched her; she was so childlike. It was hard for me to fathom that she would be getting married in the morning. In this candid moment, I wondered if she truly understood what she'd be doing on the following day.

"So, what's the ice cream doing for you?" I leaned into the table and rested my chin on the bridge formed by my linked fingers.

Caroline looked confused, but after a brief pause, something stirred in her. "Trinity, have you ever done anything because it seemed right, even though you didn't understand it?

Her eyes revealed confusion, even melancholy. I nodded my head in response to her question.

"Simon truly loves me," she continued. "I didn't grow up seeing the kind of love he's given me. I mean, my mom and my dad always made sure I was taken care of. They met my wants and my needs. They made sure I was happy." She paused, holding a spoonful of ice cream that began to melt. "But I always wondered if they were happy together."

"You don't think they were happy?" I asked.

She put the spoon in her mouth. A drop of ice cream fell into the pint. "I don't really know," Caroline said. "They seemed to do things because that's what they were supposed to do, but I don't know if they wanted to do it."

I dropped my head and put my hands in my lap, running my thumb across the cuticle of my right index finger.

"I want to be happy, Trinity."

She had my full attention.

"Simon loves me and that makes me happy."

I tried to gather my thoughts. I did not want the words to come out wrong. "Well, does his loving you make you happy *or* is it the love you have for each other that makes you happy?"

"What do you mean?" Caroline applied a subtle but effective jab to the ice cream in the carton to loosen it up.

"I mean... in Detroit, you told me you loved him. You didn't say that you loved him just now. You didn't say you loved him at the rehearsal dinner. I'm just wondering if you love him or if you love that he loves you?"

"Cousin, you're confusing me."

"I am?" I was truly trying to communicate with her, so confusion was not what I was going for.

Caroline sat back in the chair and pulled her knees to her chest. Her sock-covered feet hung halfway off the edge of the chair.

"When I was little, I asked for someone to love me... just as I am. Now I've got that... in Simon. And that's all I ever wanted."

"If that's all you've ever wanted, what void are you trying to fill with that pint of Ben & Jerry's hours before your wedding?"

"I don't know. Maybe I do have nerves. Who wouldn't? What woman wouldn't find comfort in a little ice cream? Maybe it takes me away from reality for a moment, you know?"

Of course I knew. Sweets had been known to speak to me in my moments of vulnerability, but for me, the relationship had been bittersweet. I've cursed a chocolaty treat many times while on my Saturday morning jogs.

"Yes, I get it, Caroline. I just want to know that it's not an excuse for ignoring a much bigger issue."

"A bigger issue?" She leaned across the table to grab one of my hands in both of hers. "I know that Simon is a forgiving man. I know that he accepts me as I am. I know that he won't keep me waiting up at all hours of the night while he's..." She held up her right hand. In a quick motion, she moved her index and middle finger up and down as she said "working late." She removed her left hand from mine and took another scoop of the ice cream. "And that," she licked the spoon, "I love."

The microwave dinged. I had forgotten about the popcorn despite the fact that the aroma and the popping should have drawn my attention. I pulled the bag from the microwave and grabbed a paper towel. Caroline continued to indulge in her ice cream as I sat across from her and ate the popcorn. Only a few more words were exchanged for the rest of the night, but it was clear that I had connected with my little cousin, however troubled the conversation left me.

Regardless of what my mom or anyone else said, Caroline had been affected by her father's marital indiscretions. I could see that she was so desperate not to be like her mother, she found a man to play her mom's role; Caroline felt safer playing her dad's role. Simon would adore and honor Caroline, despite her flaws and her actions. At that moment it was clear to me that just as Uncle Jonathon's adultery had been apparent to Caroline, her unfaithfulness was evident to Simon on some level. He knew who she was and it did not matter to him.

I knew that Caroline was not just the phlegmatic person I saw in Detroit; she was a woman who was searching for happiness. I could see that despite her experiences, despite her fortunate background and despite being raised in Barrington, Illinois, she wasn't much different than a twenty-two-year-old who grew up in the projects of Chicago's west side—she wanted to be loved.

I wondered if Caroline would be able to show Simon the same love and respect he'd given her. It seemed impossible—especially since she wasn't in love with him. Then I realized that it *was* possible. God may have placed Simon in Caroline's life to teach her through his actions what it meant to love unconditionally. Maybe her relationship with Simon could be used to bring Caroline closer to Jesus.

I glanced up at her across the table. She was looking at me as she scraped the bottom of the ice cream carton. She grinned, and I grinned back. We engaged in a brief conversation without words. I told her I understood her a little bit more, and I hoped she'd find the happiness she was looking for. She thanked me and said she appreciated my concern—even when she acted like I was butting into her life. Satisfied, I wiped my hands on a paper towel and threw it away with the popcorn bag.

I looked at my watch. "Looks like it's time to turn in. The last thing we want is for you to have puffy eyes tomorrow."

"Yeah, you're right." She pitched the carton and extended her arms to the ceiling in a stretch. "I better take advantage of what's left of my beauty sleep."

We headed upstairs and said goodnight to one another before retiring to separate rooms. It was 1:20 a.m. and I still wasn't sleepy, but I figured it was time to go to bed. Even though I wasn't in the wedding, I didn't want puffy eyes, either.

My mother was a sound sleeper, so my walking around didn't wake her. I changed my clothes and took care of my hair, face and teeth, then climbed into bed, kissing my mom on the cheek. I closed my eyes and prayed that Caroline would learn how to love and love truly despite her upbringing, and I prayed that she'd gain the wisdom to recognize that what she was searching for could not be found in the solace of another person. I knew she had to search her soul, and I hoped she would find the Lord there.

Chapter Seventeen

At one o'clock the next afternoon, I sat in a pew of a historic Catholic church. My dad sat next to me as I periodically glanced toward the sanctuary doors. I rested my feet on the kneeling bench for a moment when it occurred to me that my Protestant upbringing may have painted me as a complete ignoramus. I planted my feet on the ground and glanced at my watch. 1:05.

"I'm sure they'll be starting at any second." My dad covered my watch with his hand.

"I'm sure you're right. I was just wondering if I should go back there to see if Lydia and Mom needed help with the kids."

"With your mom back there, I'm sure that things are under control."

He was right. I took his calming words at face value and looked around the church. The presider's chair, lectern and altar table stood empty at the front of the sanctuary. Dwarfing the pulpit was an enormous statue of Jesus on the cross that pulled away from the wall. Stained glass windows depicted scenes from the Bible and told the story of Christ's passion. All of the faces on the window were the color of porcelain with European features. It was a peculiar depiction of a people who were indigenous to Africa and the Middle East.

The ceremony began nine minutes after its scheduled time. The priest entered from a side door and made his way to the pulpit, draped in his alb and chasuble. Simon followed him, standing to his left. He wore a black tuxedo with a reddish-pink vest and bow tie. According to Caroline, the official name of the vest and tie color was honeysuckle. Simon's hair was trimmed to the top of his ear and was more orderly than it had been at the dinner, just the night before. He crossed his arms in front of him as he waited for his bride.

The family was seated. Only one set of Simon's grandparents was living, and according to Caroline, they were too frail to make the flight from England. Our maternal grandmother's absence was painfully obvious, though Ma Lo succumbed to cancer before I was a teenager and while Caroline was still in grade school. Her husband, Papa Theo, passed when I was too young to remember much about him.

The four bridesmaids and four groomsmen entered, one couple at a time. The groomsmen were dressed like Simon. The bridesmaids were wearing honeysuckle, sleeveless Vera Wang dresses that cupped the bosom and flowed loosely from their waistlines to the floor. They held bouquets filled with flowers that looked like they were plucked from a hillside. Dark pink mini calla lilies and melon roses were accented by golden Asiatic lilies.

Aaron walked toward the front of the sanctuary in a shrunken version of the groomsmen's tuxes and held a melon-colored ring pillow. The pained look on his face revealed his gapped front teeth and tiny bottom teeth. Someone had obviously told him to smile. This was his concerted effort.

Autumn began her walk down the aisle. Reddish and orange flowers lined the bottom of her cream colored satin and organza dress. Spiral curls replaced her signature pigtails and a rhinestone crown adorned her head. She held a satin basket accented with Swarovski crystals. Methodically, she tossed deep red rose petals onto the runner, looked to the guests with a smile and dipped her hand into the basket before repeating her actions.

Once the cooing over the children stopped, all eyes were on the doorway. Caroline appeared with Uncle Jonathan just as a violinist and a cellist began to play the "Wedding March." Caroline looked composed, and her demeanor was matched by her appearance. Her unruly hair had been tamed into flowing, loose curls that were swept into an up-do. Her loud lipstick was replaced by a subtle flesh-colored choice with a pink tint. Earth-toned eye shadow and blush added warmth to her complexion. Caroline's jewelry was stunning in its simplicity—diamond-stud earrings and a delicate white-gold chain that supported a diamond heart. Her strapless, ball-gown-styled Vera Wang dress was the color of champagne diamonds. The satin bodice was lined with large rows of crystals that extended from the neckline to the bottom of her bust where there was a row of dangling pearls. At her tiny waistline, soft layers of bridal tulle hung like giant teardrops that glistened as she approached the threshold. Her bouquet held vibrant flowers that poured over the sides.

After an opening prayer and a scripture reading from Genesis about the creation of man and woman, the priest led the guests in a responsorial psalm. He sang a verse from the Book of Psalms and we responded, "I will bless the Lord at all times." The call and response tradition was strangely intriguing. I was determined to get the timing of the response right since this ritual was new to me.

After several more ceremonial traditions, Caroline and Simon said their vows. His voice wavered as he repeated the priest's words. Caroline's words were much steadier, but were quiet and lacked her usual bubbly enthusiasm. Once they exchanged rings, one verse in the final blessing gave me pause.

"May your heart's first desire be always the good things waiting for you in the life of heaven," the priest said before the guests responded with "Amen." I wondered about the first desire of Caroline's heart. She'd said that Simon was good for her, but did she desire to have a Godly marriage with him? He seemed committed to Caroline and their relationship, but his bride-to-be lacked a moral compass.

I thought about the desires of my own heart and realized that they were selfish. I had not shaped them around God and I had no idea what His plan was for me. I just wanted to follow the path I designed.

The priest told Simon he could kiss his bride and after a lingering lip-lock between bride and groom, the cheering guests were introduced to Mr. Simon Clarke and Mrs. Caroline Hill-Clarke. It was then that I realized that my cousin and I had something in common. Neither of us wanted to admit that something inside was missing that could not be filled by any worldly accomplishment or treasure.

After the ceremony, we followed Caroline and Simon to the front steps of the church where they released three doves that dipped, rose and danced before flying off to the east. When they were nearly out of sight, I turned back to Caroline and Simon, who were gazing into each other's eyes.

There seemed to be so much bliss between them. Both sets of parents watched from a side of the church steps.

Simon's father comforted his mother, who watched the event through a steady stream of tears that she desperately tried to wipe away with a tissue. Uncle Jonathan stood behind Aunt Georgia at the opposite end of the steps, rubbing his wife's shoulders. She, too, clung to a tissue, dabbing her face, trying not to smudge her makeup. While both women cried, their emotions were visibly different. My aunt shed tears of joy, while the tears of Simon's mother dripped in sorrow.

All of the guests headed over to the Chicago Botanic Garden for the reception. We followed a broad bridge, passing small, still lakes and colorful meadows of plants and flowers. The air was rich with the natural aroma of the garden—a smell that was easily forgotten by those of us who lived in the city.

Everyone passed through the gates of the Rose Garden. I walked a few paces ahead of my parents. At the entrance, deep shades of red roses intermingled with evergreens and vines. Floral shrubs formed a protective wall around the garden. A winding path led toward a tremendous, clear-span white tent. The colors of the roses changed as if I was looking through a kaleidoscope, moving from orange to red, saffron, pale pink and violet. I imagined that my spectacular view was much like the one that Eve saw in the Garden of Eden.

Inside the tent, I was drawn to a cathedral-style ceiling and ivory-colored Greek columns that stood tall like unwavering trees. Each was topped with a set of scrolls that curved like the horns of a ram. The columns eased toward a dark wooden floor with reddish tones. I ran my hand down one of the pillars.

Yep. It's marble.

"Isn't this beautiful?" My mom stood behind my left shoulder, next to my father. "You know, your aunt had these floors imported from Indonesia. They are teak," she said.

Teak? Should I know what that is?

Lights hung down from the rafters and changed colors every few minutes, projecting warm jewel tones. Beyond the tent, a harpist played angelic music near a magnificent fountain. I approached it to get a better look. My father was at my side. At the center of the fountain was a chiseled cement rose, large enough for someone to lie across. From its center, water spewed upward and brawny streams fell into the surrounding pool.

My dad squeezed my shoulder. "It's almost as beautiful as you."

If anyone else had uttered those words, I would not have thought twice about dismissing any sincerity, but coming from my daddy, the words were golden.

"Why, thank you." I turned to him with a girlish curtsy.

"I don't care what your mother says. I'm not worried one bit about you finding a man. You *should* be picky, sweetie. There are a whole lot of knuckleheads out here." He leaned down to kiss me on the cheek, making sure to complete the gesture with a kissing noise.

We continued to walk around, taking in the scenery—not just the garden but the people, too. I did a quick inventory to determine the guests' association with Caroline or Simon. According to my assessment, the majority of the 500 guests were Caroline's—actually, her parents' guests. It was an interesting dynamic that simply confirmed my ideas that social climbing was a priority for my aunt and my uncle.

My family's birthright did not provide the type of status my aunt and uncle desired. Uncle Jonathan had built his way up from nothing and it appeared that Simon had the potential to do the same. Therefore, his family brought nothing to Aunt Georgia or Uncle Jonathan in the way of status. I supposed they were confident that Simon would provide for Caroline in at least the same way Uncle Jonathan had provided for Aunt Georgia. If Simon didn't deliver, I was sure that a nice "back-to-daddy" account was awaiting Caroline.

My father accepted a glass of champagne from a waiter and took a sip. "Trinity, we should probably get our place cards," he said.

"I'll get them."

I went to the hostess table and picked up the cards for our table. Fanning through them, I found that most of us had chosen the stuffed chicken breast. According to the card, it was filled with broccoli, ricotta and sun-dried tomato, all "lovingly rolled in a bed of breadcrumbs." Uncle Jimmy had chosen the beef tenderloin, "tastefully marinated in a Cabernet sauvignon sauce and surrounded by a bed of fresh, grilled vegetables."

I placed each card at a seat at our table, which was draped with a melon tablecloth that dusted the wood flooring. Instead of traditional table centerpieces, flowers hung from the rafters and hovered about three feet above the middle of each table. Several long strands of crystals looped around a bowl-shaped fixture filled with an explosion of monochromatic flowers. Every table featured flowers with either honeysuckle or melon colors.

I laid my wrap in my seat and walked around the rest of the reception area. An open dance floor was at the rear of the tent, so dancers had a beautiful view of the rose fountain. On one side, a live jazz band played a rendition of "What a Wonderful World" by Louis Armstrong. On the other side was a table with five magnificent tiered cakes that looked more like gifts than food.

The center cake sat higher than the others and had cream-colored frosting with one-inch gold trim around the base of each layer. Flowers in red, orange and dark pink were nestled into the melon bows at each level of the cake.

Opposite the dance floor, an open bar had attracted Uncle Jimmy, who had assumed a position holding a full brandy glass. He was trying his luck with one of Aunt Georgia's sorority sisters who was polite but looked all too uninterested. My father made his way to Uncle Jimmy, distracting him long enough for the woman to slip away. It wasn't long before the wedding party arrived, making their grand entrance to resounding applause, standing ovations and spotlights fit for an acceptance speech at the Oscars. As the wedding coordinator announced everyone's name and affiliation to Caroline or Simon, it was clear that part two of the "Caroline Hill-Clarke Production" was well underway.

Mom and Lydia joined the rest of us at the table we shared with two of Uncle Jonathan's law associates and their wives. When dinner was served, Uncle Jimmy barely looked up from his plate of beef tenderloin and vegetables, all of which he'd covered in a visible layer of salt.

As the sun set and dinner wrapped up, the guests were asked to direct their attention to the dance floor. Caroline and Simon walked to the center of the floor. As they faced one another and locked fingers, a row of water jets that, until then, remained unnoticed fixtures on the other side of the windows, ejected water twenty feet into the air. The band began to play "At Last" by Etta James. Simon and Caroline danced, with spewing water and mesmerized guests as their backdrop. When they finished, the coordinator called for the father/ daughter dance and the mother/son dance. It wasn't long before the part I dreaded was upon us.

"May I please have all the single ladies to the dance floor?" The singer of the band, a voluptuous woman wearing a black sequined dress, tossed her long dark hair as she scanned the room, seeming to await a response to her call. Women began to converge onto the dance floor as the band played "I'm Coming Out" by Diana Ross. The singer continued her cattle call.

Oh, great.

I tried to slip my chair back for a subtle escape, but my mom was too quick for me.

"Baby, go up there!" she insisted.

"I'm going." I grabbed my purse.

I didn't say where I was going.

"How are you going to catch the bouquet with a purse," she asked, reaching for it.

I channeled Barry Sanders—from the era when the Detroit Lions seemed to always be in the playoffs—and gripped my purse to my chest like a football, trying to prevent a fumble.

"Oh, no. I'm fine." By this time, I was drawing the eyes of people at the table—exactly what I did not want.

I managed to slip into the crowd of single women who were making their way toward the dance floor, but I made a quick beeline toward the door that led to the building where the restrooms were. I found a bench beyond the fountain, out of the view of the guests, and sat down. I realized I'd made it to the end zone and placed the purse on the bench beside me.

Smiling, I listened to the cheering and the "one-two-three" counts from inside. So often, I had done the wedding guest thing, and I knew I was hearing reactions to several fake bouquet tosses. The fake-outs had been followed by an actual toss of the bouquet into the first row of women while even those in the last row would dive into one another, breaking nails, taking scratches and ruffling clothes, all for some silly sign that would temporarily pacify them on their quest for the perfect man. It wasn't for me.

I tuned out the activity in the tent and focused on the fountain in the near distance, illuminated with lights that gradually changed from orange to blue to purple. Closing my eyes and clearing my head of all thoughts, I listened to the rhythmic sound of the falling water. With several deep breaths, I inhaled the calming fragrance of the flowers. If only for a brief moment, I had achieved serenity and I wanted to stay awhile.

A pulsation on my leg startled me. The purse I had tried so desperately to keep out of my mom's hands was vibrating. I opened the purse and looked at the screen on my cell phone. Malik was calling. I held the phone for a few seconds before turning it off and slipping it back into my purse. I was spending time with Trinity, and I wanted to enjoy me, if only for a moment longer.

❦

Back inside, the poor guy who'd inevitably been forced into catching the garter was slipping it onto the leg of a bridesmaid, who had apparently caught the bouquet. Everyone had returned to their seats, and I went back to mine.

"I couldn't see you up there," my mom said.

"Did you see how many women there were? I could barely see my own hands."

"What took you so long to get back?" she badgered.

"I went to the restroom. That's why I wanted my purse." I held up my purse before tucking it in the side of my seat.

"Oh," my mom said. She didn't sound convinced by my story.

The deejay opened the dance floor to all guests, so I used dancing as an opportunity to end the conversation that had me lying to my mother twice in a matter of seconds. "Uncle Jimmy," I said. "Care to dance?" I stood and extended my hand.

"Sure, sweetie." I think I had him at "Uncle Jimmy." He loved to dance.

He grabbed my hand, and we went on the dance floor. He whirled me around, showing off his Chicago-step moves while everyone watched. I really didn't know what I was doing, but he had been ballroom stepping for so long, he made me look good. We danced for a couple of songs before my three-hour shoes gave out on me. I'd had them on for five hours, so I headed back to the table. Uncle Jimmy searched for his next dance partner.

There was cake cutting, conversations with guests, and many glimpses of Simon and Caroline. They both looked happy. I only wondered what life would be like when the guests went home and the ceremony was merely a memory.

As the crowd thinned, my family headed outside to the valet area where, drunk with the wine of the world, some of the guests were quite candid in their conversations with one another. Several people had gathered to wait for their cars. While my family was talking among themselves, trying to figure out who had Aaron's tie and determining who would sit where in Uncle Jimmy's SUV, I noticed that Simon's parents were waiting nearby. Then I heard what was only meant for Simon's mother's ears. His father leaned into his wife and said, "I know this isn't how you wanted it to be, but it's done. Now we've got to be supportive."

My eyebrow rose as I watched them shuffle toward a silver Buick Regal. "Cheerio!" Simon's dad yelled and waved to the guests who were still waiting on their cars. Within seconds, they were gone—gone before I could even ask anyone if they'd heard what Simon's dad said. When I turned around, I knew they hadn't. They were so wrapped up in their own conversations, they had not noticed anyone else. It seemed that I was the only one who'd heard the comment. While I had no proof of the context, my suspicions about his mom's tears at the ceremony had just been confirmed. Given my family's history of reacting to things, I knew that my best option was to keep what I heard to myself.

Chapter Eighteen

The fall season was approaching with significant rainfall. It rained every other day since I'd been back from Chicago. The humidity was doing wonders for my skin but wreaking havoc on my hair, which seemed to swell with each hour of the day.

On a quiet Friday, my mom cooked her famous chili then called me at work to invite me to dinner and a movie that night. My dad and Ron were on their way to Cleveland to look at a commercial property, thinking they might open a restaurant down there. I knew Mom was lonely and hated being in the house without my father—even with Chi Chi there.

When I got to the house, I found that she'd rented *Breakfast at Tiffany's*, because she knew I liked old movies. We ate and watched the movie, before she went into the kitchen to do the dishes. I wiped down the TV trays and wandered into the kitchen behind her. I put the chili and the cheese in the refrigerator and returned the crackers to the pantry before sitting at the table and watching her load the dishwasher. At that moment, I realized how pretty she was, despite her discomfort with her God-given beauty. She had beautiful streaks of gray that her hairdresser covered with dye every few weeks, hereditary freckles that she covered with foundation, and curves that were swallowed by her oversized clothes. I began to think of the less visible parts of her being that she also covered up day after day. Specifically, I thought of my brother.

"Mom, I need to ask you a question." She looked up from her task and swept her forehead with the back of her hand.

"What is it, baby?" She wiped down the countertop.

My heart began to race as I tried to make my words come together.

"Why don't you ever talk about Bashaye?"

She rinsed a glass, then dried off her hands.

"What do you mean?" She turned to face me.

"I mean, it's as if it's taboo to talk about him. Even being in the house... unless you go upstairs to his room, there's no evidence that he ever existed."

A silence fell over the house while the rest of the world moved on. The bass vibrations from the music of a passing car tickled my feet. Chi-Chi released a timid bark from upstairs. Mom was still pondering my initial question.

I broke the silence. "Shouldn't we be keeping him alive through talking about him, through keeping evidence of him throughout the house, not just in that... shrine?"

"Shrine?" She hung on to my last word.

She walked over to the table and sat down beside me, waiting for clarification.

"His room is like the living room at every black family's house," I continued. "You don't go in there unless you have a dust rag and a vacuum cleaner."

"Oh, Trinee." She shifted her weight and rolled her eyes.

"Okay," I said, ready to make a point. "Just consider this: Why aren't there any pictures of him in any other rooms of the house? Why aren't his trophies by mine in the den? Why are his clothes still in the closet? When you and Daddy remodeled, you did every room *but* Bashaye's, and you even locked his room when the workers were in the house."

Mom shook her head as if my words had no merit.

"Mom, there have been so many times that I remembered things he used to do or say and I wanted to talk about him so badly and share all of my stories, but I didn't... because no one else did."

"Everyone deals with death in a different way, Trinity."

"But who deals with the death of a child as if it never happened? I was there in the morgue when you and Daddy identified his body after the car accident. I was there when the coroner called to say that alcohol was in Bashaye's system. I was there at the funeral. I know that despite the fact that it appears to be waiting for him, Bashaye is not hiding somewhere in that room." I paused. "There may as well have been an altar in there with candles. Clearly, that is not normal."

"Normal?" she asked. Repeating my words was turning into some sort of a pattern. "What is normal, Trinity? I didn't get a manual on what to do when your child dies."

In that instant, I felt like an ass. Was I really that insensitive? I didn't know what to say.

"When people get married and have children, they think about what their kids will be like at each stage of their lives." She shook her head and stared at her clasped hands. "They envision all of the awards they'll bring home, and look forward to all of the height marks on the inside of the pantry door. They think of listening to their children's names being called at high school and college graduations. Then they dream of the weddings that mark their babies moving on to new chapters where they will build successful careers, make grandbabies and do better than their parents had ever imagined."

I could pinpoint the moment the gleam in her eye disappeared. My mother stared off into space and steadied herself in the chair, as if to prepare herself for what she had to say next. "They don't think about getting a call to identify the body, picking out a casket or laying a child in the ground who was not given the chance to live." I could tell there were more words on her heart, so I listened, allowing her words to saturate my soul.

"As children grow, you do all you can to protect them while trying to find a way to begin to let go. You give them what they need to make it in life, then hope they will take heed and blaze their own trails." She pushed her hands upward. "That's all you can do. But when life takes a different course—when God says I'm taking your child back—there's a bitter reminder that life is not your own."

For so many years I assumed my mother's smile, her warm touch, and her conscious or unconscious decision not to talk about my brother, were indications that she no longer struggled with his being gone. I thought that her grieving process was over, and that I was the only person with rancor in my heart. But today gave me the first inkling that the inner struggle may not have belonged to me alone.

"Mom, I could never imagine what it must be like to lose a child. I lost a brother and my best friend. It was more pain than I could ever imagine. I know it *had* to hurt you to the core. Why didn't you let that show?"

"I had to be strong for you and your dad." She searched for something in my eyes. "Trinee, if the way I handled this hurt you that badly, why didn't you ever come to me about it?"

"Because I watched you and Dad move on, and I knew in my heart that I had not. I thought something was wrong with me. So I pretended to be over it, too.

"What would you have said if I told you I slept in his bed for a year, waiting for him to come back? How about if I told you that to this day, every time I walk in this house, I wait for him to come down the stairs?"

She looked confused.

"That's right. You would have taken me straight to the loony bin."

"Trinity, Bashaye's death is something we'll never get over. Your father and I had to find a way to get through it. I had no idea that you hadn't been able to do that, too. I'm so sorry if I took for granted that—"

"Mom, you don't have to apologize. I'm not mad at you. Just disappointed in myself because I haven't been able to be strong about this."

"Trinity, if I've never told you this, you should know that you are the strongest person I know. Baby, I tried to let you grieve in your own way, and I thought that you had done that, so I let his memory rest where it was. I'm so sorry. You seemed so..."

"Adjusted? I guess I just know how to fake it." I grinned and looked at the floor. My heart sank as if it had followed my line of sight.

"Trinity, understand that the Lord giveth and the Lord taketh away. I will do all I can to help you, but know that He is all you need."

I nodded my head to let her know I heard her, but all I could think about was the day I realized my prayer would go unanswered.

"I remember you and Daddy taking us to church twice a week. I learned that when the faithful prayed, God heard and answered those prayers. So I tried to do that.

When Bashaye died, I prayed that it wasn't him in that car accident. When I waited with you in that morgue to identify his body, I prayed for Him to bring Bashaye back, just like Jesus did for Jairus' daughter. Then I prayed for Him to take away the pain. I've been praying for that for fifteen years, and guess what? It still hurts."

I crossed my arms and pulled them to my body. My confession was draining.

"Maybe it's time you changed your prayer," my mom said.

Her desperate eyes revealed a mother who wanted to shield her child from the world, but unbeknownst to her, the world had long since crept in and corrupted her offspring.

I opened my mouth to speak, but her words echoed in my mind so loudly that I could not talk. She got up from the table, squeezed into my chair and wrapped herself around me. Neither of us spoke. We sat there in a moment unlike any we'd shared since I was a little girl, unable to offer everything we'd been given, but willing to give every bit of what we had left.

Chapter Nineteen

The conversation with my mom had triggered the passionate desire to figure out how I'd arrived at the place where I stood, emotionally. I knew that Bashaye's alcohol-related death was the reason that I didn't drink. I knew that my fears of people leaving me drove my standoffish nature. And after I spoke with Mom, I realized something else about myself. There were layers to my pain and each one helped to shape the person I'd become. One of those layers was secured in my collegiate days.

Diori and I had one date that changed the course of our relationship. We had dinner downtown at the Capitol Grille and saw a play at the African Continuum Theatre Company in D.C. He planned the evening to celebrate the anniversary of our first date. When we got back to his apartment, he poured each of us a glass of champagne, despite the fact that I did not drink alcohol. He said it was for toasting purposes, so I obliged. Diori put on his favorite Dinah Washington CD and proposed a toast to our relationship. He had shown me nothing but consideration and respect, and I had always given the same back to him.

My feet were pounding from walking all night in cute, sidewalk-unfriendly shoes. He slipped off my shoes and massaged my feet on the couch, and I let my entire body fall into a state of relaxation. His hands traveled up my legs, massaging my calves and thighs. Diori picked me up and carried me into the bedroom. He laid me down on the bed and he crawled over me, kissing me gently from my mouth to my navel. Soon, I felt him inside of me, gently, and I became one with his flesh for the first time. I closed my eyes, trying to absorb all of him, but when I opened my eyes, I saw Tony.

Petrified with fear, I clenched my fists and thrust them at Diori's chest, repeatedly. I screamed at him to get off me. Diori jumped up, and held his hands beside his ears, as if to say he had no weapon and meant no harm. I'd frightened him, but I did not have the mindset to calm him down. Snatching the comforter from the bed, I wrapped myself in it and sought refuge in the only corner of the room that was bare. I sat in that corner, crying. Diori sat next to me, trying to console me, apologizing profusely. I clasped my knees and tried to get Tony's image out of my mind. Diori wanted to know what he did wrong. I tried to say, "It wasn't you. Someone else did this to me before we met," but I couldn't coerce the words from the tip of my tongue. Seeing Tony's face in Diori was more than I could handle.

Eventually I lay down on the floor and fell asleep. Diori never left my side. He waited for me to tell him what caused me to snap, but I couldn't—not that night or any other night that followed. I was ashamed—ashamed that I could not control the situation with Tony; ashamed that despite what Diori thought, he had not been the first man to touch me in that way.

I knew my decision to be intimate with Diori stemmed from the desire to erase what Tony had done to me. I had already lost my virginity to Tony, even though it wasn't a willful decision. If I could no longer offer that to my husband as I had planned, then I might as well have been with someone I loved. In my mind, being with someone I was truly in love with would make the past simply disappear. My rationalization did not take into account the fact that I had not faced my feelings about the rape, the pregnancy or the abortion. After my breakdown, Diori and I tried to go on. I believed that if I pretended nothing had transpired, we could live our lives as if it never happened. Only, Diori was not as eager as I to live out my fantasy. He couldn't take the mystery, and probably questioned my sanity. I could not blame him. How could I be willing to risk all that I had found in this man for something that had festered in my memory?

To this day, I don't know how I could have been willing to lose Diori. All I know is that I *was* willing. I pushed Diori away by changing the subject any time he brought up that night. I found every excuse to avoid intimacy with him out of fear that it would happen again. I made him feel as if he had done something wrong, but the only thing Diori was guilty of was loving me. I loved him, too. He was the first man I had ever loved. As it turned out, I loved life as I had once known it, more. So I left.

One month later, I received my MBA in Marketing. After the ceremony, I packed up my bags and moved back home, though I had convinced Diori I was only visiting. I said my move was temporary and that I just needed to be around my family for a while. But when I got in my car, I knew I had no intention of going back. I knew I would not be able to face Diori again.

I made a futile attempt to start over in Detroit. Diori realized I wasn't going back to D.C. and mailed me a box of things he had accumulated during the relationship. While losing him hurt more than words could say, I just wanted to create a new life. I got my job with Keemer and Dewitt and found my condo community.

More than six months had passed when I met Angel at a networking event. He was sitting with Leo Talbert, an acquaintance from high school. Leo introduced Angel to me. There was something alluring about his personality and his looks. His face was so symmetrical, his physique so sculpted that he seemed more like the work of an artist rather than the result of two flawed human beings. That should have been my first clue to leave him alone.

Our relationship started off simply enough. I often met him and his friends for a couple games of bowling or at someone's house for a few hands of Spades. We were just hanging out and my feelings for him were kept well under wraps. I just enjoyed being around him.

Things remained that way for months until he invited me to a company party where he, among several other colleagues, was being recognized for top pharmaceutical sales. It was the first time I had actually spent time with him alone. When the night ended, I'd had such a good time with him that I didn't think twice about going back to his house. After all, I had done it many times before. Only this time, his countless friends were not around.

When things heated up, I didn't stop him. The plan I'd held to since I was ten to wait until marriage had been abandoned with Tony and confirmed with Diori. So I did what I wanted to do with Angel that night, as well as on several other nights. But sleeping with Angel was not an act that stemmed from the desire to merely have sex; it was an embedded desire to free myself of my past.

Not long after my relationship with Angel became intimate, it became clear to me just how casual our relationship was. When Ramona attacked him on his sexual prowess during the Spades game, she was determined to make me feel as if I were just another notch in Angel's headboard. As they sat around the kitchen table, flinging Spades and passing insults, Ramona and her piercing words shredded everything that bonded me to Angel. Those feelings of embarrassment and devaluation triggered the decision to change my life. It was only now that I realized I went about it in the wrong way.

I had decided to do things differently after that Spades game. In my mind, the key to accomplishing that began with sex. I looked at sex as the common denominator in the demise of each relationship with the three men in my past. When I told my friends I had decided to be celibate, they said things like, "Girl, I couldn't do it," and "I hope you have a vibrator," but none of them knew my true reasons for giving up sex. All assumed that it was because the girl who grew up in the church was returning to her roots. How I wished my celibacy was a testimony of my faith and a symbol of my love for Jesus Christ. I should have used my celibacy as an opportunity to see my life through His eyes, but as reality had it, the only thing I truly accomplished through celibacy was a little bit of self assurance.

Without dating, I could reduce the likelihood of date rape. Without sex, I was assured that I could not get pregnant. Removing sex let me be free of wondering if he'd call the next morning or getting attached to the wrong person. Without sex, I didn't have to pop pills, ask if he had a condom or be concerned that a humiliating or even debilitating disease might make its way into my system and nest there either temporarily or for the rest of my days.

From a physical standpoint, giving up sex was not a major issue for me. I had only willingly had sex with Diori and Angel, and while the experiences with both were memorable, neither Diori nor Angel introduced me to the "Big O." I was not one of those women who wanted to cuddle afterwards and talk about where our relationship was going. When it was over, the only thing I wanted to do was get in the shower and wash the man-sweat from my body. The thought of ridding myself of sexual afterthoughts was overwhelmingly refreshing. Symbolically, it would take me to a time when my life was easier, purer, clearer.

I believed that if my friends looked deep enough, they'd have seen past my barren smiles and discover the truth, not only about my celibacy, but also about all of the things I'd been hiding.

I always felt that there would be someone who would see beneath my mask, but so far, no one had discovered my act. So I continued to hide under the mask, content that I had perfected my role as Trinity Joi Porter, actress.

We see people day in and day out, hear their words and watch the corners of their mouths curl to reveal brilliant smiles. We pass them each day, exchange niceties and go on our way. We envy the upstanding people we think they are. We even live in their homes, share their beds and confess our deepest love for them. Yet, there is often a window or a door that we have never opened—one that leads to the truth of who they are; one that they pray is left undiscovered.

My window was death—of my grandmother, my brother and my spirit. It was the inability to forgive God. It was the inability to forgive Bashaye. It was rape. My door was avoidance—of love, intimacy and memory. I felt as if my window had been busted and my door flung open in rage. I was no longer able to shut out these feelings, and I did not know how to handle them.

A week had passed since my conversation with Mom. I woke up early on that Sunday morning and could not go back to sleep. It was as if I had been pulled out of a hypnotized state rather than awakened from slumber. Unlike most mornings, I was neither tired nor groggy.

I sat up with revelations about the masquerade I'd been cultivating for more years than I cared to count. My attempts to be the person I thought I should be and the person who I was taught to be were suffocating the woman I had become. I had been my own enemy by hindering my growth as the woman I really was.

My epiphany was so real, its emergence seemed to pick me up and slam me into a wall, releasing strongholds and leaving behind someone I didn't truly know. My body trembled as I sat erect in my bed. The only light penetrating the darkness of my room was from a street light that stood about fifty feet from my window. It created a subtle glow that seeped through the corner of my mini blinds.

I climbed out of my bed and fell to my knees. The old Bible that lay on the end table shelf was beside me. I pulled it out and opened it to the dedication page, asking the Lord to show me what it meant. Then I prayed like I hadn't prayed before. I couldn't remember what I prayed for. I just prayed, opening my heart and my mind to the Lord. I wasn't sure how long I had been on my knees, but once I rose, I saw that the street-light that tiptoed into my window had been replaced by sunlight.

Two hours later, I found myself sitting in the sixth pew. My watch ticked to 10:23. I patiently waited for service to begin. I found the scripture reading in the bulletin, then flipped to it in my Bible. The scripture was Mark 11:22-24. "So Jesus answered and said to them, 'Have faith in God. For assuredly, I say to you, whoever says to this mountain, "Be removed and be cast into the sea," and does not doubt in his head, but believes that those things he says will be done, he will have whatever he says. Therefore I say to you, whatever things you ask when you pray, believe that you will receive them, and you will have them.'"

The concept of moving mountains reminded me of my childhood. Once, I read that scripture and stood outside for hours trying to make bikes, cars, houses, trees and modest hills move. These were my alternatives, as you wouldn't find any mountains in Detroit.

I smiled at the thought of those futile attempts. I hadn't realized that the church was filling rapidly. My pew was nearly full and a glance behind me showed a residual effect. The choir marched down the center aisle, and Reverend Smiley sat in the pulpit.

When it was time for the sermon, Reverend Smiley assumed his position at the podium. He reread the scripture then asked, "Did you know that a mountain can be any thing that stands in your way? Hmm?" He searched the faces of the congregation. The question was one I had never entertained.

"This mountain can be a person, an experience, an idea. Whatever it is, when you stand face to face with it, it appears steadfast and immovable." He paused to wipe his forehead, which had already begun to perspire under the lighting.

"I know instinct sometimes tells us to avoid things that stand in our way, but think about what would happen if you were to work your way around a mountain."

Reverend Smiley grabbed the microphone and stepped down from the pulpit to interact with the congregation.

"If you try to go around it, it will always be on at least one side of you. If you go through it, one false move will cause you to run directly into it, whether it is to the front, side, top or bottom of the mountain. It's... still... there," he said, looking at a different area of the congregation with each word.

"If you don't climb, you won't conquer. Mountains, my friends, are meant to be conquered."

I thought about the way I had lived my life and dealt with my problems. Each time I faced adversity, I tried to bury what I knew was reality in a hollow grave that was too small to hold the problem. It never went away. It just lay dormant for a while. When the storms came, the rain washed away all of my efforts to cover the problem.

"People want to curse mountains in anger, frustration or exhaustion, but when you get tired, remember this: He did not bring you this far to leave you."

"Amen!" several men and women shouted in unison.

Reverend Smiley headed back to the podium, where he took a sip of water. "We all get weak sometimes, but be encouraged.

"Do the names Reverend F.C. Barnes and Reverend Janice Brown ring a bell for you?"

I glanced at Sister Moore, who was sitting next to me, to see her reaction to the question. I felt as if I should know who Reverends Barnes and Brown were, but I did not; at least not by name.

"No? Some of you seasoned Christians know who I am talking about," Pastor continued. Sister Moore, who was in her sixties, chuckled. I knew she was one step ahead of me.

Reverend Smiley leaned into the microphone. "Well if you don't know the names, you certainly know the song." He sang, "I'm com-in' up... on the rough siiiide, of the moun-tain."

"Well!" Sister Moore said with rising intonation, offering a testimony through one simple word.

Reverend Smiley drew me in. "Have you ever stopped to think of why it's the rough side that they sing about? Hmm? Think about it. It's because that's the only side where you can get a grip.

"Don't you know there is reward in climbing your mountains? Don't you understand that the higher you climb, the smaller the mountain gets? Don't you understand that God wants you to climb so that you can clearly see Him, without distraction? Don't you see that we are given these mountains so that God can teach us about ourselves and teach us about Him? Don't you know that He will help you climb?"

I knew that my mountains had developed years ago after unanswered prayers for Ma Lo and Bashaye, as well as myself after the rape and the abortion. The seemingly empty results of those prayers only fed my anger toward God. He had let me down. It was only now that I'd begun to realize that God's children face obstacles they don't seem to deserve, but I also realized that God may not have answered some of my prayer because I had not been a faithful servant. Yes, I went to church, served on committees and prayed, but my faith had been shattered long ago. I didn't live for Jesus. I lived, and I fit Him in. The reason was one that I had denied for years and it lay in a jagged pill: I knew that the God I prayed to was the same God I held contempt for.

When I began to understand this, it was clear that my faith, or lack of faith, was what God had been trying to restore in me. I had put so much faith in the Lord healing Ma Lo, restoring Bashaye's life and turning my nonconsensual liaison with Tony into a bad dream, that religion became ritualistic rather than life altering.

When Reverend Smiley finished his sermon and opened the doors of the church, a rejuvenating sensation ran through my body. When the reverend called, I no longer felt as if a force confined me to the pew. Instead, I had been liberated. Walking down the center aisle without a second thought, I stood at the front of the church as the congregation clapped and sang "Standing in the Need of Prayer." Several more people made their way to the altar as something moved inside of me. I struggled to keep my composure.

Though he was rows away from where I stood, Tony's image was clear. For the first time in years, seeing him had no effect on me. I didn't care what Tony or anyone else thought. When the congregation finished singing, a woman stood to my left and a man and his son stood to my right. The woman was a widow who was transferring membership. The others were a single father and his young son, and both were new to Christianity.

The nurturer handed me the microphone, and my fingertips began to tremble. I spoke, attempting to settle my nerves. "My name is Trinity Porter. Some of you know me, as I've been a member for two years." I took a second to gather my thoughts. "I stand before you committing myself to God; to Jesus; to the will of the Lord.

"I've always been in the church." I pulled the microphone away from my mouth to clear my throat. "But I haven't always been of it."

"Take your time," an usher said from the distance.

Suddenly, my words flowed. "Reverend Smiley has been speaking to me for weeks, even months. We haven't had a conversation, but he's been speaking to me through the Word. I suspect God used him." I felt my eyes watering up, so I put my head back, determined not to cry. "I suspect God used Reverend Smiley because I wasn't ready to listen to Him directly. I realized that I've been holding onto baggage and anger for years."

Raising my head was no longer a successful method to fight the tears and I could not stop them from falling from my eyes. I pointed to my face. "I've fought these tears for years, because I never wanted to be vulnerable. I had to be a pillar of strength. But through that process, I forgot who I was. I forgot... *whose* I was."

"All right!" I heard from a woman I heard but did not see.

"There is a scripture—Jeremiah 1:5—that begins, 'Before I formed you in the womb I knew you, before you were born I set you apart.' I've been trying to understand what that passage means to me. I'm clearly not a prophet like Jeremiah, but I believe that scripture has a meaning just for me.

"Early this morning, God revealed to me that each of us is created by design. He knows our strengths, our weaknesses, our character. He wants to use us, despite the way we see ourselves. He sees us worthy of serving Him even when we've allowed our free will to take us down paths that don't lead to *His* will. So in spite of myself, I'm ready to recognize my place as a child of God. I'm ready to invite the Holy Spirit into my heart."

"A-men!" A man's voice rang out from the first pew.

"I'm ready to let go; to forgive; to move my mountains. I am ready... to be saved."

"Hallelujah!" a woman with a baritone voice belted out.

I gathered my thoughts and closed my eyes with a final thought. "I am a vessel, but I'm broken. Still, I'm encouraged because I know that God wants to use me... even in my brokenness."

A series of "Amens" accompanied applause as I handed the microphone back to the nurturer who hugged me and wiped my tears with a tissue.

The pastor said the sinner's prayer with me, the man and his son, and implored the congregation to support us in our new walk with Jesus. Standing there with the will in my heart to serve as I should, I was reminded of a beautiful passage that my grandmother used to read to me. It was Ecclesiastes 3 and it read:

To everything there is a season,
A time for every purpose under heaven:
A time to be born,
And a time to die;
A time to plant,
And a time to pluck what is planted;
A time to kill,
And a time to heal;
A time to break down,
And a time to build up;
A time to weep,
And a time to laugh;
A time to mourn,
And a time to dance;
A time to cast away stones,
And a time to gather stones;
A time to embrace,
And a time to refrain from embracing;
A time to gain,
And a time to lose;
A time to keep,

And a time to throw away;
A time to tear,
And a time to sew;
A time to keep silence,
And a time to speak;
A time to love,
And a time to hate;
A time of war;
And a time of peace.

When Ma Lo read it to me, I remember being amazed that the Bible had poetry. My age and lack of life experience kept me from understanding its meaning.

But now I knew that my time had come to comprehend the passage. I had my season of laughter, my season of mourning; my season of innocence and my season of worldliness; my time to sit back and observe and my time to fight; my time to gather and my time to purge. I knew that I was broken and it was time to rebuild. In order to get the strength to do that, I had to embrace peace; peace with the hand I was dealt, the choices I had made and the lessons I'd learned. It was my time to be at peace with who I was and what I was.

Everything I'd gone through made me the person I'd become. I did not understand why God chose to teach me about myself through those lessons, but I did understand that it was time to release my feelings of hatred, anger, and disillusionment. This day I would follow my mom's advice and change my prayer, moving on without looking back.

God had something in store for me. It was time for my breakthrough. I knew that I was not who I used to be. More importantly, I knew that I was not yet who I *would* be.

The End

2280600R00205

Made in the USA
San Bernardino, CA
02 April 2013